Critical Acclaim for J. M...
*Never Knew An...*
Book One in the Dogsland Trilogy

"McDermott has a flair for subtle world-building. His fantasy settings and associated systems, cultural, magical, and otherwise, are as integral to his novels as his plots and characters; indeed, the three are so tightly interwoven as to be aspects of the same thing. Dogsland is one of those rare fantasies that must not only be read, it must be deciphered, translated, absorbed. In short, learned. Those are the fantasies that stick with me, that I keep coming back to, and that I keep searching for as a reader."

—Paul Witcover, *Realms of Fantasy*

"*Never Knew Another* is a raw and compelling look at people driven by loneliness and a desire for a better life warring with their darker impulses. The ending is a bit abrupt and might not be satisfying for some, but seeing as it's the first in this trilogy by J. M. McDermott, here's hoping the next installment will continue in just such a powerful fashion."

—Josh Vogt, *National Speculative Fiction*

"An unconventional—and somewhat non-linear—narrative that borders on the surreal. A narrative that could have been dreamed up by someone like Charlie Kaufman or Christopher Nolan. Recognizable fantasy elements are integrated into the unconventional narrative to create something that seems familiar—and therefore accessible—but is actually refreshingly different."

—*Fantasy Book Critic*

"A dense, elaborate, amazing novel that begs for re-reading. McDermott has, from page one, a powerful and clear storytelling voice, and a strong control over his language. You leave the book utterly invested in all the people you've just met. "

—*SF Signal*

"*Never Knew Another* is a weird but perfectly formed koan of identity, memory, loss and loneliness. Dark, moving, and unique."

—Felix Gilman, author of *Thunderer* and *The Half-Made World*

# WHEN WE WERE EXECUTIONERS

# WHEN WE WERE EXECUTIONERS

## BOOK TWO OF THE DOGSLAND TRILOGY

J.M. MCDERMOTT

NIGHT SHADE BOOKS
SAN FRANCISCO

**First Edition**

ISBN 978-1-59780-338-0

**Night Shade Books**
Please visit us on the web at
http://www.nightshadebooks.com

*This book is dedicated to the early visitors*
*in the streets of Dogsland, who each took time*
*to make the city and people there more true:*
*Nancy Holder, James Patrick Kelly, Michelle Muenzler,*
*Sharon Maas, and Juliet Ulman.*
*Juliet, in particular, moved mountains.*

# CHAPTER I

I dream of dead men.

The skull that rests upon a lip in the cave pollutes my mind, in sleep. Corporal Jona, the Lord of Joni, died in the woods. My husband and I found him there, polluting the ground with the stain of the demon in Jona's blood.

For days we cleaned the ruin, there, and called upon the Goddess Erin for the mind of the dead. When it came upon us, it came to me in a flood. *Where is my body... Where is Rachel...* I wept for the dead, and the loneliness.

I wrote it all down. All that I could peel away from the mind inside of mine became ink on paper, handed off to my husband that together we could find the living remains of the demon stain.

The city spurned us. Sabachthani demands the demon-stained for his abominations, and his wicked magics. No one stops him, not even us.

We left, my husband and me, for the hills, on the trail of old stains, searching for clues.

Finding none, we slept.

And, in sleep, I dream of dead men.

❦

Corporal Tripoli sits alone at a table. He is a handsome enough man, with huge, strong hands. He cracks peanuts between thumb and forefinger without looking up. He isn't eating the nuts. He's placing them on one side of the table, away from the shells. He looks up. He nods at Jona, his fellow king's man, watching Tripoli crack the shells. He picks up one of the nuts and tosses it at Jona, the Lord of Joni. Jona's a corporal in the king's men, too. He catches the nut and eats it. Tripoli's face is bony in the tavern light. His thinning hair looks like a skull. His eyes are hollowed out. He's a dead man, already sick.

Jona reaches over to take another nut. When he looks up, Tripoli is gone, like he was never there. The pile of peanuts cracked and sorted is all that's left of him.

The tavern is the same as it was before. The city is the same as it was before.

Tripoli's death was like nothing had happened.

Save us from these cities of men, Blessed Erin. Howl in the night like wolves for the dead. Let their souls travel across the mournful wails, riding the painful prayers to Erin's mercy.

I dream of dead men.

Oh, but he isn't dead, yet. Still, I know he will be dead, soon. The ones who die, most of them, cloud into Jona's memory. He had time to forget them. He had time to believe in their absence.

Their names fade. Jona knew Tripoli's first name, and I do not. He had a father, so I know it could not be Tripola.

My husband whispers in my ear.

*Restless dream, my love? I have brought the quill and parchment. Write it down. Maybe there will be a clue in the dream.*

And, I do.

I dream, still.

Jona was asking Rachel a question.

I don't know where they were. I can't smell the location inside his skull, only the words. Maybe they were in his dark bedroom, clinging to each other, so it smelled like nothing to him because it smelled like him and her but mostly him.

"How do you learn how to be a Senta?" he said, to her.

"You breathe," Rachel said. "How do you learn to be a noble?"

"I guess you just breathe, too. What about all those tricks?"

"The greatest Senta never discover such things. The greatest Senta—the Seers—see through them. Dreamcasting is an expression of that path. I struggle to touch that Unity, Jona. Our skin, mine more than yours, they are only partially made of the world of light above Elishta. The other part is an absence that even light ignores. Senta—dreamcasting Senta—see right through me with glowing eyes of light. I can't see that way. I try but, I can't. I am a novice's novice."

"I've seen you freeze two buckets on a whim."

"The Unity is greater than two buckets, Jona, and much smaller than a single crystal of ice."

"Now you're just tossing me. You're trying to sound wise."

"You're just listening. I'm saying nothing. We're both saying nothing. This is all a ruse because what we really want is to kiss. But do not kiss me now. Let's stay a while just like this. Don't move."

Aggie, in her cell, her hands slowly turning black where her fingers leaned back in her pallet. "Are you all right?"

"Who, me?" said Jona.

She rolled away from him, her back to him. She looked at the wall. Aggie had been Salvatore's beloved. Once she had committed one sin, he had abandoned her. And, Jona was to blame that she was in a cell, with an infection in her nose.

"You just going to sit there like that?" said Jona.

"I didn't ask for you to come here," said Aggie. "I don't want you here. The last time you came here, I was sick. I couldn't tell you to leave. Now I'm telling you to leave."

"Feeling better, though, right?"

"Of course not. They're burning me alive as soon as the church mother signs the form."

"Ain't dead yet, though."

"No."

"Salvatore's going to get here, soon. I promise. He'll get you out."

"I don't believe anything you say."

Jona stood in her cell, looking down on her, her back to him and she was feigning sleep. He had brought her food. He had brought her some better water than they have in the prison. There were vomit stains along the wall by her pallet. She had been puking in her sleep. Her neck was flush. She must have been running a fever.

"Tell Salvatore..." She started to cry.

I dream of dead men.

I dream of dead men, all night long.

Geek steps into an open sewer grate as if swallowed. His uniform vomits up in dirty water overflowing from the rains. In the dream, he is standing at the bottom of a sewer grate, looking up, reaching his hand up for the light above the flood. The rains come again, and flood the ground with muddy water. It pours over Geek, staining him in mud, and pushing him away until he's gone. Flowing in the water, all the lost boys with their broken crowns, and all the girls in their dresses and cracked jars and porcelain, lime-white skin of Rachel's brothels and all the animals moved from boat to killing floor in the abbatoir dismembered and thrown into the brack.

Bad dreams, from two minds blurred in sleep.

I woke up in a cold sweat, half-woman, half-wolf, thrashing around in the dark. Blessings of Erin, they are difficult things. Goddesses do not ask us to do easy things. In life, he was a king's man, a lord of Dogsland, fallen into poverty after the failure of his father. In death, he was a blight below a bluff, where toxic mushrooms sprouted in his acidic demon blood.

I could smell Jona's skull in the cave. I could feel its empty eyes upon me, as if he could see though dead. I'm the one who sees through his eyes. The dead see nothing. His skull was dead weight, and toxic, but the smell of it helped me see through his eyes.

When we finish the hunt, we will leave it with the Temple of Erin in the city, and it will be easier to keep my dreams away from his.

Salvatore, the thief, eluded us in the city with the aid of his masters. Rachel Nolander, a nomad all her life, had been running north beyond our territory when Jona died. All the places they had touched and corrupted in our territory must be cleaned of the stain.

This blessing of Erin, that I might see and smell the world inside Jona's memories, walk down the paths that a Walker can read in the signs of things, read the patterns of a life like Senta dreamcasting, it all fills me up in the dark. At night, this blessing makes it hard to sleep. Last night, I turned over and over again enough to drive my husband to another corner of the cave. I woke up afraid, reaching for him, because I was dreaming with memories that were both mine and not mine. My husband was not there.

I searched for a body that was not my own in between the three bodies I knew. I was only supposed to have two: I am wolf and I am woman. The third, Jona's body from Jona's memories, was never mine except in dreams. Those first moments awake were as unreal to me as a dream.

*Breathe...*

My husband came to my side. I calmed. I wondered how long until the demon child's mind might fade away into the distant hum of old memories. My husband carried a demon child's mind, too, and he never seemed so anxious as me. He had had so many years to think the bad dreams through to quietude. He licked my face. His long whiskers tickled me, and I laughed from it. I was a woman, and laughed like a woman. He had the wolf skin pulled over his back.

*Don't lose yourself in him.*

I joined my husband in the early morning dawn outside the cave. He flicked his ears at the small insects that liked this dry cave upon a small mountain. I let them land. I liked how they felt in my ears. The itch was my own, and helped me recover from the dream. The wind over my fur. The ground beneath my paws. I was a Walker of Erin, and I knew my mind from Jona's.

I stretched. I walked into the early dawn. "I'm getting breakfast."

My husband ran on ahead into the forested places down the side of the little mountain.

*Easier like this.*

I paused to watch the sunrise. Every hill is a mountain dying or being born; every mountain is a hill upon a hill upon a hill. From where I stood, I could see over the trees to a rising sun. It looked like the hills were on fire.

I started a fire of my own. Without the wolfskin on my back I was cold, but I had human hands, and I could build fires. My husband yawned awake, flashing his predator teeth. He wanted meat for breakfast, and he did not want to eat bread like we did in the city. He spoke to me.

*What do you remember?*

"Everything."

*I remember many things I had forgotten, just being here, where he lived long ago. I have seen nothing new in the demon child's mind that leads to our enemies. Had Jona ever come here? Do you remember him here?*

"Jona only left the city twice in his life. Once to train with the king's men, and once more to die. We should find Sergeant Calipari, again. He knows the streets, the way criminals hide in pieces of paper. We can force him to lead us to Jona's mother."

*We can ask anyone. Jona should have known such things. Other people should know them. Where did she work? He knows where she worked, doesn't he?*

The sun cracked over the treeline, light like fire everywhere, and rain clouds in a haze, deep grey like smoke.

"Yes and no. There are too many places that he remembers. If we found precisely his street, we'd find his house. If she has left her house, sold it off perhaps... We'd need to purify the ground, still. I need the streets below my feet to find it, more time study-ing his skull. I can't get his mind in order outside of the city."

*What I remember of this one from the cave is so old. Even were they my own memories, it would be hard to find anything new to unravel Sabachthani.*

"We have to go back."

My husband pulled the wolf skin from his back. He stood up, on two legs—man's legs—and he held his hands to my fire. "Lady Sabachthani? What would Jona do about her?"

"I think... If I were Jona, I would write to her father."

My husband growled deep in his throat. The red valley was Lord Sabachthani's legacy, at the northern boundary of the kingdom. Two of the three skulls we kept with us were from the demon children's, them only just children, and bones we stole from his estate. *He will kill us faster than she.*

*We don't know that.*

*He is our enemy more than she is.*

*We don't know that, either.*

He snarled. He pulled the wolf skin over his back, gathered up our three skulls, and howled a mournful song of death. We would return to the city.

Three skulls: two deformed children and Corporal Jona Lord Joni. Both of us had taken the children's skulls from Sabach-thani's estate, stolen from the shape that his wicked magic had twisted them to enslaved abominations. Inside their minds, their memories would be only confusion and pain and a void where a soul might have been. We suspected their father's name, and that was enough. Jona's skull was mine, alone. We had found his dead body near the north, and found the stain of his death. We took his skull from the body. With the blessings of Erin, his memories came to me, and I carry them still. I'll carry them, and his skull, all the days of my life.

I buried our fire with rocks and sand. I gathered all the maps and letters we had accumulated from both Sergeant Calipari and my own quill pouring out the memories inside of me. We had packed them away in oilskin and stones to keep them dry and away from mice. We needed them, now. I pulled the wolf skin over my back.

We would travel slower back to the city than when we had run to here. We were going to be cautious, this time, with Lady Sabachthani watching for us.

Down the hill, through the trees and valleys until we reached the roads. A small rain storm came. I closed my eyes, rolled onto my back and opened my mouth for the drink.

I carry his mind. It pushes into my own, like a kept sea. His whole world was mine, with my senses, the Blessings of Erin, a wolf's nose for scent, and the wisdom of the wild places, I dive deep inside his memories.

I remember looking up into the storm from Jona's mind, where the falling raindrops appeared spontaneously from the mysterious depths of sky. They appeared like magic from the grey depths, and tasted clean as magic as they pooled on the tongue.

Erin, bless us, your loyal Walkers, that we may be swift in our hunt, and make peace with Sabachthani that we may lay the wicked low.

Raining, again, and Jona, I remember you in every rainstorm because of the smell of the rain so close to the ocean is the only rain you knew.

❈

Salvatore is still alive. I do not dream of him. He's running through empty sewer lines, and slipping into windows in the dark. Slipping into bedrooms, into beds, into the hearts of lonely women in the night.

The skulls of the dead, deformed demon children, plucked from Sabachthani's monstrous abominations: they are Salvatore's children.

Alive, and alive and always alive, and spreading his life without remembering the purposes of life except to live.

I do not dream of him.

❈

Rachel and Jona were lovers, but not quite yet.

Windows closed nearly all at once when homebound women saw the sunlight darken and return and darken again with the salt smell of sea rain and the strong winds. Jona did not close Rachel's window. He leaned out backwards as far as he could with his boots hooked under a bed. He looked straight up into the silver clouds, all of them lambent from the swallowed sun.

"What are you doing?" said Rachel.

"Just looking," he said, "I want to see the rain fall."

"Your tea is getting cold."

"Fate worse than death."

Rachel stood up. She touched his stomach with her gloved hand. He looked down his body, back into the room, where she touched him. Then, he looked into into her face. A raindrop landed on his forehead. He smiled.

"How many days you get off a week?" she asked.

"Just one or two," he said, "Unless they need me and I don't get any."

"So come in here and drink tea with me. Watch the rain on the king's time. You woke me up for this."

"Yeah." He pulled himself in from the window. He turned around and closed the shutters. Her hands straightened his uniform at his shoulders.

"You wearing this on your day off?"

He shrugged. "Keeps me out of trouble," he said, "You ever give the Senta stuff a break?"

"Of course not," she said, "I'm wearing all the clothes I own."

"Yeah," he said. He nodded at her. He sat down at the little table under the window. "Yeah, I know. I wasn't trying to... I'm just saying that me out of this uniform is like you out of your Senta stuff. Anyhow, tough fellows might like to find me out of it, no bells to call my brothers-in-arms down. I wear the uniform. I bleed for the city, all the blood I got in my body, in my heart. All of us king's men do. We swear an oath like that."

She sat down across from him. There were teacups, with tea. They were supposed to be drinking it. Rachel and Jona both stared down into the brown pools of stale tea, and their restless hands upon the cups.

Rachel yawned. She spoke to her tea, not him. "Do you know anything about hearts, Jona? The Senta know hearts. Hearts are not one organ. Inside a mother's womb, two pulsing bags of blood seek their eternal mate."

Her hand reached out to his. She opened his palm, and traced a finger down his lifeline, then his loveline. She lifted it up to her own face. She placed it on her cheek.

"Lungs are fine apart," she said, "Hands do not need another but to clap. Brains gnarl like roots in the nothing of soul, and guts spin in knots around the nothing of hunger. But hearts are made by two complete parts merging together. Once the two pieces sense each other in the blood flow, they cross every bloody cliff inside of us. The arteries bind the halves close. The veins make love to each other in the life pulse that makes all life from love entwined."

She let go of his hand. He let it linger on her face.

"Your tea is getting cold, Jona."

"Fate worse than death," he said. He did not move his hand from her face. Then, he moved his hand. It went down to the table. He stood up. "I have to go," he said.

"Don't you want tea?"

He shook his head. "No... I did, but..."

"Sit down. You're making me nervous."

"Right," he said. He sat back down. He picked up the teacup, and sniffed at it. He sipped a little. "It's good," he said.

"So, what do you want to talk about?"

"I don't know," he said. "I just wanted to see you. Was that one of the koans?"

"No. It's just something my mother taught me before she died." Her face, the way she looked at him, makes me happy, because Jona was loved by someone before he died.

❦

My husband and I feasted in the night on stolen meat. A sheep heavy with lamb, it slowed her down. We dragged her into the woods while the shepherds' dogs cowered away from us.

From the raw mutton, I showed this Senta wisdom to my husband, from the heart of the aborted lamb.

In the daylight, we searched fetal birds peeled from their shells —their tiny grey bodies limp in our human palms, all blood and fluids and dying tissues. Just beneath the translucent skin, the organs pulsed and died in two distinct pieces that would no longer fully merge.

He said nothing to me, nor I to him, after we proved this to ourselves. We ate what we had killed.

*Say something, my husband.*

*I regret returning to the city because it means you will not be completely yours, completely mine. Too many bad smells. All of them his.*

*That is not our place to choose. If Erin wills it…*

*…we die on this trail. Eat, beloved, for tomorrow we may face Sabachthani's executioners.*

As wolves we dashed into the city, not priest and priestess. We ran like wild dogs, snarling and biting and blood on our teeth.

For three days we lived in the alleys like dogs. We slept in mud, and ate in the mud and snarled at everything that came near, all our skulls and papers always hidden deep under our fur. We had to slink our way through the streets to a small temple of Erin, near the harbor. We scratched at the back door until we were discovered and could enter in hiding, make arrangements for our stay. After dark, we slipped into a rented room dressed like foreign thieves. The innkeeper, greedy enough to have no curiosity, was paid to ignore us. Not even a maid came to our little room.

We wrote to Lord Sabachthani by addressing the king, though the king would do nothing for us. We waited, hunting nothing. We told Lord Sabachthani that we would not hunt without his permission—only wait for word through a liaison of the temple.

Wait and wait, then. So much paper arrived at a man's door. He ruled this city while the king was too old, and too tired to take the reins of state. Our small concerns were nothing to the diplomacy and negotiations of all these crowded districts, and all the cities of the world.

Patience, then, and wait. Close my eyes and see with my eyes, smell with my nose, deep into the streets and buildings Jona's memory.

Three crowns, painted on doors and archways, lined up in a row like winning at cards, and Calipari didn't like it. Nobody liked it. New marks on the walls meant fighting. Newcomers meant upsetting the balance. The king's men were sent to find the new markers of things, drag them in before anything changed. Vandalism, at least, and more if they could beat anything out of them.

Jona and Geek found a porter they knew eating sausage from a street vendor. Sweat pooled at the porter's armpits and spilled down the front of his dirty shirt.

Geek whistled and stuck out his hand in friendship.

The porter smiled with food jammed in every gap in his teeth. The porter took Geek's hand, but cringed when Geek clamped down for the shake. Geek had powerful hands. He was reminding the porter that Geek was not here in friendship.

After the handshake, Geek showed his palm to Jona. Sweaty blood was all over Geek's hand. The porter rubbed at his, trying to force a smile at the king's men come to push him for something. Geek showed his dirty palm to the porter, too, like it was the porter's fault.

"Sorry," he said, to Geek. He wiped his blood-soaked palms along his leg. It wasn't going to get cleaner on his bloody pants. "I've been pushing meat from the killing floor to the river. Forgot about it."

"Nothing on it," said Geek. "Me and my boy," Geek pointed his bloody thumb at Jona, "We are on a tear looking for a few fellows."

"They in trouble?"

Geek whistled and shook his head. "They will be if we don't find them."

"Who?"

"Don't know the names. Some foreigner moving the pink demon weed around like he's somebody, but he ain't anybody. Who knows where he's getting his supply? Can't be good for his health. Dunnlander, I hear, dressed in red. Got a couple fellows on his side, drawing three crowns on things. They set up shop a day, maybe an hour. Then, they run somewhere new. Dunnlander finds the new spot, the supplies find their way in from who knows where, and these two other fellows go watch-out-man or touting or something else."

"Always something," said the porter, "I see that stuff coming in off the ships and lots of my boys plucking it for someone else. Don't know anybody doing it for new people. Nasty stuff, I think. Wish you could drive it all out, but it would just find its way back again. Leastways keep it in order, right? Keep any trouble off the streets."

Jona's eyes narrowed. The porter wouldn't be so friendly with Geek if he hadn't spent some time in a room negotiating mercy with Sergeant Calipari. He was hiding something.

Geek touched Jona's arm, pulling him back. "Hey, I forgot to ask," said Geek, "How's that wife of yours doing? You ever see this fellow's wife, Jona?"

The porter looked over his shoulder, his face a mask. He was feeling the fear, now. "We got a boy coming, soon. I hope it's a boy. She's big as a sow."

"This ugly fellow's going to be a father?" said Jona. "I was doubting Imam all morning. Now I have faith in miracles."

The porter smiled wide with ragged teeth like a broken, yellow fence spilling sausage bits down his shirt. "I gotta get back," he said, "But, I do hear a Dunnlander's running with ragpickers. Mudskippers are the only ones not scared enough to know better. Those kids'll cut your throat for your boots if you're asleep in an alley. None of them half as old as the mongrels that follow them for scraps."

"Got a name for us?"

"I don't know nobody. I know he's got some rowdy friends."

"How rowdy?"

"Rowdy, but, you know, not rowdy enough for what they're doing. And not enough of them."

Jona had a vision of them, then. A few foreigners scrambling what they could, skimming off the top of other people's shipments, maybe jumping people in alleys for their product. They would have to be moving around a lot. They probably wouldn't use the same place more than a day. It was no wonder their marks were up all over, in and out of the Pens.

Geek tossed the porter a coin. "Thanks," he said. The porter winked and turned. He lumbered through the bustle back to the main slaughterhouse of the Pens.

Geek looked around the street for ragpickers. "You know any ragpickers?" he asked.

"I hate street kids," said Jona, "You?"

"Not yet." Geek tossed a coin to the same food vendor the porter had used. The vendor said nothing, about it, and handed Geek a sausage. Geek offered Jona a sausage. Jona shrugged, and paid for his own.

The sausage came wrapped in bread. When Geek was eating, the sweaty blood left on his hand got on the bread and he didn't seem to care. Jona watched and it made him a little sick every time the red bread disappeared into Geek's mouth. Jona thought about his blood. Then, he threw his own food into a sewer grate. "Guess I ain't so hungry," he said.

Geek wiped his dirty hands off on the vendor's apron.

The vendor hated it, but he said nothing. The vendor looked at the two king's men like they were chasing off business just by standing in front of the man—which is exactly what they were doing.

"What?" said Jona, to the vendor.

"Nothing," said the vendor.

"We'll stay here long as we want," said Jona. "Nice and safe with us around."

The vendor nodded his assent. His eyes burned. The vendor pulled out a glass flask half-full. "You king's men thirsty after your meal? Maybe you take this brandy somewhere people don't see you drinking it? Rainstorm coming. Hard enough to sell anything in the rain without you two blocking up the view."

Geek took the flask with his bloody hand, nodding.

The two king's men walked away down the street without a word more about it.

Pens district streets coiled like muddy vipers. With so many boot prints and wheel-tracks, an empty stretch of avenue looked like a swarm of muddy vipers lying asleep in the sun. These muddy vipers grabbed at boots and held on. They hissed in the suck when the boot pulled loose.

Jona left Geek to searching out the ragpickers among all those twisting veins of mud. He said he had someone he needed to talk to, and the two men separated. Jona went to Rachel's apartment. He hesitated there, wondering if he should knock or not knock. He pressed his ear against it. He heard nothing. He thought about leaving, then.

He lifted his knuckles to the door. He took a breath.

"Djoss isn't here."

"Yeah? Good."

"Jona?"

"Yeah."

"Oh."

The door opened. She looked at him, up and down. Her hair was mussed. She had been sleeping. "What is it?"

"I… It's going to rain soon. Can I come in?"

"You woke me up," she said. "Want some tea?"

He didn't want tea. He didn't want to enter. He didn't want to leave. He didn't want anything. But, he wanted something, and he knew it was something with her and only her, wherever she might be.

The rainstorm came, at last, washing up from the water. He leaned back out the window, deliriously happy to see the rain falling down, right into his face.

# CHAPTER II

Inn beds acquired too many old smells for wolf noses. In this little room, a thousand lovers have left the ghosts of their affections in the sheets. With the loamy soap smell and the sea wind and the maid sweat from all the trips down the stairs, through the wash, onto the line, and back again for more lovers, I'd only dream of the mechanical motion of anonymous lovers and anonymous maids like clock hands tearing at the white linen skin of the sheets. I'd wake up dizzy.

We slept, my husband and me, on the floor near the iron stove. We rested our wolf noses in a light film of coal ash that had drifted here with hair and dead skin. Tea leaves that had escaped the boiling pot curled like desiccated ants in the lint and dust near the baseboards. We smelled it all, as we slept, seeing everything.

When we woke, my husband and me, we woke up hungry.

His eyes opened first, with the songs of the birds. He pulled the wolfskin off his back to make himself a man. He lit a single candle near the stove. He scratched behind my ears.

*Not yet.*

He yawned. *I'm hungry.*

I stretched, and I yawned. I felt the papers beneath my back when I rolled over. I pulled the wolfskin off completely. *Me, too. It is my turn, isn't it?*

*Yes, it is. Hurry up. I'm hungry.*

When I stood, I faced the mantle. Three demon skulls in wicker boxes slept there. When we finished with the skulls, we'd leave them with the church for servants of Erin to study. Imam's inquisitors have already requested the skulls, but they must wait.

Our paper map filled most of the floor. Wax landmarks followed our daily paths through the room where our candles had spilled.

From outside, I heard the bird songs of sunrise. Inside, we lived in darkness. We did not want windows. A curious eye might see our map across the floor from another window, and our papers. City folk frowned upon different households so close to their own beds.

When I found my way to the street, there was rain.

The good men and women of Dogsland hid below parasols. Some wore wide hats to keep the rain off their faces.

I bought soggy bread from a skinny girl no taller than my hip. She should have been at home, but she was out working. She had a sheet of canvas over her cart that was too old to keep the rain out. She probably didn't notice because she had trouble seeing through the sheets of rain in her eyes. I touched her cheek. Her skin felt so cold. She shoved my hand away. She held one hand up over her eyes. "Don't touch me, lady."

I laughed at her. I stepped into the street. I opened my arms and praised Erin for the blessing.

"Lady, ain't you got the head to get out of the rain?"

What was rain to me? If Ela Sabachthani found my husband and me in her city, we'd be dead by nightfall.

I bowed to the shop girl. I went inside with the sopping bread that tasted like the blessed rain and the blessed waters were all over me. I handed the wet food through the door to my husband. I stood in the hall until I was dry. I didn't want to get the maps wet.

When I was dry enough, I went inside to lie with him and wait among the papers and ink. I'd write what I could remember, if I hadn't written it, yet.

Rachel sat on Jona's lap. Her dark smell was more intoxicating than the ale—cheap soap, dirty leather, and her demon blood beneath like wet brimstone.

Jona wanted to say something. He didn't know what to say. Her gloves ran through his hair. Her Senta leathers scratched at his bare neck.

Jona wanted to fill this silence. She listened while staring out the window. They whispered in each other's ear about the forbidden thing.

Fathers.

"My father wrapped his fortune in running the enemy blockade so we could get more coal," said Jona, "Every ship was lost. Pissed the king off big, so he tried to blame the loss on my father's sabotage."

Rachel kissed Jona under his ear.

"King offed a bunch of nobles by commanding they do the impossible. Called it treason when they failed," whispered Jona, "He took our lands along the rivers. He took most of our estate in the city. When I was a boy, our house was surrounded with a beautiful garden full of pine trees that you could always smell first thing in the morning."

Teeth pulled gently at Jona's earlobe.

Jona breathed in, hard. "King sold the grounds out from under us. Got buildings pressed right up to the windows. Nothing left but the house. Can't rent out rooms on account of... Well, you know."

"That's awful," said Rachel. Her hot breath on Jona's neck. She kissed him under his ear again.

"Wasn't the only family it happened to. King needed the money. He did what he had to do to fight the war and build his city. Sure, I hate his guts, but he's still the king," said Jona.

Jona fingered the frayed edges of her Senta leather collar as if these ragged places were fine lace.

"Maybe my father was a traitor," he said. "Who knows? Maybe he was an evil demon and should've burned for his sins and this was all they could catch him doing."

Rachel kissed his temple. "We won't talk about him anymore," she said. "We don't need to talk about it. I mean, if he was like us, then he couldn't have been so bad, right?"

Jona pulled away. He cocked his head at her. "What was your father like?"

Rachel smiled, sadly. "My brother's father, I've heard he was a nice man until he was possessed by the doeppelgaenger. I was born after. The demon entered his nose, devoured his brain, and coiled on his spine. The demon stole anything he wanted, and did anything he wanted to anybody. My family traveled because my father made it so we had to flee. It wasn't some grand scheme, either. It was petty stuff. Theft, murder, rape."

"Elishta…" said Jona, "Bloody Elishta…"

Rachel kept talking like Jona hadn't said anything. "My brother poisoned my father and killed the demon with a club, and don't you forget that about him if you ever meet him. He did it for Ma and me. My father was… I never called him my father. He was something horrible. Something worse than us. So much worse. So, my brother took me to find our mother, but the body was found too soon. We hid. She was so sick. She couldn't have run far. Djoss took care of me after that."

"That's… Good for him," said Jona. "Good for him, yeah? Ain't as bad as all that, then? Demon's dead, and your brother's looking out for you."

Rachel shrugged. "It's my life," she said, "Not everybody gets to be happy and... We make the best of it, Djoss and me."

"Still..."

"We can't change the circumstances," she said, "We just do the best we can." She turned away from him. "I have to go home," she said.

"Yeah."

"I'll find you later, okay?"

"Yeah.

⁂

We were in for the night, my husband and me, carefully blowing out candles and holding down papers with stones and bricks.

Someone knocked on the door. My husband coiled behind the door and pulled the wolfskin over his back. *If anything happens, fall into the room.*

I listened at the door a moment, hearing breathing, cloth, no steel chains or armor. I held up a lit candle and cracked the door.

A Sabachthani servant, armed only with an envelope, bowed gracefully to us, and presented to me his envelope. An official invitation from Lord Sabachthani. I took the paper. "How long has he been making us squat in here like cats?"

The servant smiled, mercurial and polite. She offered to send us a basket of fresh fruit, which I refused.

In the morning, my husband and I left for the noblemen's little island. We crossed the city. We took ferries over rivers, and carts over mud-patches. On the last ferry to the Island, we stood between the horses of two fine carriages.

I touched the neck of a white horse. The horse told me about a strange smell on the ferry. I smelled it, too. I recognized it. I smelled the old blood, urine, and alcohol in the air. A wicked man stood behind us, hiding among the carriages. My husband

and I did not make this journey unobserved.

The ferry landed uneventfully.

Two sleepy king's men sat on chairs and waved at everyone to pass. We stepped onto the smooth cobblestones of wealth, power, and glory, cut away from the city by a man-made canal. How could they not see the destruction of the ground, the disconnection of power from place, and the dissolution of the city in this way of noblemen and kings? The commoners saw it. They talked of this place as if it were foreign soil.

Once we arrived at Lord Sabachthani's estate, he did not waste our time posturing through his seneschal as if Erin's Walkers were as irrelevant as Corporal Jona Lord Joni and Sergeant Calipari. We were led directly up the main stairway, to Lord Sabachthani's bedroom in the center of the hall. We had a private audience with him, an honor long overdue to us.

We entered the room together. We saw the man who ruled this city in the king's dotage. Lord Sabachthani had grown fat in his old age. He was poured into a large chair in front of an empty fireplace. His huge stomach rose and fell in little bursts like a slow tremble. It was breathing. He could barely breathe. He lifted a white hand. He gestured at us to step forward.

His chamber smelled like the ocean. My ear wanted for the sound of gulls and water, but there was none. Magic, then. Illegal magic, and a blight on the natural world of Erin's Holy Law. I heard the Lord's labored breathing instead.

Paper upon paper in neat stacks smothered every empty surface. He could not rule, in his condition, strolling from meetings to meetings. All had to be done on papers, from this chamber.

I sniffed hard at the sea air, seeking the source in this windowless room. My husband coughed in the heresy as if it were smoke. I managed to hold back my own indignant disgust.

This magic caused us pain to breathe it.

"The salty air helps my lungs," said Lord Sabachthani, then, after a breath, "It's harmless."

My husband walked to the fireplace, smelling after a source. He plucked a painted seashell from the mantle. He placed the shell in the hall. He closed the door behind us.

The ocean smell faded. Candle-smoke, then, but this was also not real. I also smelled some tiny darkness hidden in the flames that must have burned eternally with small carvings of demon bones, not wicks. My husband and I blew them out.

"I don't have windows," said the lord. "We'll be forced to sit in the dark."

After the last candle was snuffed, I lit a match. I threw a handful of fireseeds into the fireplace, and stacks of his accumulated papers as fuel. I lit them with my match. He didn't say anything about the papers he had lost. He had only watched me, calmly, burning requests and commands. It was fair price for his attempt to expose us to heretic magic.

The flicker bounced around the crevices in the lord's face, like a shadow dancing on a ghost. He was too calm to be anything but an adversary.

"That will be enough light for us," I said. "This light is natural. It will not slowly poison the lungs with the stain of Elishta."

"How little you know of what I do," said Lord Sabachthani. "Did you bring me a present? Usually visiting dignitaries come bearing gifts."

"We did not bring back the skulls from your mechanicals. Nor will our Church pay you for destroying your shameful creations," I said. "Our gift to you is allowing you to remain a free man, and not under arrest for your sins. This is more than you deserve."

He smirked. "I could still use those skulls for something, even if my guardians are gone. No one got sick from my creations. I made those beasts during the war, you know. Thirty years and no one's sick from them."

"Those were children, not veterans. Where did you find them, I wonder? You are still engaged in illegal magic."

"My work is more academic these days. I have been trying to extend my life."

"You will fail."

"I have not been successful, I admit, but the research is young, yet."

"Abandon this path of sin, before it is too late for your soul, and the city that needs you."

"No," he said. "Does your holy mandate extend to hunting down where I acquired my guardians?"

We said nothing.

"I see," he said. "I should let Ela have her way with you."

My husband growled under his breath. I remained silent and still.

"What do you want, exactly?" he asked. "Why have you come bothering us? We don't need your kind here. The Church of Imam can deal with this problem of yours."

From my robes, I lifted a corncob wrapped in rags with a red-yarn smile, and rose-colored cheeks. "It's for your daughter," I said.

"You bring gifts for her, but not for me? How unkind." He held out his hand for it, and caught his breath before speaking again. He took his time. I did not hand over the doll to him. "Lady Sabachthani's a little too old for dolls," he said. "She'll be lucky to bear my heir at her age."

I adjusted the yarn hair. "Not with your illegal magic," I replied. "You test the magic on yourself to give to her, don't you?"

He pulled his hand away. "Throw the doll in the fire," he said. "That's what she'll do when she sees it."

I placed the doll on the mantle. "Enemies you make now may not fear your daughter as they fear you. Erin's church and Imam's both have longer memories than city courts of law. This doll is a baby girl."

"I have no grandchildren, yet. I don't even have a son-in-law. Is this what you came to me for, Walker? Petty threats?"

"We came to speak of Lord Joni," I replied. "I have seen into his mind."

"I heard about Lord Joni."

"You knew before?"

He snorted. "I never bothered to check," he said. He took a deep breath, and then another. "If Ela did, that's her business, not mine. Lord Joni was a crasher of parties, and nothing more. If it wasn't for his uniform, we'd never let him in uninvited. Ela said he was useful to her because of it. I've already purified the grounds as best I could and encouraged my former guests to drink a little more holy water for a while. I'm not stupid. I know what a demon stain can do to a man. I take serious precautions. I always have."

He would have continued talking but for the coughing.

"We did not come here to persecute you or your daughter, nor influence your interests. That is city business, as long as it stays away from our hunt. I carry Lord Joni's mind with me now," I said. "We search for two creatures of demon blood. One that Lord Joni loved, a demon child named Rachel Nolander. She called herself a Senta, and even mastered some of their smaller tricks. We have found no trace of her current location in Jona's mind, or on these city streets."

He smiled at me, with bright white teeth—far too white for a hoary, old man. They looked foreign in his mouth. "My daughter tells me you refuse to search for her."

"She is not completely correct. There is another demon child of more urgency."

"Ela needs him, for now. He is useful."

"What is a petty criminal to you, even a very talented one, when you could gain the support of the Church of Erin when the king dies?"

"Long live the king."

"We are unconcerned about the throne, and have no interest in your illegal activities. We care only for the demon children. Give them to us, all of them, and we will support whomever you wish."

"This city worships Imam more than you. What use is your faithful to me?"

"Is it more useful than a single thief?"

He laughed. "You learn to negotiate with lords in your forest?"

"In a wolf pack, the insurrection is always one meal away. Who rules the pack can change in a single swipe of antlers. Every wolf hunts. Every wolf dies."

"I never liked wolves. What I would give for your powers, Walker," he said, "To wear the skins of beasts, and see through the eyes of the dead."

I curled my nose at him. "You could never trade, take, or challenge for our path," I said. "If you desired Her Blessing for power, you would never merge with Erin's Will."

"I will not live long enough to find a way," he said. "Perhaps my daughter will take that from you. Perhaps the little moppet on the mantle will learn of your powers."

"Perhaps we will return for their heads," I said. "What of this city? You know we will not leave until we have purified this place of the stain of demons."

Lord Sabachthani took three long, hard breaths. He coughed. While he spoke he fidgeted with his hands. He had a handkerchief that he used to wipe his fingernails. The handkerchief stank of vinegar so strongly that I smelled it from where I stood.

"I knew the last real Lord Joni, Jona's father, during the war," said Lord Sabachthani. "If Jona got his blood from anyone, it was his mother. Lord Severa Joni was a fine man, for a traitor. His wife was an opportunistic harpy. She ruined a good man with a pretty face."

"We will find that out for ourselves. Your daughter wanted to marry Jona."

"Nothing surprises me about my daughter. Personally, I was hoping for the commoner, Mishle, but he wasn't much of a swimmer when they threw him in the bay. Nor was Lord Elitrean's useless son."

"Lord Joni killed both of those men," I said.

Sabachthani snorted laughter, then paused, recovering his lungs. "Yes, Ela thought he was useful. Jona must've been a fine prospect for the throne. Resourceful, obedient, ruthless, and, he'd know his city streets like a king's man." Lord Sabachthani yawned. He scratched his neck. "Too bad he died in your woods."

I narrowed my gaze at the man. "If you were wiser, you'd protect your daughter from the children of demons and this city's throne."

"If you were wiser, you'd never come to my city at all," said Lord Sabachthani. He coughed once, into his vinegar-laced handkerchief. The cough was wet, and probably had bits of blood. Lord Sabachthani waved his handkerchief at my husband. "That man of yours, he hasn't said a word to me."

"Be glad of that," I said.

"He spoke to me before, long ago. Before you were born, I suspect." The Lord smirked like a sinner. He turned his fake, brilliant smile upon my husband. "How is my valley doing, Walker?"

My husband moved across the room fast and fluid. He slapped Sabachthani, hard. The white teeth banged loose from the glue in the Lord's gums.

"Be glad I do not wear the wolf skin when I swipe at you, fiend," he growled, "Your lands and your laws cannot protect you from Erin when you are dead." A red welt rose on the Lord's white cheek.

Lord Sabachthani did not touch his teeth. He spoke through them. His words were muffled, but we understood them, fine. "I'm not dead, yet, Walker," he said. Tears welled up in his eyes.

He choked them down. We are the only two creatures on earth that would dare raise a hand against him. I imagine he'd never been struck in his life. His lip curled. He fixed his teeth with just his tongue. He clamped his jaw shut to hold them down.

We waited for him to finish re-attaching his teeth. We let him speak again, correctly.

"Be careful lest I hand the whole forest over to the street rats. Farms for everyone, free of charge, to honor a dying king's dream of public prosperity."

I pulled the wolf skin across my back, but I did not wear it full. I let my eyes and spine remain human. I was mostly wolf, but tall and proud and terrible. I leaned over him like kissing a lover, so I could shove my maw into his face and let him smell the death in my hot breath. I growled at him. *Send the dogs to their death if you must, but it is on dogs that you have built your daughter's throne. When all the dogs are dead, nothing will stand between your family's throats and my teeth.*

He smiled at us. He nodded his head, respectfully, as if he understood me. He might have. "I think we have threatened each other enough. A pleasure, children of Erin. May you find everyone and everything you seek, and leave Dogsland forever," he said. "My daughter will be informed to stay out of your affairs. I advise you stay out of hers as well, but I will not stop you."

Sabachthani snapped his fingers. The hall servant, seashell in hand, opened the door behind us. The candles flicked on again, in a burst of light. The fireplace smoldered down to steamy wisps of smoke.

My husband and I left.

In my husband's pocket, he had collected loose paper while the Lord stared into my teeth. We took that paper and gave it to our church, that we may gain advantages against our enemies here.

He had made a deal with wolves. He would be true to his word.

Wolves do not honor agreements with men like him. When we are ready to strike against him, we will.

By evening twilight, I prowled the streets with my husband. I still saw the faded paint in the Pens District. Three crowns in a row brushed in ragged ink hid in alleys and broken crates and ruined stone walls.

I touched the ink. Dog, Djoss, and Turco had painted these signs before his mind died. This was one of their abandoned demon weed dens.

✵

My husband and I spent weeks wandering the streets in day and night—the wolfskin pulled over us in the dark—sniffing out the stain of the demons. We had to find them, if they were still in the city. I carried the mind of Jona Lord Joni, found dead in the woods, inside my own. We carried his skull in blessed wicker wrapped in leather and paper and cloth to keep all hands away from accidental contact with the demon stain.

I needed his scent, from his skull, to sift his world of his memories and see through them, into his world as if into my own. I needed to be close enough to smell the bones to feed my studies of the demon child's consciousness inside of my own mind, where the blessings of Erin have opened the mysteries of his life and death to me, with his mind's memories.

My husband says that the woods will need us soon, and we must hurry. But, there is nothing to hurry. A demon stain is more dangerous than a blighted tree or an animal spreading diseases for a while, or even a farmer casting sins upon his land. The care of the souls of farmers, who are mostly good men without our aid, was trivial to this.

That is what I tell my husband. He tells me the moon fattens and fades while we stumble through darkness, howling into the corners of the sewers of the city after the stain of Elishta.

When we woke up at last, we left in the dark and returned in the dark, and scoured the sewers in the dark. We slept without bothering to return to our human skins. We didn't sleep in the bed.

☙

The main temple of Erin was far from the Pens. We sent runners ahead so we would not have to wait for our supplies. Holy water, fireseeds, kerosene, candles, quills, ink and coins waited for us. Sometimes we requested dandelion wine, or matches, or pieces of the woods to soothe our restless wolf soul: a slip of moss, the lost bark of trees, anything to remind us of home.

We take to the temples these papers that I write, and give them to the temple druids. Scribes spread these words to you, that we may find Rachel and Djoss before they escape beyond our eyes.

We did not take paper from the temple. We bought paper to get close to the ragmen of the Pens, unchallenged.

☙

My husband and I bought paper from a ragman that tugged on his beard and muttered under his breath in a foreign tongue. He refused to speak to us at all.

His alley was contaminated with Jona's stain.

I don't remember what had happened here.

A stain smothered the mossy brick walls and tracked through the mud and washed with the rain into the sewer grates, into the bay where people caught fish at the grates to pickle with dill. The fish was sold cheap to the ragpickers that couldn't afford better, and they ate more of this awful stain. The boys came back to the ragman and the stained alley, a little queasy from Elishta's touch, and the boys puked on the stained walls, and the pollution rose like flood water in the alley.

My husband and I came here to pour holy water on the walls and the ground. We brought temple fruit to bless and purify the boys.

These boys wore old sacks more than clothes. They looked like tree roots with legs. When they smiled their teeth were brown stones. They huddled in the angled places—the shadows, the empty stairwells and empty doorways. They observed us two strange outsiders pouring water on the walls like cats watching wolves.

An older boy sneered at us with his broken teeth. "Why you doing that?" he said. "You washing that wall or something?"

"We are," I said.

He smacked at the boy next to him. "You know we're peeing on that wall soon as you leave, right?" The two boys smiled like thieves.

I smiled back at him. "We do what we must," I said. I pulled a blessed apple from my belt. I held it up so the boy could see it. "Tell me, Mudskipper, did you know a fellow that couldn't speak and everybody called him 'Dog'?"

"Yeah," he said, "I won't tell you nothing, though."

"I guess I'll have to eat this apple myself. I was going to give it to Dog's friend, Djoss."

The boy started to laugh, but a cough cut him short. "Djoss is dead," he said. "What do I gotta do for that apple?"

"Tell me something I don't already know about someone who is dead."

My husband walked the perimeter while I spoke with the boys. He glared off anything that looked like trouble.

And this is how my husband and I learned of the Three Kings of Dogsland. I didn't have enough apples for everyone, but I told these boys that I'd return for more paper, and I'd have more apples, and I'd want to know all I could about these men who are all dead, anyway.

I smelled Jona slithering under their rotten breath. Erin only knows exactly how many illnesses his demon-stain had caused. Most weren't fatal. Sometimes another illness struck with strength while the body was weak from the stain of Elishta.

The ragpickers told me a few stories about boys that had died horribly out of nowhere, like Corporal Tripoli.

Everyone's fine and fine for weeks. Then, one morning, some threshold breaks inside of one body, and death pours through them like cholera, or worse.

But, we'll speak to that later. I say this so you may know this: we approached the knowledge of the Three Kings of Dogsland from the mouths of the ragpickers. With Jona, later on, I sought them from the other side.

⚜

When the summer rains fell, Rachel came to Dogsland with her brother, Djoss. They were Nolanders, with nothing to their name.

Corporal Jona Lord Joni, a King's man and a killer, lived for months in the same city streets, unknown to his beloved Rachel. When Rachel and Jona finally met and knew each other for what they were, they spun together like threads beneath a weaver's thumb.

Beasts always seek to merge into tribes from instincts more primal than sublime.

Sometimes this becomes love.

⚜

Rachel was watching from a window. She looked down at him, unable to sleep. She saw the children of the neighborhood part. She ducked back inside the shadows of her window before he could see her. She waited a few minutes. She didn't know what she was afraid of, but she didn't want him to see her. When she thought she was being stupid, she went back to the window, and he hadn't even looked up to her building. He probably didn't know where she lived, yet.

Jona walked the rounds with a dangerous-looking hooked halberd. When he found a dead body, he dragged it on the hook to the nearest large sewer grate. He hooked the grate open. Jona tugged the body into the grate, and closed it shut. The bodies piled up inside the sewers. In other neighborhoods, a body might be checked for identifying things—jewelry or papers—and perhaps the family would be contacted. In the Pens district—and the Warehouses and anywhere else the working poor might call home—bodies were pulled into the sewers before anyone got sick with the diseases of the poor.

This time of year, only light drizzle poured in off the bay. Without the powerful spring rains, the stench of the streets and the sickness never washed away.

When the bodies stank strong enough to reach a lamper high on his stilts, the lamper poured some of his noxious whale oil and kerosene into the sewer. He tossed a match behind the liquid, and let the oil stink melt away the body stink.

Bodies burned, shit burned, and discarded pieces of rotting meat burned, but no paper, no wood, and no clothes ever burned.

Ragpickers found their way into the underground, before any fires came. They plucked anything fibrous for the ragmen making paper by the river.

The fires stank. But, the fires burned down the worst of the stink. Fires never burned down enough stink.

Rachel, at her window, was used to the smell, by now. She watched Jona's back. He was cheerfully moving through the streets, sweeping away the dead, as if they were never there. Any violence that claimed a man in the street was his own problem if a king's man didn't see it. It was at once comforting to Rachel, and frightening when she thought about it that way. Still, she was glad she was friends with a king's man, if they were friends.

She was sure they were friends.

# CHAPTER III

J ona and Tripoli dragged in three men stoned and naked in mid-morning from the middle of the street. Real pinkers didn't move much when they hit the pipes, but eaters didn't get strong enough hits to fall so far. They were just chewing on leaves, not smoking the old, dried dung-like balls of the weed heavy with the pink stain from the flowers. These three eaters were still naked. When they came down from bliss in the prison cell, they'd think about how to get home unashamed.

Tripoli led the three pinkers with their hands tied to the same long rope towards the interrogation room.

Calipari jumped up and grabbed the rope between two naked eaters. "Nope," said Calipari, "Just toss them in the tank. The king doesn't need to know why they're are naked. We already know. Third cell's open."

"Aye, sir," said Tripoli.

Jona stuck his thumb out at the closed door. "Got anything good, Sergeant?"

Calipari sat back down. He looked at the report he was writing. "Ugliest bird you ever saw in your life," he said, "Tougher than you boys, too."

Jona laughed. "Tougher than us? Who's tougher than us? This is the Pens," said Jona. He puffed out his chest. "We scare blood monkeys. Night King shivers from us."

Calipari salted his page. He pushed the paper aside, and grabbed a clean sheet. "Night King's just street talk," said Calipari. "Real trouble coming when the Chief Engineer gets here to dig up everything. Don't even know what he's doing down here. Got a letter say he's coming here to work. What I want to know is why now? What's he planning? People like that don't come here for real. Lord Sabachthani don't come visiting, what's this fellow like him doing? Troublesome stuff, that's what."

Jona reached over to a scrivener's hand and swiped a quill straight from the scribbling fingers. Jona handed the inked and ready goose-feather to Calipari. The scrivener shouted at Jona for the theft.

Jona ignored the scrivener. "Who you got in the room?"

Calipari shushed the scrivener with one look. "Thanks," he said. He scratched numbers on his page.

Jona leaned over the desk to see what precisely Nicola wrote, but all Jona saw were numbers.

"Well?" said Jona.

Calipari harrumphed. "Right," he said. "Big Jess bounces down in this dive with a bunch of the sailor and slaughterhouse girls," said Calipari. "Whores hear all kinds of stuff. So, Jess hears it. She's no flower, our Jess. She's a fighter, big as an ox."

"My kind of girl," said Jona, "What's she singing?"

"You hear about a porter name of Umberti?"

"I heard he was running pinks for that Dunnlander on the side. What's that Dunnlander's name? He's more gangly than ganger. Too pink to last long."

"Turco," said Calipari. "Turns out Umberti is pulling a little off the top of someone else's stuff, and slipping it out on the side, and Big Jess heard about it from one of her girls who heard it from a stevedore who works it with Umberti. Word spreads quick on a skimmer, true or not. If we don't pull Umberti soon, he'll roll with no help from us, and we won't get our hands on the Dunnlander fast enough to hang him."

"We're just rolling him to the noose for smuggling, right?"

Calipari shrugged. "Find Umberti before his bosses figure it out, and maybe we get some push. Nothing makes a good bird like the king's shield. If he's too tough, we'll roll him to the noose with Turco beside him. If he's smart, he'll give us the foreigner."

Jona cracked his neck. He looked over at the closed door behind which Big Jess and Geek talked about the streets. "Do I get to meet the contact?" he asked. Jona had a goofy smile on his face like begging.

Calipari rolled his eyes. "No, you don't get to meet Big Jess. This is Geek's show. You got that of-demon girl for Sabachthani and the Anchorites. That's the stuff you need for the fleur-de-lis, Lieutenant Lord Joni. Geek just wants Sergeant stripes, and he needs this stuff for it. Foreign gangers hang for Sergeants, and no one cares but us." A piece of paper moved from one side of the Sergeant's desk to the other, full of numbers. "I want you and Jaime to hit Bone 'n Cleaver and the Dead Goat, for sure. Ask around for Umberti and Turco for Geek."

"*Dead Goat?*" said Jona. He shook his head. "That's no porter pub," said Jona, "That's deep in the pink. Too deep. You want riot bells, you send us in there alone."

Calipari brushed off Jona's words with a wave of his hand. "Jaime knows a fellow who'll let you in back," said Calipari, "as long as you promise only one guy and only talk. Talk Umberti—or Turco—to leave alone with our protection. Guilty or not, the word's out. They're both safer here than at the Dead Goat."

"I'll do it," said Jona, "but I'm carrying two bells in case one gets palmed."

Calipari nodded. "Hurry up, then." He scribbled at his papers, and scribbled at his papers, and scribbled at his papers, and he didn't say one more word. Jona heard laughter through the walls. It wasn't a woman laughing. It was a man, in there, with a hard laugh. It wasn't Geek. It wasn't some woman from a brothel.

The laugh was familiar, too. It could have been the carpenter.

Sergeant Calipari was lying about the person in that room.

Jaime grabbed Jona's sleeve. "Come on, let's go. I ain't going down there alone."

Calipari wouldn't lie without a reason. Jona looked over at Calipari, looking at him hard, trying to read him. Calipari shook his head. He pointed to the door with his quill before going back to writing, and shook his head. *Don't.* Jaime was already halfway outside.

Jona and Jaime went out again looking for Turco and Umberti, but the Bone 'n Cleaver was empty during the day when porters and killers were working for their ale money at the Pens' abattoir. At the Dead Goat—named for the dead goat on a pike rotting over the broken door, replaced weekly—the fellow Jaime used to know had been dropped bleeding into the river a week ago. The folks at the Dead Goat's back door looked ready to pull teeth at uniforms asking after the dead.

Jona and Jaime backed off. Instead, they walked about the Pens asking people they knew about Umberti and Turco. Nobody heard a thing. They never did.

Then, a fight broke out beside a brothel. Then, this noble's seneschal got lost looking for a particular warehouse and the two king's men helped him find his way.

And that's the rest of the king's men's day.

Most days were just a fuzz of faces passing through the streets. No one looked a king's man in the eye. Everyone lied with their eyes, saying that they weren't there with their averted faces. Jona stared them in the face, like he wanted them to look away. He was lying with his eyes, too.

The way Jona figured it, something was up with Jaime, or Nicola had heard about the things Jona had been doing for the Night King.

Jona had placed an unsigned form in the pile. It said only that the Night King was real, and hiding in an accounting ledger. Enclosed with the unsigned note was the ledger sheets from the desk of a dead man that Jona had killed because a carpenter told him to do it, and that carpenter was working for the King of the Night. All those people dropped into the canals and rivers, and none of the deaths made any sense to Jona. He had only wanted Calipari to make sense of all those deaths. Calipari was good at looking into books. That's all Jona had wanted.

# CHAPTER IV

The prison was a repurposed warehouse and still looked like a warehouse. The windows had bars. Archers on the roof congregated near mounted bells. The archers were bored, hot, sitting in the sun, and didn't even glance up at Jona walking towards them. Jona waved at one that looked familiar. The archer waved back. In training, Jona had failed archery. Veterans recommended failing it, so the new recruits wouldn't get stuck on a roof in the sun. Jona would rather be in the Pens every day, where the close buildings kept the streets in shadows and every horse trough was good for a splash of water on the neck.

The prison guards didn't even make Jona leave his gear at the door. A Pens guard should be able to take care of himself with locked up men, and some girl that hasn't done anything but cry and bleed infected blood from a broken nose. He kept his bell. He kept his club and meat pie.

Jona had brought her food.

In the prison, Aggie was in this cell at the end of an empty hall. She was in this cell because Jona had to put her there to protect Salvatore Fidelio from the consequences of his own actions. Salvatore worked for the Night King, somehow, and somehow Salvatore was a child of a demon, like Jona. Somehow, Aggie had loved him enough to burn at the stake to protect Salvatore, even if she didn't know what her beloved really was. Light slipped in from a few slivers in the ceiling where sun and sometimes rain poured in from the sky. The heat was awful. The whole room baked behind the bricks.

Jona brought her some pinks hidden in the slits of a blood pie. He had hid a few drops of his own blood in the pie, as well, to pass on the demon-stain and keep it in her. She might be tested again. He didn't know if it would work like that, but it might. She had survived so long with the stain from Salvatore's lovemaking that she might live longer with only some smoldering blood. From his perspective, no one had died, yet. Besides, she hadn't eaten anything for two days. Demon fever and gangrene had her body now, but they weren't as dangerous as starvation, now.

Her eyes were sunk into her face. Her lips were grey as charcoal. Her nose was still bandaged up, but nobody had changed the bandage in a week. The cloth was a green and black, like a snail in a burlap shell on her face. It wasn't demon stain infecting her nose, just gangrene.

She growled at Jona.

Jona put the pie in front of her. "Best blood pie in the Pens, for you."

Aggie stared at the pie. She looked up at Jona, with this terrible fear all over her face.

Jona pulled a handkerchief from his pocket. "Next time I come down here, I'm bringing something for your nose, too."

Aggie didn't say anything at all. She clutched at her stomach. She rocked forward and back.

Jona reached for her face with the handkerchief over his hand. She backed away, slapping his hand.

He snorted. "Not much I can do to you now." He reached for her again.

She pulled away from him.

Jona huffed at her. "I wanted to make sure you had a nice bite and a clean bandage. Looks like they haven't brought you any new bandages in a while. It's like that here. Nobody cares if you live or die, and nobody wants to expose themselves to the demon stain." Jona rubbed at the thin wrappings under his own black glove.

Her eyes closed.

"There's this friend of mine, I think you know him. He says I should come by and help. He's a good fellow to me," said Jona. "I spend every day chasing after cut thieves and rollers and rapists and killers and smugglers that'd drown you and your mother over a bag of nothing. Foreigners coming here, causing real trouble, crowding out all the decent folk in the Pens. Small timers like him are nothing to me. Sabachthani's sure going red over this, right? A stupid dog, and he wants to burn you for it? Search me on that one, girl. And this foreign friend of mine, Salvatore Fidelio, he's asked for my help."

Her hands clenched hard at her own body. Her eyes remained shut.

Jona's hand finally reached her face. He peeled the putrid bandage off her skin.

Her teeth clenched, but she didn't fight him.

Bits of greened wool tore off from the stained bandage. Her nose stank of rotting flesh stronger than the stink of the cells.

"I'm going to get you some hot water," said Jona, "and we'll talk about how we're going to help you when I get back."

Air moved over her aching, infected nose. Her jaw dropped. Her eyes opened and rolled in pain. Tears turned to mud at the corners of her eyes.

Jona went up to the kitchen, and got the cooks to boil some water for him. He asked if they had any medicine for a prisoner. They told him they didn't. Jona handed them coins one at a time until they had a bottle of wicked alcohol so cheap a whiff watered Jona's eyes like a strong onion.

When Jona got back to Aggie, the blood pie was gone, and the demon weed he had shoved into the pie had her eyes rolling like marbles. She tried to sit up. She tried to focus on him.

"Hey, Aggie," said Jona, "You okay?"

Aggie managed to speak a little, but her words slurred, and bits of spittle and pie dribbled down her chin. Her lip curled. "You're lying," she snarled. Her eyes rolled back into her head. She collapsed in her bed.

Jona was glad the demon weed in the pie had knocked her out, because the alcohol was going to burn like Elishta when he poured it up her nose. The hot water was probably going to burn her, too.

He placed her head in his lap. He used the hot water first, in little trickles. He drenched his handkerchief in the hot water, and wiped away the green blood and the caked puss. He was careful not to push the nose too hard. The place where it had broken was still swollen.

When he poured the alcohol up her nose, she choked through her pink sleep. He pulled her up to sitting. He smacked her on the back.

Then, he drenched the handkerchief in brandy, and tied it around her nose like a bandanna. It would have to do. It would heal, or not.

He waited for her to wake up. He watched the rats slip in from their hidden places in the walls. They had whiffed the rot in the bandages. Jona watched them dragging the cloth into the hall. Six rats, each as big as a shoe, cautiously tugged at the bandage like sneak thieves. Other rats followed, sniffling after the smell of the food in the pan.

Jona practiced his words in his mind.

*I know Salvatore set this up, girl. He told me himself. I'm not turning my buddy over a stupid nobleman's dog. Everyone knows Sabachthani is the blood monkey on your back. We're arranging things for you, Salvatore and me. You'll be out of here as soon as we can fix it, and you won't burn, and you'll never go back to Imam, either, and it'll be just you and Salvatore. Just relax, and do what I tell you, and everything's going to be fine.*

*Salvatore will be here, soon. He just has to make some arrangement to get you out.*

*Salvatore will save you.*

Jona closed his eyes. He wasn't going to say any of these things. He was going to sit with her, and hold back how angry he was at Salvatore. This is Salvatore's fault.

Salvatore would have to fix this. Jona opened his eyes. He washed away the worst of the grime with the hot water. He tried to straighten the girl's hair. He'd have to bring her a comb.

If Salvatore did come here, it'd be better if Aggie was still beautiful.

When he looked down at her, he thought about Rachel. If this were Rachel, what would he do for her? Would he break her out? Would he burn the city down for her? Would he walk away?

Did he love her the way Salvatore was supposed to love this girl?

Did anyone love like that?

Through the drug haze, her lip curled. It must have hurt bad if she could feel it through the demon weed. All this pain, and Jona had helped cause it. He could fix it, too.

(How had she survived so long with the stain of Elishta? She had been sleeping with Salvatore, exposed to Jona's blood. Now, she lay in filth, gangrenous and weak. I ask my husband if he knows how she could survive so long. He does not know either.

We think it must be the Temple of Imam, during her days, when they washed themselves with holy water, scrubbed the floors with it. It must be something like that.)

⁕

In a street café north of the Pens in the early afternoon, where breakfast was mostly uneaten and waiting for someone to give up on it. The sun was high in an afternoon sky. Night workers had emerged, blinking, into the sun at this café, pale and bruised. The remaining pastries, coffees, and teas were sold cold and cheap. The men and women were laughing, happy pickpockets and troublemakers and thieves.

Jona walked up, and a silence fell over the room.

Jona sat down across from Salvatore.

"I was saving that seat, King's Man," said Salvatore.

Jona's face was cold. "You were saving it for me."

"I wasn't," said Salvatore, sneering like a thief, "You got nothing on me, King's Man."

"Do you remember Aggie, Salvatore?"

Salvatore squinted at Jona, and then nodded. He snorted. "I think so." Salvatore blinked. His face wasn't in pain. "She dead yet?" he asked.

"Not yet," said Jona.

"Poor kid, in over her head," said Salvatore, "Wouldn't listen, you know?" She had stolen magic from Sabachthani, and tried to plant it at her Mother Superior. It was exactly the sort of thing Jona was supposed to prevent. Salvatore was too addled by his eternity to remember much in the way of instruction.

Jona sat down across from Salvatore. He reached for Salvatore's tea. He took a sip of it. He grimaced—too sweet. He wanted Salvatore to think of his blood, his demon stain. Salvatore held his breath. Jona coughed after drinking.

"I know she wouldn't then, but she'll learn," said Jona. "She doesn't talk to king's men anymore."

"She's getting smarter." Salvatore snatched his tea back from Jona. He threw the cup on the ground, stomped on it. It shattered. "Don't drink my tea," he said.

"I want you to visit her, with me."

"I won't. I don't walk into prisons on purpose. I got friends help me stay out."

"You know their names?"

Salvatore sneered at Jona. Of course he didn't know their names. He barely knew his own.

"Will you write her a letter that I can take to her?" said Jona. "I'll even tell you what to write."

Salvatore grunted. "I don't write nothing. What am I supposed to say, anyhow? It was her doing. I'm out of it."

And the men of the café, nibbled old pastries. They all stared at Jona, in his uniform, like they were going to do something if he didn't leave. The café was dead silent. Jona touched the riot bell in his breast pocket, just to make sure it was still there. It was. He pulled it out and turned it over in his hands, like he was ready to use it.

The waiter came, and poured tea for Salvatore. He offered Jona a cup. Jona shook his head. When the waiter left, Jona leaned over. He spoke softly, because he knew the whole café would hear better, the softer he spoke. "Write a letter. Tell Aggie that you love her, and that you miss her, and that she should listen to me for a while because I'm working with you to save her."

"Sounds like you got it down. You write a letter, King's Man, and I'll sign it later," said Salvatore, "I'll meet you after a ball. 'Tis the season for balls, I think. You crash those, too, right? I've seen you at them before. I'm certain of it, actually."

"When? Which one?"

"Day after tomorrow. Sabachthani's the only one throwing them these days. You aren't burning the girl right away, are you?"

"No, she's got a few more weeks. She said she was pregnant, once. She hasn't said anything about it, since. We don't know. No one's going to check her with the demon stain. If she's pregnant we have to let her have the kid before we burn the kid, too.

Law's always weird like that, but it isn't built for of-demons. King won't make a new law for just one case. Aggie's father's raising a holy stink. He had to be tested, I hear."

Salvatore laughed. "Fool girl's not pregnant," he said, "Anchorites don't know pregnant from a stone on the street. How come she's testing pure?"

Jona glanced around at the quiet tables on this stretch of empty road. "You want me to tell you here?"

Salvatore smirked. "No," he said, "Best not."

"Yeah," said Jona. Jona looked around at the eyes in the room, staring at him like killers. Jona stood up. He tossed a few coins on the table to cover Salvatore's breakfast. "A pleasure to meet you, again, Salvatore Fidelio," said Jona. "I'll be around. Look around every corner."

Salvatore touched Jona's arm. "Will they let her with all the noise on her?" asked Salvatore. "I mean, I want to and all, I do. Just tell me, though, will they let her with all the noise on her?" He meant the Night King.

"I'm trying," said Jona. He sighed. He rubbed his temple like a headache. "I'm trying."

"Yeah? Wasting your time, then. Best thing is to kill her quick, before she can say anything about anyone else."

"If you want to put her down…?"

"No," said Salvatore. "Just no. King'll do it for us soon enough. He'll even feel good about it."

Jona looked around him at the quiet men, one last time. A thief and a king's man trying to save a girl? That had to be some kind of code. That's the rumor that spread, anyway. Jona heard it later from a birdie talking about a ship named Aggie, and Jona knew what it was right away. He rolled his eyes and told Pup not to write that one down in the report later. When Pup asked why, Jona said it was him and it was his birdy, and it wasn't a conversation about any boats.

Grabbed from the street, Jona felt the push of something in his uniform pockets. A ragpicker kid wasn't looking for spare change. He put something in and left it there. Jona grabbed his arm, but couldn't hold it long enough to stop the child's escape. The boy's arm was greasy, as if dipped in hot wax. It was all just grime, the unwashed and unclean boy. Jona walked for blocks before he touched the note. Did he even need to read it? His boots found a way to the shadow of the eaves outside the carpenter's shop. Night King always kept Jona here, with this carpenter.

A carpenter's shop was the front for the Night King's operations in the Pens. He was hard at work on a bottle of wine when Jona came in. The carpenter didn't smile. "You, again? Must not of thought too much of you handling that thing with the girl."

Jona said nothing. He folded his arms.

"Got someone for you. Seneschal is coming into the Pens looking for sausage and cheap wine. Thinks he's going to throw himself a party for his lord. The gangs in the Pens are too dangerous. Oughtta teach that seneschal to stay on his own."

"Want me to improvise?"

"Bloody Elishta, no! You do exactly what we say. To the letter. Lucky you still alive after the thing with the girl."

"I obey," he said. "For my mother's sake."

"That's right. I went down and had me a discussion with one of you king's men. Didn't see you around. Hmph. Wasn't about you. Night King said to tell you that if you see me around, it's not about you. You're nothing. You're not worth handing over, even with you blowing this opportunity you had. You're less than nothing. You see any of our people around, it ain't you."

The carpenter was as hard and knotted as the wood in the shop. His eyes looked like knots, black and deep in his skull. All Jona had to do was do the seneschal beside an abandoned brewery, and drop him in the water. That was it. Not even getting his hands dirty, or setting up the kill this time.

If Jona had any doubts he was on the outs, this would clear that up. The Night King was calling on her blood monkey again. A seneschal had to die in the Pens.

"I'll obey," said Jona. "And, you tell the Night King I am pleased to serve. I'm still keeping up with the girl, and I'm still improvising."

The carpenter snorted. "Yeah. I heard. You do that. See where it gets you."

"You tell the Night King that it's only a matter of time before Calipari figures me out. There's lots of birdies around, lots of eyes and it only takes a few loose lips."

"That's your problem, isn't it? Why don't you *improvise?*" The carpenter turned away from Jona, and started planing a cabinet top. He was shaking his head at Jona. The loyal blood monkey knew he was dismissed.

A dead man walking in a crowded street, always looking ahead at something in the distance, never seeing behind. A moment pulling him into the alley with the king's man uniform to make him obey the command. A single knife shoved up into his lung with a long cloth around the hilt to catch the blood, keep it off Jona's clothes, and the splash of meat in the water, with the knife behind it.

All of it over so fast, it was like it hadn't happened at all.

A wipe of rags on the hand where the blood spilled. A splash of it into the water.

And, like nothing had happened, Jona is back in the street, alone. He's walking away with his eyes up and cold.

He made it twenty paces before the nausea struck. He ran back to the water's edge and vomited into the canal. It came up green and orange, and floated on the water's surface like something dead and steaming. Looking at it only made him feel worse.

He didn't want to kill anybody.

❖

Jona and Rachel, out of a rainstorm in a doorway. They had both been smeared in lime. It was deep night, when all good people are asleep. There wasn't anybody good in the area. Lots of lights were burning, all over the city. It was dark, but they could see each other in the reflected light from puddles and windows.

She's leaning over his shoulder, pulling at his collar.

"Your clothes are wearing thin."

"So are yours," said Jona. "The seam is already torn at the collar. See?" He reached over and touched the collar. It needed to be rethreaded where the seams were pulling apart.

"Can you help me get new ones?"

"Maybe tonight. What about your brother? I thought he did that?"

"I saw him last night. I think he's upstairs sleeping, still. I think he's, well… He hasn't been a lot of help lately."

"I can."

"No. Nevermind. You wouldn't know where to look, would you?"

"Not a lot of Senta around here. I know where I can get some thread, maybe some cloth. I could ask my mother to make it for you."

"Definitely not. Sorry, I shouldn't have said anything. Nevermind."

"I can…"

"Just, no."

"It's all right."

"Is it? Because I don't know."

"What's wrong?"

"I'm confused about something."

"What?"

"What are we doing, Jona? What are we… doing?"

He held his hand out for the rain. It wasn't raining too hard, but it was enough to fill his palm with rainwater. He drank it, then dragged his hand along his leg. "We're staying out of the rain, that's what. Bloody Elishta, you'd think it wasn't so close to the dry season, with all the parties."

"Just staying out of the rain?"

"What else is there?"

"For us, I don't think there's much more than that."

"You see your brother, lately?"

"Yeah, but… I don't know."

"I won't roll him. Promise. I can tell you he's doing something he should worry about if you think he's up to no good. He probably is."

※

*He came to me last night before we went dancing. I got a full night's pay for it, but when he came with his friends, I was sent home. Everyone was paid and sent home.*

*That doesn't sound good.*

If they paid her to leave, she left. Whatever happened at the brothel was none of her concern if she wasn't cleaning up afterwards. Jona saw her. He ran across the street and asked her what was happening. What Rachel didn't say: Her brother had bought the place for one night, to place a pipe in the kitchen. They didn't want her around in case of trouble. What trouble? Dog sat at the hookah pipe, pushing coals underneath the water and stuffing demon weed into the bowl without a word. He smoked like he was sucking on a teat. He coughed up blood. With the blood, he painted three crowns over the door. Djoss was the watchout man. He pulled the owner aside, and pointed at his sister. *Send her home. I don't want her here. I didn't know she was going to be here.*

Turco offered to walk her home.

She said yes, because Turco had helped her, and because he was working.

She changed her mind.

Then, Jona was there, hid in a dark corner, and watching

something in a tavern where people were dancing. He stepped over to her, waving hello. She smiled. She thought to introduce Turco to Jona, but she didn't really know what to say about the men to each other. *This is the king's man I know. This is the ganger I know, smuggling demon weed.*

No matter. Turco was gone into the tavern like he wasn't there at all.

"Come on," she said, to Jona. "Let's go somewhere else."

"That your friend?"

"No. My brother's friend. He's… Well, he's all right, but I just don't… um… I don't think he wants to say hello to you."

"Yeah. We were looking for a Dunnlander."

Then she's laughing. "I'm sorry. Hard to imagine anyone looking for him. He's not much more than a dog."

"If you say so."

Turco's job, then, was a tout, if Djoss was on the door, and Dog was at the pipe, Turco was walking around, looking for people who wanted to smoke, and telling them exactly where to go. He knew the city better than Djoss. Dog had his tongue cut off, his ears mutilated, and too much weed to keep things straight. Jona pointed to the tavern Turco had entered, but Rachel shook her head.

"Anywhere else. Anywhere at all."

Jona and Rachel escaped the night in this corner café. Jona ordered plain red tea. Rachel slammed three glasses of cheap gin. Rachel laughed. She tried to cool the alcohol burning in her throat. She conjured ice from midair and tossed the balls of ice into her mouth to cool the burn. When the cold stung her, too, she pulled it out, then back in again to cool the alcohol burn.

Jona asked her if she felt beautiful when she was drunk.

She shook her head, all fuzzy. "No, but you look beautiful when I'm drunk," she said, too loud.

Music from next door bounced between the cracks in the bricks. Rachel grabbed Jona's arm.

They danced in the middle of the café to the music from next door, and the café owner shouted at them for it. Jona waltzed Rachel into the street.

Rachel grabbed at Jona's hair and dug her lips into him. He pulled away when he ran out of breath, and took her by the hand and into the streets and into an alley. She asked him if he was taking her to a secret tavern for powerful noblemen.

He said he was taking her to a secret ball for criminals and thieves, which was almost the same thing.

She asked if there'd be dancing.

He said there'd be the best dancing in Dogsland.

He tossed a coin into a hidden crack on the wall. He tugged the correct stone, and the door opened. Rachel gasped because the door had opened from the side of the café where they had just been drinking brandy.

And down below, he took her through the dank and the stink. She lit Senta fires in the air to light the way. The drumming echoed through the halls.

She asked him what that drumming was and he told her it was a temple to the Nameless where people were always dancing and pounding their souls into the drums.

"I will not worship at any temple of the Breaking," she said. "Certainly not to the Nameless Ones."

"Don't worship," said Jona. "Just dance."

❦

Rachel breathed in like she was about to scream.

Jona kissed her to silence her. He laughed and told her to re-lax. The people around her ran streaks of lime through her hair. They ran blue streaks over her face and over her grey and red Senta robes. Then, they pulled her in to join the crowd.

Jona grabbed at her and wrapped his arms around her. The drums rattled in her bones. Her ears ached. She pressed her palms over her ears.

Jona grabbed her hands away, close enough to her face he could bite at them with his teeth if he wanted to.

Bodies merged into the sound of bare palms and sticks pounding the drums. A hundred faces blurred.

Rachel grabbed at Jona. He pulled her in even closer, jumping with her. The Nameless' bodies pushed the lovers together in a swell.

Their hips moved as one entity, merging like heart halves in a fetal chest.

Blue finger streaks leaked down her face from the acidic demon sweat. Her eyes were wide, watching his ecstatic face. He laughed. She tried to jump higher, above the crowd.

She was terrified. She was going to have to clean her clothes.

She pressed herself into Jona's powerful body with all her strength.

She was full of joy.

# CHAPTER IV

Calipari's note passed from Jona's hand to the hand of a Sabachthani gate guard. They were in a tavern near the island. The city was sweltering hot, like it was as hungover as everyone else. The place was empty that afternoon. Jona had bought the man a tankard. They sat in a corner, where nobody could hear the words.

The gate guard handed the letter back with a shrug. "Can't read," he said, "I know you, though, Lord Joni. You working with Calipari, right?"

"Yeah. Calipari sent me. Tell me about the Chief Engineer," said Jona. "I hear he's coming to my streets. I hear he's Ela's people. We want to know who's coming. You know, if he's going to mess things up or leave us alone."

"That fellow? He's a commoner walking around like he's somebody, that's what."

"Anything else?"

Lady Ela Sabachthani arranged meetings with the Chief en-

gineer by breaking her own canal. She sledgehammered a re-
taining wall until it cracked. Then, she sent a runner to get the
engineers to help her with the repair.

The Chief came from the palace, with his loyal engineers on
hand to repair the breach. The Chief shared tea with Lady Sabachthani until his men finished fixing what she had broken.
The man at the gate said that the Chief was a good tipper, like
he had more money than even Lord Elitrean. He couldn't have
that kind of money unless he was dirty, and all the gate guards
agreed about that.

Jona agreed, too. Ela was probably bribing him for something. It was all related to the throne, and it was all Jona needed
to know to not ask any more questions about it.

This fellow was coming into the Pens. It had something to do
with Ela. It had something to do with kings. Nicola would want
to know that.

Calipari eyed his men at roll call. Tripoli looked hung over, bad.
Calipari pointed at Tripoli. Calipari pointed at Jona. "You two,"
said Calipari, "A city engineer wants some king's men today.
Dry season. Road work, and canals time."

"What took them so long to get down here?" said Jona.

Tripoli coughed. His face was sick white. He tried talking
again, but he kept coughing. Then he sneezed, and that cleared
his throat. "What they need us for?" said Tripoli.

Calipari shrugged. "Search me if I know," he said, "but be
good boys and do what you're told. I don't want to hear about
any problems or you'll be scrivening for a week at half pay.
Something's going on. I don't know what. I want to keep the
streets safe, regardless."

Calipari grabbed the senior scrivener—a fellow called Pup on
account of how his tongue stuck out when he was thinking.
Calipari strapped a sword to the boy's back. Pup jumped to walk

about with the Sergeant. He waved at the other scriveners, and the rest of the scriveners bit their thumbs at Pup.

Tripoli and Jona waited for the engineer in the street.

Tripoli yawned and coughed at the same time, and it sounded like an animal choking. He laughed. "I don't know what we drank last night," he said.

"We were drinking from one of those hoses, Tripoli, and I drank you into the gutter, too."

"Sounds about right," said Tripoli, "Hangovers are Elishta itself, sometimes."

"Don't blame me, you can't take the juice."

The Chief Engineer's carriage turned down the road. Black horses with golden headdresses high-stepped down the street. The side of the carriage had the hammer and the snake of the city engineers.

Only one engineer had a carriage.

Tripoli stood up fast, and straightened his uniform. Jona kept his slouch. Jona sat down in the doorway. "Relax," said Jona.

Tripoli whistled at Jona. "That's the Chief Engineer."

"I know," said Jona. Jona faked a yawn. "He's a good fellow."

"You met him before, Lord Joni?"

"Naw, but I know him. He's no noble. I can boss him around easy. Why you think Calipari volunteers me on him. Relax."

Tripoli ignored Jona. Tripoli stood with a straight back, and watched the carriage with large, black horses coming down the avenue.

The Chief Engineer's carriage crawled to a stop in front of the guard post. Tripoli reached for the handle of the door. Tripoli pulled it open like a coachman.

"Thanks," said Jona, to Tripoli. Jona jumped through the door.

Inside, Jona had to let his eyes adjust to the dark. He held still in silence, blinking his eyes until he could see.

Then, Jona saw the man inside. The man had leaned back,

surprised by Jona.

"Hello, Chief!" said Jona. Jona shoved his hand into the old man's face. "We've met here or there, but I don't think we've been formally proper about it. I'm Lord Joni, Corporal Jona Lord Joni. Nice ride you brought us."

The Chief Engineer was a tall, thin man. He looked like he had more bones than muscle. His white hair, rakishly swooped around a saggy, loose face. His lips pursed to hide an amused grin. He was trying to be serious.

He took Jona's hand, shook politely, and gestured to the street. "The pleasure is all mine. Mishle Leva, Keeper of the Keys and the Chief Engineer of the city. Please, meet me outside, Corporal."

Jona stepped back outside, beside Tripoli.

The Chief Engineer peeled himself from the carriage seats. He planted his cane on the ground before he stuck his feet out. "And who else is working with us, today?" asked the Chief.

Tripoli threw up onto his boots.

"Don't mind Corporal Tripoli," said Jona, "He's a little sick. That's why he got stuck with us."

"How come you got stuck with us, Lord Joni?" said the Chief.

Jona laughed. "I volunteered, Chief," said Jona, "I hate to see Lady Sabachthani's friends down here with just him for protection."

The Chief nodded.

The Chief pulled a large, lumpy sack from the inside of the carriage. He reached inside, and rummaged through rolls of blueprints.

The smaller of the two coachmen jumped down from the high carriage seat. He pulled a strange contraption from a side compartment of the carriage. This device was an odd mass of springs and slats, like a large, crushed cricket. The couchman strapped the device across his shoulders like a backpack. He adjusted a spring. Large boards opened like wings. From his belt, two hinged rods pushed the board out and up into a drafting table. All the fellow had to do was stand still. The Chief spread the blueprints onto his walking desk. Little springs and teeth held the paper against the wind. The servant held ink in one hand and a series of quills in his pocket. He dipped a quill in ink, and handed it back over his shoulder to the Chief.

The Chief took the quill. His hands moved over the blueprint. He scribbled furiously. His old knees trembled, but his hands were musician still.

Tripoli cocked his head at the contraption. "Don't show that to Calipari or the scriveners'll never forgive us."

The Chief nodded his head. "I'll keep that in mind," he said. He didn't look up from his sketching.

Jona walked around to the blueprint. He peered over the Chief's shoulder. He recognized the sewer but he pretended that he didn't. "Where do you want us to take you?" said Jona.

The Chief Engineer pointed at a juncture in the lines and numbers. The Chief's finger paused as if Jona would say something. Jona didn't say anything.

"We'll be closing off… none of the streets have names here, do they? Can't afford street names… Well, we're going to dig a small canal out of some old sewer lines," said the Chief. "We'll make an island out of all that slaughterhouse nonsense and animal storage, to promote the cleanliness of the Pens District. Butchers'll have to take their meat directly onto the canals instead of the streets."

Jona snorted. "This district'll never be clean. You and the rest wouldn't set one suede boot down here." He looked down to Tripoli's boots, covered in regurgitated meat and bread. "Can't say I blame you, either."

Tripoli scraped his boots one at a time against the carriage wheel to clean them off. "Shit Island's better than Shit District, I guess, but it won't keep the streets clean for long. Not as long as there's horse shit and dry season."

The engineer gestured quickly to one of his servants. The man gently pulled Tripoli away from the carriage wheel. Tripoli nodded, and looked down at his boots, shamed.

The Chief Engineer kept scribbling on his blueprints. "St. Lorraina Island, actually. She's the patron of butchers, and all blessings to Imam's flock for donating this name. Shit Island is where most of the fullers work, north of town. That's what I call it, anyway. You ever been there?"

"No," said Jona.

"Avoid it if you can," said the Chief. "Makes this place smell like a rose."

"I'll keep that in mind," said Jona.

"I can't just wall off the fullers with a canal. They're up in the country past the wall, working along the beachheads. Ever been to the beaches?"

"Can't say I've been anywhere, Chief," said Jona.

"Well, the only place worth going in the whole city is Sabach-thani's estate. Nothing else is worth the trouble."

Jona nodded.

# CHAPTER V

A maid drank too much in a tavern near the eastern wall. She thought Jona was a suitor sent by her father to spare her the horror of work. Jona walked in, saw her eyes light up, and sat down. If her suitor was coming, he'd have trouble finding her with another king's man in front of her. She asked Jona if her father had sent him, and Jona said yes because she was dressed like a maid. She had blue eyes, pale as daylight, and she never seemed to smile. She drank and she told everything Jona asked about everything, drinking and drinking on Jona's coin until she could barely keep here blue eyes open. She told Jona about Mishle Levi.

The chief engineer, Mishle Levi, had a weekly meeting with the king, which had become pure ceremony.

The chief engineer poured the king's tea, helped the king drink his tea, and talked about the king's sons as if the boys were still alive. The chief forged the king's signature on anything he needed. He sent them to Lord Sabachthani, and if it came back, it was approved.

Every branch of service was like that. The Captain of the Guard answered to no one, not even Sabachthani, just clearing his budget with the tax officials. The generals trained their men in seclusion in the forests, while noblemen vied for the loyalty of the soldiers. The bureaucrats moved papers from one end of the city to the other, collecting stamps and coins and stamps and coins, passing the coins up into an unknown aether somewhere above their heads.

Foreign nations sent envoys to Lord Sabachthani. Nobles roamed unchecked in the streets, with no authority to pressure away their foolish intrigues.

✠

Tripoli's hands shook when he walked. The Chief pointed at Tripoli's hands and Jona shrugged. Jona made the universal gesture of drinking alcohol. Jona took the hook off Tripoli's back and carried both of the hooks for the grates, one on each shoulder.

Tripoli clambered down the steel ladders into the darkness carrying the knotted measuring rope to the bottom of the sewer. He had to stick his hand into the lowest point of the sewer. His arm emerged brown to the shoulder after the grate at the bottom of a hill.

After that sewer, he was coughing and choking and trying to crack a joke about what he had just done. He acted like he was about to throw an arm around Jona. Jona kicked Tripoli in the shin, and jumped away. Tripoli laughed, waving his filthy arm at the people walking past. They pulled away from Tripoli, some shouting curses to raise the dead.

Then, Tripoli walked hurriedly—no explanation—away from the men. Tripoli stepped into this alley between two larger pens full of cattle. He ducked behind a pile of bones and bloody papers. He threw his pants down to his ankles. He aimed at the fence.

Jona winced at the sounds—like a bucket dumping water

from a high window.

Tripoli coughed and cursed.

Pedestrians—rowdies and gangers, all of them—shouted encouragement.

"You can do it! Don't give up!"

"Breathe! You'll get it out!"

"Be sure to name her after your ma!"

Tripoli shouted at the people to toss off. He cursed Imam and Erin. He cursed his mother, his father. He cursed his own name, then his wicked ways. Tripoli's voice cracked in a raw scream. Tripoli fell over, clawing at the ground.

The engineers who had been trying not to look couldn't help it, now. Tripoli clawed at the ground. His face looked like dying. His mouth gasped like dying.

And he was dying.

Jona ran to him.

Tripoli flopped in this puddle. A pool of pink blood collected around his ankles. His intestines, blown inside out, twitched in a purple shit blood stew from his body.

Jona cried out for help.

Tripoli clutched at Jona's leg, gasping for air and bleeding. Wet shit and purple blood spurted out of the bloody funnels that hung out of Tripoli's body like sausages being aborted.

Jona tried to hold Tripoli. Jona tried to pick Tripoli up and hold him, and hold him still so he wouldn't bleed so much.

Then Tripoli was very still....

Mishle Levi, the Chief City Engineer of Dogsland, pulled Jona away.

The Chief tried to light fire to the body with anything he could find. "That's strong as demon fever," said the Chief, "Typhoid, and bad. Worse than plague, that strong."

Jona's stomach turned. It was because of him. "He must have picked it up from that girl we found, the nun," said Jona, his stomach turning thinking about every time he and Tripoli had handed a flask between them.

The Chief patted Jona's back. "Maybe. Jona, you'd better burn that uniform tonight and bathe alone. Go find a temple and see if you can get some holy water or something to bathe in. We all will soon as we can."

One of the journeyman engineers produced a small keg of kerosene. He poured it all over the ruined body. Jona didn't watch them burn the worst of the stain away. The mess burned like wood, but it was meat and it shouldn't have burned like that. What remained, blackened and unrecognizable, was still whole, still human. That's what a demon stain can do to a man, a real man, if there's too much of it inside of him.

The Chief sent for Sergeant Calipari, and pulled Jona away from the alley.

Jona's hands shook. His eyes were closed. He was thinking about all the times he and his fellows had handed a flask between them, and how many times someone had gotten a little sick but not really gotten sick enough to matter.

And now Tripoli's blown inside out, and burned on the street like a rabid dog.

✠

Jona and Rachel were taking a break from dancing, and Jona was sweating, and Rachel was using her Senta winds to wick the sweat off her body before it started to pool in her clothes, melt them faster than they would otherwise melt from her demon stain. She hated how she smelled when she was sweating, like she could smell the clothes burning a little.

Then the song changed, and they both needed a drink, and they went to the penny pot. One penny down, and they could drink as much as they could from this big rubber hose without stopping for air. Before they got drunk, they didn't take the hose because they didn't want to make anyone sick. After they got drunk, they figured everyone drinking at the hose was already drinking themselves sick, so why not drink at the hose?

Rachel went first, and got enough down to make her eyes water. Jona didn't drink much right then. He was trying to keep his head together.

Jona tried to tell her she was beautiful.

She smacked his arm. She told him to cut that out.

"Why?" said Jona.

"I just want you to, okay."

"Something else, then. Did you hear the criers? Big ship went down in the bay. Foul play suspected."

"I didn't hear anything," she said, "What happened?"

Jona flung another penny at the barman, and handed the tube to Rachel. She listened while she drank.

Jona looked past the bar, to the water far beyond the smoky room. "This big ship was coming in loaded down with all kinds of fancy wood. Somebody started a fire. Whole thing down in the bay, and everyone on board a dead man. King's men in the Low Sticks were pulling bodies out of the water all morning. The sailors wouldn't go down with the ship. They jumped— most of them on fire—right into the water, but they couldn't swim far all burned up like that. No one was going to risk getting close to a burning ship, so nobody saved them."

Rachel choked, and shoved the tube spilling cheap alcohol at the barman. She wiped her sleeve over her arm, and gasped for air. She said, breathless, "No one got out?"

Jona smiled, sadly. "No," he said, "It was fast. Spread real quick. She must've been covered in something. Looks juiced, you know, but the ship never even anchored in the bay. Ship's owned by foreigners. We checked up on the sailors a bit, and the people who were expecting some nice wood. Didn't find a thing."

"That's it? You just ask a few questions and all these sailors died?"

"People die all the time for nothing," said Jona, "So, I'd rather talk about how beautiful you are, okay?"

Rachel threw another penny down, and shoved the rubber hose at Jona's face. "Only if we're red drunk," she said, "Red, red drunk!"

Jona bit the hose with his teeth. "You're beautiful," he mumbled.

⊗

Tripoli's folks came in from vineyards in the north hills. Tripoli's father built casks for new wine. When Tripoli's father got to town, he already had a casket for his son's ashy remains, hand-made from solid oak, and far bigger than the blackened bones needed.

The Lieutenant got some of the other districts to cover the Pens, so all of Calipari's boys could attend the service.

Tripoli's parents were Imam's folks. An Imam Priest preached of paradise, and ashes to ashes, water to water, and bliss. Each soul that fell away from the flesh returned again to life, un-til the lessons of immortality taught the paradox of the Break-ing, where the heavens tore to pieces while the earth remained whole.

(Rachel frowned when Jona told her that. "The false break-ing," she said, correcting him.)

Jona stared at the casket. Jona wondered if his soul would be reborn among the demons, deep below the skin of the earth, over and over, until he understood the true power of evil.

Tripoli's father led the cart with his son down to the water. His wife, wailing beside him, didn't exist to that old man. His jaw—he looked just like Tripoli, too—clamped like a steel trap against the grief. He stared off to where the water dropped be-low the horizon.

The casket shoved off from the funeral dock near the temple. The priest lit the arrowhead on fire. The priest drew his bow, aimed up, and loosed the arrow. The shot arced like riding an invisible rainbow. The arrow smacked the casket on the first shot. The arrow trembled. The casket rocked. The fire crawled down the arrowhead like falling down a mast. Then, the deck of the casket burned all over the top, and then down to the center of Tripoli's ashen body.

Jona glanced at the priest. The priest couldn't hide his satisfaction with the shot. Usually took priests a few to get a hit, and sometimes they couldn't hit it at all, and the casket just rolled away into the water.

Jona frowned at that. People shouldn't look proud now.

Tripoli's landlord never showed his face for the ceremony, or in the flat afterwards. After what happened to the furniture, no one had expected him to show his face.

Thieves had already stolen everything inside the apartment.

Landlords liked how fast sneak thieves worked. A word here or there with the local toughs, and a room unlocked in the dark, and the room's ready to rent again in hours.

Tripoli's parents didn't seem to mind.

Everybody had brought some kind of food, and Calipari put his coat on the ground, so they'd have somewhere to spread the food out, like a picnic. People ate, but nobody talked. Tripoli's folks didn't know these city toughs and these city toughs didn't want to really talk about Tripoli in front of his parents. They all just ate.

The dingy yellow walls echoed every little sound. Jona was afraid to eat too loud. He didn't want to be heard.

After the food was gone, everybody went into the street. The old man walked through the king's men, shaking hands and thanking the boys for looking out for Tripoli when he was alive.

Then, the old woman leaned on her husband's shoulder. She reached up to old man's stony face.

And that got him.

The man, standing by the funeral dock, crumpled into his wife's arms like they were holding each other up now, but neither one should have been standing at all because both were broken.

Jona turned away. He thought about how beautiful Rachel was by candlelight. He thought about how it couldn't have been his fault because Tripoli had gotten a little sick now and then, but never this sick.

But it was Jona's fault.

The boys were drinking hard for four nights and tossing any street toughs hard. Word spread fast that king's men were in a black mood. The district was dead quiet.

Private Pup became Corporal Pup.

A new private showed up a few days later, fresh from the guard posts along the southern frontier and ecstatic to be back in Dogsland. Two days scrivening, and he wasn't ecstatic anymore.

Three weeks later, Jona looked around the station house at morning muster, waiting for the graveyard crew to cut back and report out. Everybody was there, laughing and up for a kick except for Tripoli.

Jona couldn't, for the life of him, imagine what it was like to have Tripoli there instead of Pup. Black tears swelled in Jona's gut thinking about that. Jona clamped the tears down until the urge passed.

His tears were poison, after all.

Chief Engineer Mishle Leva didn't stop on the day that Tripoli died. Jona had to take over the sewer diving while a kid from an alley was paid to get the Sergeant. Another kid stood over the smoldering body to keep the ragpickers off the toxic corpse.

The rain was gone for such a short window, and no time could be spared over just one death. Jona understood that. (In his mind, he thought about how the Night King might want the Chief Engineer killed.)

Underground in his first sewer dive, tired men looked up at Jona from pallets spread on the damp ground. They didn't say anything. The light slanted down from the open grate onto the shriveled heads and the men there looked like bones in burlap.

Jona tossed them a few coins. "Things are changing, soon, fellows. Find somewhere new."

One of the men picked up the coins from the ground. This fellow used both hands to hold the coins up, one at a time, like touching something holy. He passed the coins, one at a time, back to the other men.

The men collected their things quietly. They walked into the dark.

Jona called up to the engineers for the measuring line. He held it down to the bottom of the sewer, and felt the rope tugged taut from above.

❈

Workmen came the day after Tripoli's funeral.

The Chief Engineer, in his wisdom, had designed heavier equipment that sneak thieves couldn't carry alone, and nobody could fence easy. Two strong men, each holding half a forked handle, slammed huge picks into the stones. Two strong men pulled the mud into iron wheelbarrows with giant shovels.

They sang while they worked, and the streets filled with the weary baritones of the birth of the new canal.

Shopgirls spun their own singsong into the songs of the workmen.

*Fresh-faced girl with the restless palms*

*I've got apples in my palms*
*Tossed me off for all I own*
*Fresh flowers for the lady left at home*
*Now I work all day and night long*
*Apples fresh as the dawn*
*Because my girl gave me a son*
*Sweet corn here, hot as the sun*

Jona stood on the roof in the morning light, waiting for his uniform to dry. He watched the men with their giant equipment and their tiny, shirtless bodies, a few blocks away over the rooftops. He listened to the songs from the street. Somebody had a drum and beat the rhythm for the digging men.

And Jona listened, his uniforms like flags on the line drying in the sea breeze.

# CHAPTER VI

The ragmen's kids picked through the trash. The ragmen made cheap paper from the ragpickers' recovered trash. This paper, the ragmen sold to the temples and businessmen of the district. The temples and businessmen used the ragman's paper as receipts and cheap scratch paper. The receipts, the items bought, and the notepaper fell back into the trash piles on the street. The ragmen's kids recovered the fibers and brought them to the ragmen.

The forest has the cycle of leaves. The city has the cycle of paper.

I write this down, to remind my husband and me to see this world as it is, to help us search with Erin's guidance and understanding.

The ragpickers tell us what they know of the dead. They are too afraid of my husband because he is a man, with steel grey hair, and a body as hard as a wolf's. I must go with him to search it out, give them apples and dried figs.

Salvatore is missing from these pages, but maybe he will be found if I pass through them all. I see into the way of the streets, and the men who lived among them. I smell their blood spilling, and pouring from their ruined skin.

He wakes with the night fall. He keeps nothing in his room but his hammock. His tools are hidden in the street stones, loose bricks, and sewers of the city. He is immortal, and must be killed. He has lived too long. His mind can't hold the memories of his moments. He is patterns and shapes of a man. He loves until it is no longer easy, then he cannot remember her name for long, for she is gone from his mind.

Take a piece of paper, and write upon it seven times, along the same lines. Write again and again, for centuries. In time, the paper is destroyed. The ink remains, carrying the shape of the letters in the strokes, but only where so many brushstrokes have moved.

To seduce a lonely woman in the night, to find a way to use her hands for thievery, to take something innocent and bend it away until it is lost.

Aggie waits in her cell for him. All he has to do is show up and she will walk away with him, out of the prison and into life. She won't leave without Salvatore. She won't believe in anything but death without him.

And she is dead. He never came for her.

I write this down because I wish for her soul to know that my husband and I will come for Salvatore. We will come for him, and there will be peace for her, in his death. I write down my wish because I feel it, and in writing what I feel, I can move beyond it, to other felt things inside the memories.

We search the streets where a weed rules even the king's men, who would rather push out new gangs than fight the old ones. No one can stop it, and no matter what the Captain of the Guard says, it's better to have demon weed quietly than to beat it back to the ships in a pool of blood, for it only to return and return and return. Would that my husband and I could find the fields of the flowers, and burn them to the ground. Even then, the men on the streets would pay for it.

There are women who carry mattresses on their backs. They run after the ships that are coming in to port. They shout for the men to pay them for a trip into an alley. All they have to do is lean back, with the dirty mattress to catch their fall.

Ragpickers run after them, shout names at them and throw rocks and bricks at the mattresses. When they're older, they'll know a few by name. Probably, they'll find a few of them dead coughing, bleeding from the lungs, with the pink blood and fluid seeping out of their pores that eats their skin from the inside out. Pink mattresses from the blood, and black from the mud.

People will buy anything they want. It cannot be stopped.

The trees of our woodlands wait. They do not mind the axes of the farmers, for the farmers will fall down and feed the roots of trees. The roofs will fall. The wolves will return to rule the streets, and eat the dogs that remain to gnaw on the festering corpses of their masters.

And Salvatore, who would live longer than this city, a festering wound among the night streets, pouring his loneliness upon the loneliest girls of the city, must be laid low.

All things must die. Everything must die.

Rachel, I'm sorry.

Rachel never told Jona about the whistles of the ragpickers, and Calipari never bothered with the origin of them, either.

The whistles were a good idea, so they needed no explanation. One boy had a whistle, and blew it to call his friends for help. It worked. Everyone else acquired their own whistles. Soon, the streets were alive with whistles converging like king's man bells.

In the official city reports about this little street gang, the whistles were what first got the guards' attention. Suddenly, every ragpicking mudskipper had a whistle, and suddenly they were using them to fight back in packs against grown men.

The real smugglers—the big fellows that could arrange a meeting with the Night King—figured it was a front for something else. None of them believed the kids could be in the real business without leadership.

Calipari was getting tips from all over about the three men who ran an unaffiliated den in quick bursts, moving all over as soon as they thought someone might be looking for them. They never used the same room two nights in a row.

But, the kids were in the real business.

There wasn't a leader. There was just money. The ragpickers swarmed over someone, ripped his weed from his pockets, and sold it to Turco. The only leader was hunger. Street kids didn't make enough money to sleep off the street. If they wanted to eat, they had to steal.

This blighted place needed orphanages. It needed schools and farms and parks.

Dogsland, I smell your ruin on the wind. The patterns and weights of this city carve away at the foundations, until all towers will crumble, all rich men will flee or die.

✦

Rachel never knew the origin of the gang's name to tell it to Jona. Neither did Sergeant Calipari. Neither did Salvatore. No one knew but Turco, Djoss, and Dog. Turco's dead. Dog is as good as dead. And Djoss is one whom we seek, either dead or alive.

If you seek to know the source, than find Djoss alive and ask him. We seek him out for answers about demons, like Salvatore and Rachel. We do not concern ourselves with the etymologies of street gangs. I know what I can see and smell and know from the memories of Jona. I see with my eyes into his world, and see what I see, know what I know.

✦

Jona heard it said, while walking around his streets on the Night King's business, looking for a fellow that needed a knife in his back. Jona heard it from an alley. He peeked around, and Turco was there with a ragman against a wall, a knife against the ragman's cheek.

Turco said it. "You and your mudskippers helping us? We're the Three Kings of Dogsland. We got our signs all over."

And Jona kept walking because he was on the Night King's business.

Three Kings was a simple gang, for simple folk.

✦

I'm in this alley, sniffing out the stink of Salvatore's paths, dropping holy water wherever the mud collects an evil strength. Maybe Salvatore pissed behind this particular crate when he was alive. Maybe Salvatore lost blood there.

Smell Salvatore in the dirt, pour the holy water in a ring around the stink. Burn the center with good kerosene.

In front of me is a tribal scrawl in faded black. The Three Kings' crowns stare back. I touch the ink, and think about Dog.

Djoss tried to get Dog to stop painting crowns, because Djoss knew the fastest way to lose turf is to claim it. Dog grunted. Dog kept stealing ink or paint and putting crowns up everywhere he went. He used his thumb if he couldn't find a rag or a stick.

Turco didn't seem to care either way, because the money was good.

✦

Djoss came back with decent food from a different district that didn't carry the stink of the Pens. Rachel was in bed, looking up at her brother with all this food.

"Hey," she said.

Djoss didn't look at her right away, busy hiding food in the cupboards. "Don't say anything," he said.

"I didn't."

Djoss turned around, with a loaf of bread in his hands that was so fresh it was still steaming. "It's like this," said Djoss, "Only way to protect yourself from the bigger dogs is to be one."

He handed her the hot loaf of bread.

Rachel passed the hot bread from one hand to the other. "Or, not to be a dog at all. Be careful, Djoss," said Rachel. She was talking about the hot bread in her hands. "We should leave the city."

"You see something I don't?" Djoss reached down to the loaf. He tore off a piece of the bread. He shoved it into his mouth, steaming hot. Crumbs fell all on her bed.

"Sometimes I do," said Rachel.

Djoss shoved the rest of the bread into his mouth. "What do you see?" Crumbs spilled down his shirt when he talked, like snow from his scruffy beard. He needed a shave, a haircut, clean clothes. Instead, he had bought food.

"I don't know what it means," said Rachel, "and I don't think you'd stop even if I told you what I saw. You like the money. You like being important to those kids." She stared at crumbs like snow falling all over him, and all over the floor.

"If you know something, or think something I need to know…?"

"Djoss, I see lots of women dying all around me," said Rachel, "these women I work with are always dying. I hope none of them are really visions of us hiding behind the skin of foolish bliss."

"Where would we go if we left here? How would we get out?"

"I don't know, Djoss. I don't want to leave the city. I like it here, too. I have… I have friends here. A friend here. I can be alone in a crowded room with him. I can move with the whores

among the different houses whenever I think someone is looking too close. I wish you had safer work."

"It's safe as anything. Safe as walking down that street. Kids
are running in packs like dogs. Mudskippers get teeth, now."

✦

*It's not safe. What he's doing is dangerous, Jona. But, what else can
we do?*

*I got nothing for him. He could go birdie on his crew. A few coin
in that, and he's out forever.*

*No. Never that. They'd kill him. Anyone would kill him.*

Rachel stitched a gash shut along her brother's back. She didn't
want to talk about the injury. She asked about what caused the
injury, instead. "Where does this stuff come from, anyway?

"Stevedores get it from the crates. Mudskippers lift it. We're
secondhand thieves. First, the stevedores and killing floor cut-
ters are lifting their cut of the stuff out of the meat. Mudskippers are after them. They got whistles, now. Hard to stop a
whole bunch of them. They don't have Turco's connections to
do anything with it. We buy it, and we can set it up somewhere
with a pipe. Turco has a pipe. Or Dog. I don't know. I watch the
door. They come and they pay and all I have to do is watch."

Rachel poured hot wine over the wound. Djoss gasped.

"I knew that already," she said. "It's a weed, right?"

"That's what they call it," said Djoss.

"So, where does it come from? What kind of plant is this, and
where does it come from?"

"I don't know," said Djoss. "It comes from the stevedores,"
said Djoss. "They drop it off. I cut it into smaller packages. We
give it to the mudskippers and the ragmen. Who cares where it
comes from? All we have to know is where it's going."

Rachel keeps this thought she reserved for Jona, when they
curled together, briefly, in the morning light. *But where is Turco
going, Djoss?* A creature stepped off the ships one day, and the

world behind him remained as mysterious as the weed that fed his desires.

The Unity ignored Turco's past, for his death. She looked at him sometimes, and she saw no hands, and no feet. She saw his legs moving, and his arms moving, but the man was like a ghost to her, floating through the air, unable to touch the world where he moved. Hands are the things that make a man. Hands are what helps him control his world. Without hands, without feet, just a hunger on the street, grinding down and going nowhere.

When Turco spoke, she couldn't hear anything from his lips but a gust of wind that blew in from the water and left as empty as it came.

❈

My hand touched a large cobblestone.

I looked around me at the road signs and the doors. I knew exactly where I was, in a flash of borrowed memories. There, the zig-zag path to the animal pits. There, the tobacco shop. That way, the red brick ruin of the old brewery. Six steps backwards and I was in the Pens District's new canal, that had made this awful place an island. Six steps forward and old wheel-ruts from dozens of carriages that had stopped in this field of mud remained like statues until the rain melted the old ruts away in new mud.

My husband asked me why I had stopped.

I told him that I stood where Jona had killed the Chief Engineer.

# CHAPTER VII

Jona was on his own with a sword on his belt in case of trouble. He was supposed to watch the killing floor door to see if anybody came out without blood all over them. Nobody came off the abattoir clean unless they were dirty.

Calipari had Jona doing this, looking for the smugglers the same way the mudskippers looked for them.

In the distance, Jona heard the sound of a scrivener running closer. Street vendors in the distance shouted out to a king's man, "Hello, king's man! Hello!" Jona heard the king's man shouting back, but didn't recognize the voice. The voice was winded. This king's man was running. Jona looked down the road to the sound of the vendors shouting.

The private's stomach bounced when he ran. He looked like a taller, heavier version of Geek without the muscle hidden under his flesh.

"Sergeant made you run, didn't he?" said Jona.

The Private planted his hands on his knees. He gasped for air.

He nodded.

"Those street rats shouting hello at you?" said Jona. "Next time any fellow says hello to you like that, punch him in the face hard as you can. Don't care if it's your own mother."

"What?" said the Private.

"They're doing that to warn people you're coming," said Jona.

The Private looked down at his boots. He pulled a cloth from his pocket and padded sweat off his face. His other hand pulled out a note for Jona.

Jona held the note gingerly because it was sweaty, too. He read the note—the ink all bled from sweat like a printed mumble from Calipari's clean hand. Calipari told Jona to head to Station 12. Jona scratched his head. "What's your name, private?"

"Sir?"

"Your name."

"Kessleri, sir."

"Private Kessleri, you know where Station 12 is?"

"Yes, sir."

"How far away is it?"

"Far, sir. It's north and east. Bunch of merchant homes. A few good markets. My brother lives around there."

"Did Calipari tell you why we're going up there?"

"We, sir?"

"Yup. Did he tell you why we're going up there?"

"No, sir. I have other duties, Corporal."

"Then we'd better hop a cart. How much coin you got?"

"Not much."

"I got a bit."

Jona jumped into the street at a meatcart. He threw his hands up at the driver. "Hey, driver!" shouted Jona, "Where you headed?"

The driver reigned in his horses. He tightened his grip and scowled. The driver was about as old as Kessleri, but the driver was small as a child. He didn't look like he'd keep his bench in a strong breeze. "You king's men?" said the driver.

"Yeah, but all we want's a ride if you're heading the right way. No trouble and no peeking where you don't want us. Where're you headed?"

"You tell me where you're headed," said the driver.

Jona laughed. He glanced sideways at Kessleri and nodded encouragement. *Go on, Private.*

Kessleri curled his lip. "Don't work that way," he said. Kessleri put a palm on his pocket to push out a hard round thing like he was carrying a blackjack there. Jona knew that Kessleri was bluffing. It was probably a bottle of ink.

The driver nodded. "I'm heading north," he said, "I've got to make the far wall by sundown and stop a few times by and by."

Kessleri laughed. "North and which way," he said.

"What?"

Kessleri pointed out the three directions with the hand that wasn't holding his imaginary blackjack. "North and east, north and west, or north and north?"

The driver shook his head. "I don't know. Look, just get on, king's men. We're wasting time. I'll take you north a ways, and you can steal another ride when you know which way I'm headed."

Kessleri nodded at Jona. Jona hopped on after Kessleri. Jona sat on one side of the driver, and Kessleri sat on the other.

The driver snorted. "Safest cart in the Pens," he said, barely under his breath.

❧

After the ferry, the driver turned to the west. Kessleri and Jona gestured at the driver to slow down, and they jumped off. Kessleri pointed to the western road. "We can head this way a bit. We're close."

"I thought you said the place was far," said Jona.

"Yeah, and we went far, didn't we?" said Kessleri, "Look, we're almost there. We just need to head west towards the second wall."

"We should've walked," said Jona.

Kessleri shrugged.

Jona walked through the door and saluted the sergeant. "Corporal Lord Joni, and Private Kessleri" said Jona, "We're here from the Pens. Calipari didn't tell me anything."

The sergeant pointed over his shoulder at the cells. "Somebody show these Pens boys our little prize," he shouted. The scriveners ignored the order, and kept their heads down over their papers. "Mopper," said the sergeant, "Take the Corporal to the cell."

A skinny private with a harelip stood up. He looked like he was always grinning with that harelip, but his eyes were pissed.

Kessleri looked at Jona like the Kessleri didn't know what was going on. Jona gave away nothing. Jona stared Mopper down.

Mopper, with the harelip, handed Jona a key. He pointed back to the last cell in the station. "We got your smuggler, Umberti, carrying enough pinks to cheese-for-brains three bulls and redroots, too. We wanted to roll him to the noose. Apparently Sergeant Calipari wants him, first. Now, I hear he won't pay for his crimes on account of some other fellow you're after."

"What'd he do to you?" said Kessleri.

Mopper shrugged. "He's ours. We don't come to the Pens looking after trouble. Why you come to us to get yours?"

Jona raised a hand. "It ain't about us. It's Geek's thing. You know Geek, right? Calipari wants one of us to get stripes before he retires. Geek's gotta put something together big enough to take over the station in a couple months. If it wasn't for that, Umberti'd be yours."

Mopper spit through the hole in his face. "This one started something he couldn't finish, and now we watch him walk?"

Jona nodded. "We'll finish with him quick," said Jona, "You see him again and he's yours."

"Like we need your permission," said Mopper.

Jona gestured with his head at Kessleri. Jona walked past

Mopper, and Kessleri followed.

Umberti, his face all black and blue, looked up from his cell.

"What'd you do?" said Jona.

Umberti coughed. He didn't say anything.

"We're taking you to the Pens, Umberti. My boy Geek wants to talk to you. Maybe you talk right, and you don't come back here." Jona opened the cell. He pulled a rope from his back pocket and bound Umberti. The rope didn't seem necessary. Umberti's leg was swollen up, and he could barely walk.

"I'll tell you what you want to know," said Umberti, "Just don't hit me again."

Jona laughed. "The man you're singing to is Corporal Geek. Don't even whisper a thing to us. I don't even care enough to hear it. Me and my boy, we're just mules, like you."

"There's two of them. A Dunnlander and another fellow. A big fellow. Mudskippers blowing whistles and they all came for me. Took me down, stole what I was carrying. I go back to the Pens, I'm a dead man."

That's how Djoss and his crew are getting away with it. The mules they hit are too scared to go anywhere, tell anyone. They lose their shipment, and if they're still alive, they run.

"Umberti, I don't know what delusions you living with, but you're a dead man here, and faster, too."

Out in the street, Jona made Kessleri carry Umberti like a porter with a sack of potatoes. Kessleri gasped for air and walked slow. Umberti just closed his eyes. He mumbled under his breath like he was praying to Imam.

Jona knew Sergeant Calipari would appreciate making Kessleri exert himself. The private had been scrivening too long. The three had to stop on the way back a dozen times, to let Kessleri catch his breath. Umberti said nothing. He looked at the ground with pain on his face like a bleeding pig. Eventually, Jona got impatient, and stole the services of another cart headed south.

Kessleri asked Jona what was going to happen to Umberti.

Jona looked at Kessleri sideways because the private ought to know already. "Geek's going to find Turco and his friend," said Jona, slowly, "and he's going to put the two into the two different rooms next to each other. First one to sing lives."

"Umberti's ready to sing?"

"He's just dead meat walking. He's nothing. He's a payoff to keep the real power off the mudskippers. We're throwing him to the wolves. Stuff you never see written in a report, Kessleri. You're late on the real work. And fat. I bet Calipari transfers you back out to signal fires on the outposts. I would, if I were him. Look at you."

Kessleri didn't say anything in his own defense. He stank of sweat. When the king's men returned to the Pens station with their prize, Kessleri collapsed into his scrivening chair like he was falling into a hole.

Calipari looked at Jona knowingly and pointed with his eyes at Kessleri. Jona shook his head at his Sergeant. *This private's no good.* The old soldier nodded. Jona went back out to where he was standing before he had to pull Umberti. The rest of the day he stood there, watching blood-stained men walk in and out of the killing floor.

Most days it was like that.

At shift change, Geek invited Jona and Kessleri to the Pits to celebrate the new bird with some bear-baiting. Kessleri said he was too tired to move.

Calipari pointed at Kessleri, and spoke loud so everyone in the district could here. "He keeps on like that, he'll never be more than a scrivener. Geek, you're going to have to do something with him when you're running the place."

Geek scoffed. "I'll transfer him back to signal fires," said Geek, just as loud. "Soft fellow'll leave and we'll get someone else tough enough to roll all the pinkers and drunks."

🐾

Jona was at a bear-baiting at a pit under a bridge. The giant black bear had six chains bound to two metal collars holding her in the ring. She could stand up, turn around, and move a few feet. The chains came off anchors from old ships and had a sheen of rust on them, but they were solid enough to keep the bears from charging the crowd. This bear was starved and angry and standing up on her hind legs and swiping at the air.

People behind her threw bits of trash at her. The bear spat white foam when she roared. Her voice cracked.

They probably had been boozing her up. She probably hadn't had a drink of plain water in days, and was so dehydrated she couldn't think straight.

The dogs were in a wicker cage at the edge of the pit, just as hungry and wild.

The dogs—three giant wolfhounds as big as small ponies and vicious—busted loose of the wicker and bolted around the perimeter of the pit. They circled the chained bear. They barked like they were the kings of the pits.

Jona had bet for the bear, and he already knew he was losing this bet with the drunk, weak bear and the ready dogs. Jona walked around the back of the crowd to go to the man selling bottles of warm gin from crates. The gin tasted like vinegar, camphor, and piss more than it tasted like gin, but it fuzzed a fellow's head just fine.

Jona paid for his bottle. Before he could open the bottle, a small stone smacked his back from the better seats above the rabble on the killing floor.

Jona looked up and the Chief Engineer was up there, sitting next to a veiled woman. (Jona recognized Lady Sabachthani even with the veil, but he didn't dare acknowledge her, even in his mind, lest his tongue slip while drunk.) The Chief leaned over the railing. He handed Jona a gold-embossed flask of expensive brandy. He spoke a greeting, but no one could hear anything over the crowd. *My Lord Joni,* said the Chief's mouth.

Jona smiled and shouted *Thanks*, as loud as he could. Jona handed his own piss gin from the cheap barrels up to the Chief. The Chief nodded his gratitude. He popped the top of the bottle and raised the piss gin in a toast. The Chief poured the gin down his throat like a man in a desert. Jona couldn't drink the piss gin without flinching, and the Chief did it like it was water.

The veiled noblewoman laughed.

When Jona turned back, one of the dogs had a broken back, and had fallen under the feet of the bear, whimpering and bloody and trying to crawl away with the one leg that was still working.

Jona threw the flask's liquid back so he didn't have to watch. People cheered.

One of the dogs got right up into the bear's jugular—latched onto the bear and didn't let go. The third dog was up on the bear's back, chomping and clawing on her shoulders. The bear's claws were awful, tearing at the dog at the throat, but the dead dog's teeth never let go. Jona looked away.

Men cheered. Men cursed. Men threw their tickets down. Men held their tickets up. Jona handed the flask to Geek. Geek didn't look at what he was drinking by now. He just drank as much as he could as fast as he could. Geek passed it to the guy next to him, some nameless lump of uniform—the scrivener, Kessleri or Pup or anyone at all.

The flask went to the next guy after that, and on through the crowd, and if the Chief wanted his flask back, he'd have to buy it from a fence.

Jona looked back to the match in the pit. The bear was almost dead by now. The dead dog's teeth had locked into her throat. The bear couldn't roar. She collapsed to all four feet.

The dog on her back, who had merely survived, was the victor.

Jona looked back at the Chief in the good seats, but the Chief was gone. The flask was gone, too. The only thing that made

Jona sure the Chief had been there at all was the warm aftertaste of good brandy.

Pugilists jumped into the pit and helped roll the dead bear and the dead dogs to the edge where two fat women in aprons were going to cut away the flesh of the three dead creatures and roast the meat on the spot over big cans full of hot coals.

Jona had already eaten. He looked the pugilists up and down. Ugly men with cauliflower ears threw red drunk words at each other. They were older than Calipari. Their best fights were long behind them.

Jona didn't have any more money to bet. Jona waved at a drunk Geek. Geek didn't see. Jona pushed through the crowd, crossed a field of carriages, and climbed up a small hill to get back to the streets.

It hadn't rained in three days. The summer sun was still up in the sky, right at the edge of the western skyline.

Jona passed three sailors speaking gibberish. He thought about hustling them for a bribe. He turned back, but all three had disappeared into the crowd.

(*The thing about living in this city, Rachel, is that a fellow has to walk like they're going somewhere, even when they don't know where they're going or else they'll look like a mark or like trouble and everyone will see them there, and wonder about them.*

*That may be true for men, Jona, but women linger and gossip and watch the faces in the crowd for lost boys, lost lovers, and all the men that are always walking like they're going somewhere.*

*Well, your brother had better keep his boots on in the street, else he might get a lasso around his neck. Troublesome folk are getting braver with their ropes these days.*)

Jona started walking.

A knot twisted in Jona's stomach when he thought about the flask disappearing into the crowd.

Tripoli had died of demon fever. People got sick all the time.

Rachel ran a rag down Jona's face. Little bits of blood had splattered across his face, but he hadn't noticed until she had wiped the blood away. She didn't ask about the blood. He didn't volunteer anything.

They both knew it was human.

Rachel and Jona sat in a booth drinking red tea while the sun rose behind them. She sat against the wall, and tried hard to protect her head's absent shadow from the slanting light. She was going to be late going home, and she didn't want to move about in the slanting morning light. She wanted to wait until the sun rose enough to push the shadows into puddles underfoot, and hers would just be the wad of her clothes in the crowd. They were drinking red tea, and waiting. Jona had to go to muster, soon, but he didn't care if he was late.

He pushed muster from his mind. He leaned towards Rachel's demure smile. "How do you and him get by anyway?" said Jona, "I just don't get how you can get by like that, traveling everywhere."

She smiled. "Oh, the best we can," she said, "We work. We live."

"You're sharp as daylight, and you ain't even grinding the whores?"

"When they don't ask questions, they don't look close. Sometimes, they don't look at all. They just tell me what to do, and they pay me for doing it. People like us don't get many choices. Djoss can barely read, and I can't really work during the day. I'm not so good at prophecy, so I can't read the cards well enough unless the fellow's too drunk to care what I say. So, that's my life. It's the only one I got and I just have to bloom where I land."

He stroked her face with his hand.

"I could be dead tomorrow," she said, "Someone tells your fellows on me and I can't bounce fast enough? I'm dead."

"I promise I won't roll you," he said. He leaned across the

table. He placed his face upon her hand, and he kissed her just above her wrist.

He put down his tea and brought her hand up to his nose. He breathed in her hand's smell of smoke and old bleach. He pressed his nose into her skin and tried to fill himself with that smell.

She looked at him like he was cheese-for-brains. Gingerly, her other hand touched the small hairs at the base of his skull. She traced those tiny hairs and wondered if this particular of-demon was crazy, or just sweet.

Jona pulled his head up from the table. He frowned. "I guess," he said. His eyes looked past her at the street. "I guess I have to go to work," he said.

She nodded. She waved.

❈

Jona met Rachel on her night off for lunch. Outside, rain fell in steady waves upon the parasols as if it were still early summer, and Jona and Rachel stopped to eat at this cafe because neither had a parasol, and they didn't want to walk through all that rain to the place they both knew down the road.

This café was narrow, with tables along one wall, and the owner walked up and down with a huge teapot shaped like a swamp bear bleeding red tea from a punctured paw. The owner saw Jona's City Guard uniform and perked up.

Jona pointed at one of the tables. The owner nodded. Jona waited for Rachel to sit down. He wanted her to notice his courtly manners. He gestured at the teapot, and the owner handed it to him. The owner placed a cup on the table.

"What's this?" said Rachel.

Jona popped his heels like a Lord's servant. He bowed, and poured a cup. "Milady's tea," he said. He smiled gracefully.

She cocked her head. "What's this, then?"

Jona dropped the charade. "Haven't you ever had dinner with nobility before?"

"No," she said.

"Well, you'd best be ready," said Jona, "One of these days, I'll take you to a grand ball, and you'll have to be prepared for fine manners." He poured a cup of tea for himself.

"I'm not going to any grand ball," she said, "and you look like a fellow going to get tossed."

Jona shared a quick glance with the proprietor. Jona winked at the old man, and the old man nodded.

The old man praised Rachel's beauty. She blushed.

Jona slipped the old man some coins, and sat down across from Rachel. The old man continued to praise her beauty until Jona waved the old man away.

Rachel covered her eyes. "I think my ears are burning," she said.

"I think he likes you," said Jona.

Rachel looked over Jona's shoulder at the rain falling. Outside all this rain fell on the hats and the parasols and thunder crashed and lightning slapped white fingers across the sky.

Jona tried to catch her eyes. He looked right at her—really looked at her. Her face was ashamed of his eyes. Her face spun around the room like a dancer spinning around Jona's warm spotlight, never stepping into this steady light.

She smiled at his eyes, still trying to escape them. She had crooked teeth, and Jona figured the teeth suited her face fine.

Who was Jona talking, to? Was it Rachel? Was it Pup? A man in a bar, asking Jona about the job of a king's man—some upholsterer in an aura of lost thread, leaning into his empty mug, sneering at Jona?

Jona said this to all of them.

"Take a pig," said Jona, moving his hands as if a dead pig was lying bare upon an examiner's table in front of him, "Pig's all parts. Nothing but parts." A hand touches the imaginary nose, the imaginary spleen, the imaginary everything. "These parts go to the sausage man, these parts to the good butchers all over the town, and that part goes to the soap and tabor man, and this part goes to the glue man, and these other parts go to the tanners and knife-makers and all that." He cut apart the pig with the edge of his hand, partitioning portions across the imaginary table.

"These parts go everywhere but Elishta. Since gangers are everywhere, you can't send anything anywhere in this town without guarding it, right? So a fellow hires armed guards, and calls himself a legitimate business."

Jona leaned in close, squinting a skeptical eye. "Remember how those parts go all over town?" he said, "Parts stink coming in, and stink going out. Nobody looks twice on account of the stink. So, if you're running pinks or you're a fence, you love the sight of that stinking, grunting bag of parts, right?"

Jona leaned back, away from the examining table in front of him. He points with his thumb here and there. "We got plenty of gangs in the Pens, but they just don't mark themselves like they do everywhere else, see? Most of the time, they're legitimate businessmen in the business of parts. We got our share of fences at the edges, but most of what we got is the demon weed. Pink smoke flowing through these streets like you wouldn't believe. Stop five people in the street, two of them are smuggling, two of them are using, and the last one's too scared to say a thing over it. Smugglers have guards that'll kill you surer than a street gang'll roll you for a coin. Smugglers don't just club a fellow. They'll drop a baby straight into the water like nothing.

"Any stupid gangers slip into the Pens and start trouble with smugglers, we club 'em out quick. We club gangers out, and we probably save their worthless little lives. Then, we go after the smart smugglers. We watch books. We watch carts. We watch parts. We negotiate with 'em."

He held his hands up, offering his imaginary pig to the people who heard him speak. "See?"

"I don't see anything," said Rachel. "All I see is my brother, and his friends, and they're gone all the time. Sometimes Djoss comes home bloody."

# CHAPTER VIII

*You should get out of these kinds of places. Stay off the streets a while, if you can.*

*Think I'll end up like one of the hot corn girls? I'm Senta. I can see their fate. I don't choose that for myself. I couldn't even if I wanted to.*

*That's not what I mean. I mean, try to keep off the streets a while. Something is… It's getting strange out there. Getting raw and wrong. New people trying to come up rowdy. Workmen are coming to tear up the streets, build new canals. Who knows what'll happen when the roads change, and everyone's angry about it. Not good for anyone foreign times like that.*

*Not good for you, either. You should get out of it. Marry rich. Be a lord.*

*Yeah. My mother says that.*

*I don't think you should marry anybody. I don't think you and I should ever marry anyone at all. I was just being spiteful.*

*You only get sold once when you get married. It's cleaner that way.*

A young girl—I'll call her Jess, because Rachel never knew her name—was not earning enough to pay for her room. She was too slow with them. They didn't come back for her like they were supposed to do. The owner of the building went up to Jess in her room with a new girl in tow. The owner—I shall call him nothing at all—handed Jess a bucket of hot corn. He told the girl to walk about and sing out the corn songs a while. Maybe she'd find enough young men to fill a room again.

Rachel pushed a rag from one side of the room to the other, an invisible observer like all maids. In the street, Jess came up to Rachel, and offered her some corn for free. "Just go in and give it to the cat. See if he'll eat it. Don't let him starve."

"I'm working," said Rachel. She lined sheets up along a wall. She pulled down sheets that hadn't had time to dry. "Don't steal any of these sheets. We'd know it was you."

"Please…"

"He counts the corn at the end of the night. You know he does. He counts the coin and the corn."

"He's helpless without me." Rouge cracked in river deltas beneath her tears. Polluted make-up streams stained her yellow shift.

"There are as many cats as there are women in this city. Maybe more."

"Don't you care about anyone? Please, help me."

And Rachel heard Jess crying in her head all night.

A new girl came to work in the room, and the cat was still in it. The cat hid from the new girl in Jess' old room behind a crack in the wall and yowled for Jess to come and throw this strange girl out of the cat's bed. This new girl clapped her hands over her ears, and then pulled powder out from her bag of make-up. She doused a piece of old food in the powder and threw it into the wall for the cat to eat.

Later that night, Rachel had to pull the dead cat from a crack in the wall with a long broom handle.

Rachel threw the dead cat over the wall, where the rain would come to wash the body into the sewers.

With Jess crying somewhere about her lost cat—selling hot corn among the thugs and night bruisers, paying for anything stolen—Rachel figured that the powder had done exactly what it had been made to do. The powder had killed a working girl's baby.

She never went back to that establishment. Somewhere new, always a place that needed cleaning, and Turco had long since turned a blind eye to Rachel's work. He wasn't coming around and demanding a cut like before.

Night came and there was no end to the beds in the city, and the whorehouses strung together in a chain of forgotten buildings, sheets, and the smell of them, like a swamp full of rosewater.

❈

*I want you to know who my brother is, if you see him in a crowd. He's not worth making trouble over, if you run into him. He's a good man, trying to make money for me.*

*Your brother should stay out of the demon weed.*

*He should. He won't, though. Look, just leave him alone, okay?*

Djoss was cooking when Rachel came home. He was leaning over a pot, stirring. He looked tired. She touched his shoulder. He leaned back, into a cot. He fumbled in his pockets for some money, but there wasn't any. He said, "I'm doing better. I barely touch the stuff."

"I wish you were around more often."

"I'm around, just not when you're here."

"How's Turco doing?"

"I don't know if he sleeps. I've never seen him sleep. The weed wakes him up. It gives him this huge energy. He runs all over the city to tell people where we are. I think he gives all his money to the mudskippers. Looks like he does, anyway."

"You making good money?"

"Yeah," he said. "Got rent paid. Got food. How're your clothes?"

"Not good."

"We can go get some. I can go get some tonight."

"Okay," she said. She sat down on her cot and looked up at him. He had lost weight since coming to Dogsland, and regained it in his shoulders and back. He was dressed like a local. His clothes had the sweat-stain lines, the blood stains and pink splashes as if he stepped off the killing floor where they cut and grind the meat. He had the tan of a local, no longer a pale man from the north.

"I was thinking," he said. His hand started shaking when he spoke. "I was thinking maybe we should get our coin together, and put this place behind us."

"Why?"

"Because... I don't know. We've been here almost a year. It doesn't seem right, does it?"

"I know."

"We should go."

"We will. Just, not yet."

He nodded. "The weed is something else, isn't it? I mean it really gets in your head."

"Yeah. So you need to cut it out."

"Or leave. We could go somewhere new, and I wouldn't know where it was or how to find it. Maybe it wouldn't be there at all."

"No one's found out about me. We've been here for months and we haven't had to run. No one is paying attention to us. Djoss, maybe you should start bouncing again. Maybe you should get out of it."

"We'd have to leave this place. Go somewhere cheaper."

"Yeah, but that's nothing."

"Let me think about it, then. Let me just think about it."

"I'm working at a new place again. I'm way out on the water. I have to take a ferry to work. People there're almost respectable."

"Show me."

"Tomorrow. You know you're going to leave before I do."

She was meeting Jona later. She couldn't show him anything.

❊

Rachel saw a familiar face running from a mob of little sharks—a kid's gang that claimed most of the boys on the street.

In the poor streets, this girl that we called Jess once hauled muddy rags on her back in heaps, like a hump. Rachel caught the girl's eye but she didn't look long and soon they passed each other.

When the ships unloaded their sailors, these women ran to the dock and pinched their cheeks red to look healthier, happier. They took any kind of coin you had, and not much of them. They slipped into alleys and fell back, their humpbacks like cheap mattresses. They pulled their skirts up.

Men ran past the cheap girls with ragbacks while the girls ran for the new ships—owners hate free girls—with spikes and small clubs up their sleeves. The girls ran fast with their rag bed humps always on their backs. That's why they wore them.

Jess had children chasing after her—a kid gang screaming at her humpback. They threw rocks at it.

The hump back girls stank worse than the alleys they slept in.

And these girls liked to dream back to their younger days, at the best brothels in town, wrapped in silk and flattery.

Then, the silks wore down to linens and then wools, and the men were workers with the smells of their profession—printers drenched in acrid ink, fruitmen like sweet rot, and bakers in a cloud of musty flour. Now, the sailors rolled off the ships to these used-up girls with beds on their backs for the first furious rounds of shore leave.

Sometimes the smarter girls saw the shape of their destiny and saved their coins, opened their own brothels or married an older client whose wife had passed.

The ones who married usually found themselves back on the street, when their husband passed, and the rest of the family threw her out of her own home over a few coins left in no one's name and the judication that should have saved her was bribed to throw her out.

Rachel never told the women of her brothel about their future, no matter how often they asked. Sometimes Rachel lied, if she needed the money. Sometimes, she focused on the bright spots in the black night.

She didn't like to think about her brother's future, but she knew it, too.

Inside of herself, she wondered if there was anything she could do about it. She pushed her mop, and hung the clean sheets to dry. She threw out the trash. She focused on the Unity. She dreamed of Jona....

The hot corn girl, back in from the streets with a bed and men paying for her, asked Rachel for help. The words didn't register right away. Rachel was mopping. The mop moved from one side to another. She didn't look up. The night was almost done, and then Rachel'd go home.

The girl, Jess, touched Rachel's shoulder. "Hey," she said, "Hey, Senta, can you help me?"

"What?" said Rachel.

Jess had a speculum in one hand, and a small hook in the other. "You know what this is, right? Maids and Senta do this. I'll pay you for it. Please?"

Rachel took the speculum in one hand, not knowing precisely what Jess meant. Then, Rachel saw the hook and thought for a moment about what the two together could be used to do to a working girl, and how Rachel had seen these before, all bloody.

Rachel frowned. "I don't want trouble," she said.

"Maybe you know somebody?"

"Don't *you?*"

"I've never…" Jess looked down at it. "I'm sorry. I thought you would. Everyone said to ask the maid. Ask a Senta. Ask someone."

"I don't do that. I don't want any trouble. I don't want anything."

Two days later, Jess was gone. Rachel didn't need dreamcasting to know what had happened.

# CHAPTER IX

This is how they did it in the beginning, before the kids were really involved. The mudskippers saw this, though. They saw and they told us and it sounded true to the minds inside of my head, mine and Jona's.

Turco pointed out the guy walking around like he was somebody out of his element. Turco gestured at Dog. Dog nodded. Dog had a leather rope in his pocket, and Djoss sat on the corner and watched for guards.

People walking past that knew a thing about the Pens didn't stop. Hat brims stayed low. Parasols angled out the view. This fellow in Senta leathers looked like he had a big red "A" on account of the way his stomach spilled over his waist like an apron. His belt lashed over the wrong part of the shirt, with a triangle in the center like a target. He had a big black beard that bobbed while he walked, side-to-side. Beard and stomach swayed in each heavy step. The Senta wiped his brow with a clean, white handkerchief.

Djoss raised his hand. *All clear!*

The Senta didn't see it coming.

Dog flipped the leather rope around the man's throat. Turco flanked the huge outsider, pushing him into an alley with a dagger pressed into the triangle in the victim's belly. Did the Senta live or die? Did it matter after his clothes were gone?

Djoss didn't watch. He didn't want to know. He walked away.

At the last stop, Djoss met up with Dog and Turco, and poured the money on the ground in front of Turco and Dog. The clothes were there, too, for Rachel.

Djoss got a closer look at Turco's palms when Turco counted out the money between the three of them. His sweat was actually a thin sheen of blood, pink like demon weed. Djoss blinked.

Turco sneered. "What? You look like you thought of something."

"I did but it's nothing," he said, "I just noticed something."

"What?"

"You've got blood on your hands, and it's coming out of your fingernails."

"Yeah," said Turco, "It's mostly mine."

Then, the three went to a tavern to dance at the tavern where Djoss was bouncing because Djoss slipped Turco and Dog in free of charge.

⁂

Rachel walked to work in the dark. She dragged ragged sheets across the line. She pushed a mop from one side of the room to another. She poured the filthy water into a sewer grate. She filled the bucket from a pump in the yard. She poured chamber pots into a large slop bucket, and mopped out the pots. She hung the two large slop buckets from two ends of an old broomstick. She dumped the buckets into the same sewer grate.

She walked home alone, undisturbed. She fell asleep in silence.

Through the building walls and windows, a woman yelled at

her children. Elsewhere, the sound of skin slapping skin pre-
ceded loud howls of animal bliss—nothing else to do in the
long, slow days without any money. In another room, a woman
had died, and her family was mourning her and people came
and went to offer condolences and food. Women were wailing
there, too, as loud as lovers.

Rachel closed her eyes, and fought hard to find her brother in
between the lines of the koans.

She cleared her mind with breathing.

*Since none can look into the sun's light, none can see the sun's
darkness.*

She held it in her mind.

*Since all can gaze in peace upon the moon, all can see the moon's
shining light.*

She drifted into a light doze, when time faded still, but the
sounds of the city lingered at the lambent edge of her dreamless
mind. Women talked, and children sang out games and laughter
and men walking to work or walking home singing hellos and
good-byes and a key—Djoss is home—jangling in the lock.

Djoss shoved the door open. He ran to her bedside, and
grabbed her arms. "Hey, Rachel!"

She groaned.

"Are you okay?" he said.

She cringed out of his hands. "I'm fine," she said, "I'm sleeping. Are you okay?"

"I heard a few Sentas got rolled," said Djoss, "It's all over the
city."

"Well, it wasn't me."

"Turco seems to think there's a Senta that's really a demon
child. There's this demon child that's going to burn for stealing some dog, and everyone's saying her accomplice is wearing
Senta leathers to hide."

Rachel fell back in her bed. "Well, I don't know anything
about that. We're not leaving," she said, "The rumor will pass.

No one's been looking at me twice. The king's men couldn't care less about you and me. I haven't seen Sparrow or her little thugs anywhere, and I don't think they can put two and two together about anything."

"I've seen those little thugs. They don't even talk about it. They couldn't care less. Just be careful, okay?"

"I'll be careful," she said. She touched her brother's nose. "You be careful, too," she said, "You're walking a bad way and don't think I don't know it."

"I'm careful," said Djoss, "I'm always careful. We have to get ready to run. Need coin for that."

❦

Jona rowed, and Rachel ran her hands through the lake. She couldn't really see herself in the rippling reflection, only her clothes, and pieces of her face like a ghost's mangled shadow. She hadn't seen herself in a mirror in a long time. "What do I look like, Jona?"

"What?" said Jona.

"What does my face look like? Am I beautiful?"

"You're beautiful."

"You always say that. How beautiful? Who do I look like to you?"

"You don't look like anyone I know. You're just you."

"Well, if you see someone who looks like me, let me know. I don't know what I look like."

"I will if I can," said Jona.

When the boat reached the edge of the construction, Jona pulled into the construction site where they had borrowed the boat. The site's night watchman waved at Jona. Jona thanked him for the boat and pressed a coin into the man's palm.

The watchman handed Jona a black feather. "Oh," said Jona, "Hey, Rachel? I have to go. Can you get home by yourself?"

"What's wrong?"

"Nothing. This is from someone I know. I have to go help him."

"Okay," she said. She frowned. She cocked her head. This had never happened to them before. "Who?" she said.

"I got my birdies and my brothers. Sometimes they need my help, is all. Dead men don't face king's justice, you know?"

"What?"

He frowned. "This feather's a cry for help. I've got to go help. I can't really explain who it is, okay?"

"Okay," said Rachel, "Be safe. I hope your friend is safe."

"It'll be fine," said Jona, "I just have to go fast."

He walked away confidently, holding the feather in his hands. He felt the streetlights and the passing sailors envelope him in anonymity. In a big city, a fellow could walk three blocks away from his usual places and suddenly no one knew his name, and no one remembered. Crowded cities are the only place to be a no one in a uniform. Jona turned and waved at Rachel back at the street. She blew him a kiss. He smiled at her, nodding.

He turned a corner, and turned away from Rachel. His shoulders clenched. His smile thinned into a sick sliver.

He went to a tiny tavern that took up three rowdy floors south of the Pens district. The sign was as big as the door. A giant blackbird perched on a painted minaret.

He gave the feather to one of the bouncers. The bouncer took Jona up to this fourth floor that didn't officially exist. A door opened.

Two men stood on either side of a man in Senta robes, holding him there, waiting for Jona.

The Senta had his eyes closed. He was breathing in, holding his breath, and then releasing gently with a hiss, like air leaking out of a punctured ball.

Jona stepped into the room. The door closed behind him.

"Go on," said one of the two men. "Show him what you are." Jona looked up at the fellow in the Senta leathers. He wasn't big.

In the light, his little body and little head looked like a skull, all forehead, cheekbone, and jaw.

This fellow handed Jona a little dagger.

The Senta closed his eyes. "Does the wind move," he said, "Or is it just the flag hung up in the wind? Neither really move. Motion is only the mind moving."

"Can you truly see your own demise?" asked Jona.

"Yes," said the Senta.

"How do you die, then?" said Jona, "Tell me what you see in your dreamcasting."

"I see only my mind moving," said the Senta. "I don't understand why I am here. I've done nothing."

"I don't understand it, either. I just do what I'm told. I don't ask questions. Tell me something, though, if you had to guess, what was it?"

"A demon child," he said. "I saw one with a woman. I saw them, and I tried to warn her. I tried to tell somebody."

"I see," said Jona. "What he look like? Anything like me?"

"No," said the Senta. "He was thin and pale. He was... Don't people care that the demon children are here?"

"How did you know what he was?"

"I... I just know. Dreamcasting is like that. It's a feeling I get, and I see things."

"See anything about me."

"I'm too scared to do it."

"Try."

The Senta was crying. "Please don't hurt me. I can't see anything in you. I can't concentrate when I'm this frightened."

Jona cut his own palm, not very deep, along the same healed line that he had used when he had condemned Aggie. He grabbed the Senta's ear, and shoved the prisoner's skull sideways. Blood dripped, burning like acid, into the Senta's head, exposing the skull beneath the skin.

The Senta screamed.

"I'm sorry about this," said Jona. "Believe it or not, I don't want to kill you."

The Senta didn't seem to hear anything. Jona watched his own blood burning down the side of the man's face. He watched the skin boil and singe with the demon blood, and the clothing burn where the blood ran. Jona pressed his hand into the Senta's eyes. They melted like ice cubes in the acid.

Jona watched it. He wrapped his hand in strips of the Senta's leather. He sat and watched.

The Senta stopped screaming long enough to vomit. His skin kept burning away. His blood and bone boiled with the acid. The side of the Senta's face caved in like a boiling watermelon.

Jona closed his eyes. He jammed the knife into the Senta's heart. He kicked the Senta, with his chair back to a trapdoor near the wall that opened to the old canal.

※

"What do you mean, a grudge?" said Rachel, touching Jona's bandaged palm with another question on her face.

Jona shrugged. He pulled his hand away. "Oh," he said, "I mean that people kill each other sometimes, when they get mad at them, and we catch them doing it, and they're never smart about it, and they confess right away because they did it when they were angry and can't believe they did it and telling us about it and dooming themselves is like healing them."

She touched the knife in Jona's belt. "You ever kill anyone?"

"I'm a king's man, a city guard, so I have to kill sometimes. They aren't good people, though. I kill killers, and worse."

"What's worse, children of demons?"

"No," said Jona, "I've seen a poor man spend his last coin on a single puff of the pinks, when he was supposed to be work-ing, and his whole family is on the street with nothing to eat, and nothing to do but start stealing, so then I have to arrest the thieves who were only trying to steal to eat, and maybe they stole enough to hang."

"That's horrible."

"So, when we find the smugglers, we push 'em. We do everything we can to break 'em. Then, we hang 'em high, and we put their heads on pikes along the city walls and harbors."

"That's just horrible," she said.

"It's important," he said. He stopped and let the little boat drift a minute. "You know, when you're talking about something that hurts one person, it's not so big. Lots of people get hurt, you know, and you can't stop it all. But, when something hurts lots of people and makes them hurt people, too, then you're talking about something big."

Rachel sighed. She leaned back and stared at the night sky overhead. Out in the middle of the lake, a few strong stars poked through the clouds and the lights. She recognized a constellation.

# CHAPTER X

I remember Jona's friends and fellow guardsmen falling away. Corporal Jaime's eldest daughter died. He paid the Erin priests all his savings to inter her under a picture of her because he thought she was so beautiful—so pure. He cried on duty, slipping into alleys and empty cells.

None of the other guards said anything about him crying like that.

Three weeks after the funeral, Jaime was still a mess.

Then, Jaime's wife hung herself.

Jaime disappeared a while. When he came back, his younger kids were all living with his wife's family. Just him and his eldest boy remained in this old house that had grown new echoes.

He sold the rope she had used to hang herself to a crazy old woman that probably imagined herself like Lord Sabachthani. He used most of the money to buy his eldest son an apprenticeship with a stone-mason in the Temple districts on the east river, and the boy never came home again.

Jaime had a few coins left and this house that had been in his family forever, all empty now. He blew all of the coins on a single bottle of foreign whiskey.

He brought the whiskey in to the guards to share, but not even the scriveners wanted to touch a drop of suicide-rope whiskey. So, Jaime sat in an empty cell alone and drank it all, singing rowdy songs, and screaming, and singing sad songs, and crying out his daughter's name which was the same as his wife's name. *Dacha... Oh, Dacha!*

He was still there in the morning. Calipari sent him home without pay. Calipari told Jaime to get his head right and then come back when he was ready.

Three days later Jaime came back like nothing had happened, and he wouldn't let anyone talk about it. He smiled and pushed the boys around and he was ready to walk the streets.

Two weeks ago, he had a wife, and four kids.

Aggie was not showing signs of pregnancy. The Captain was impatient, and her death was imminent.

Jona had forged a letter.

She read the letter, and cried. She crumpled it up in her palm. She threw it at Jona just like she threw words at Jona.

"How do I know this is real? How do I know it's really him? I don't believe you, king's man. I can't believe you. Why won't he come to me? Tell me why he doesn't come for me!"

Jona stroked her cheek. "He'll come when he can," said Jona, "Sneaking into a prison is not for a thief. He'll come when he's leaving with you. Until then, eat something."

"I don't want to eat! I want Salvatore!"

Jona clutched the wailing girl to his chest. He stroked her hair. He didn't try to speak. He didn't know what to say. He let her cry, and he looked over at the food he had brought her and the flies that swarmed upon the bread. He hated that Aggie wouldn't eat first. He hated seeing those flies eating her food in tiny crumbs, planting maggots in the meat.

He held the girl close.

❈

Jona stopped on his way out of the prison. He handed a bunch of tea-stained letters to the carpenter that had sent Jona off on so many killing jobs. He set up shop at the gates to catch the prison workers coming and going out the main gate. Some of the tea stains had flecks of blood. Some of them, just drops of ink.

The carpenter scanned the letters quickly. Jona watched the merchant's eyes light up. He pulled Jona into a back room.

"You know what this says?" said the carpenter. He had these tiny glasses on his eyes wrapped in cloth to hold them together. They were far too small for his huge face. He read slowly.

"I wrote it, didn't I?" said Jona. "I copied it out of Calipari's papers."

Jona had been looking for any sign that Calipari was investigating the Night King. He found nothing. He had planted another document into the pile of papers, with news of a Senta killed, and bodies tumbling into the water, for no reason. He found rumors that Mishle and Ela Sabachthani were checking the laws to see if he could be king despite being a commoner. In this, Jona saw a life for Aggie.

"We don't like Mishle," said the carpenter.

"I'll do what I have to do," said Jona. "I'm hoping for a different kind of payment."

"Commoner's shouldn't try to be the king, you know," said the merchant, "Ain't right."

"He's a good man," said Jona. "I want something good in exchange.

"He's not *our* man."

"Give me Aggie. I'm doing right. I'm earning my keep, ain't I?

I killed that Senta for you."

"We'll arrange Mishle for you quick. Keeping an eye out for our interests is smart. Maybe the Night King'll give you a pretty little prize for your sharp eyes. Maybe."

"If Ela doesn't go for the Chief, she's going to be married to Elitrean's son, right?"

"Rumors say so, even if she hates the boy. We can rumor them together, make it look good. He's our boy. He's better for us."

"I guess he would be."

"The Chief is impossible. He's owned by the lords, not by us."

"He is impossible. No commoner should be king while a lord like me is nothing but a blood monkey. You can always count on me. I don't think Sabachthani'll be the queen. Sabachthani's too smart to want the throne. She's smart enough to know where power really is."

"Yeah? Where's that?"

"This city is built on mud. You and me, and all the people like us. We're the mud. We're holding everything up and wiggling around, pushing things up out of the mud and pulling 'em back down again. Night King is the power of the mud."

"You're mud. You're not even that. You're bloody Elishta. Don't be getting any ideas. You don't deserve to be alive, and don't you forget it."

The carpenter looked down at Jona's papers like staring into a fire. "We got mud, but we got something else. We got the King, and the Night King. Everyone in between the kings got nothing."

Jona took out his knife. "We'll see how the Chief feels about mud like us when I gut him like a hog."

"I'll send a boy for you," he said. "This might be dirty. We didn't expect this. We don't have a plan in place."

"I'm ready when you're ready," said Jona.

"Good lad," said the carpenter. "And all you want is that girl, Aggie? Never pegged you for the type to want another demon's used up whores."

Jona felt no anger, anymore. He felt nothing. All he felt was tired. He wondered what it was about killing people that made him want to sit in a dark room, by himself, and never come out.

✦

*Do you want to go to one?*

*What? Of course not.*

*Why not?*

*They'd kill me!*

*They'll bounce you. But, they won't bounce you with me around. I'm the one who introduces you, so I'm the one they'd be shaming if they bounce you.*

*Then I don't want to shame you. Why do you want me to go to one of these horrible things, anyway?*

*I just think it might be fun, you know. You love to dance. We'll go, and you can dance with men who dance for a living. It might be fun.*

*It might get me killed.*

*Aren't even a little curious? We'll go, and just watch.*

*What do you mean, just watch?*

*We'll hang out in the trees and we'll be in the shadows, and I'll pretend like I snuck you back there for a tryst and no one would stop us, and we could just hang out forever and watch and listen.*

*I don't know. Maybe.*

✦

Jona slipped a coin into the palm of a coachman, with a little note. The coachman slipped the note into his pocket. He pointed up to the wall next to his couch.

Jona led Rachel to the back of the couch. "Climb up," he said.

She looked at him like he was crazy.

He jumped up to the back bumper of the carriage, clinging

to the golden luggage rack on top with one hand. He held his other hand out to her.

She frowned. She took his palm, and let him pull her up to the bumper. He planted a boot on the wheel just beside him. The carriage lurched and pulled back, but he was able to pull himself all the way to the top. Rachel didn't try that. She held up her hand. "Pull me up," she said.

He took her wrist in both hands. He leaned back, and tugged her up to the top.

The coachman shouted. "Best be quiet up there, else someone'll see."

Jona rolled his eyes. "Thanks for the warning," he said.

From where they sat, they had a good vantage point on the garden beyond the wall. Two musicians played a stringed instrument that sounded like a peacock's mournful wail. One man pushed down black and white keys, plucking long strings of a harp. The other man gently pulled the bow across the strings. The pitches bent and warped at the edges. Below them, dresses as delicate as Fabergé eggs twisted in a painted whirlpool. Luxury vessels pushed to the center in time to the song. The passengers—young women, all, and as pretty as wealth could buy them—hummed along to the music.

Jona looked at Rachel's face. Her jaw hung open. Her eyes were as big as two white moons.

A drum beat kicked into the end of the women's music. The men cheered. They could return to the dance, at last. Jona caught a familiar angle from the corner of his eye. One of the men collected his siren from the clumped center and twirled her into the new song. Jona sucked wind in from his teeth.

*Salvatore.*

A new young woman, with red hair and a laugh like huge splashes of water—she wasn't a noble and she didn't belong here and when she laughed anyone could see that. The young woman and Salvatore spun around the floor for a few measures until

Salvatore danced apart, into the arms of an older woman.

"Something wrong?" said Rachel.

"Nothing," said Jona, "I just remembered something, is all."

"What?"

"See how everyone's dancing?"

"Of course. It's beautiful."

"Well, nobody ever dances with the person they really want to dance with. You never dance with the person you came to the party with, unless you're married."

"That's stupid."

"That's how it is. These only look like fun. But they're work. Two fellows meet for a drink, and negotiate a treaty that opens new ports for new products. Two fellows fight over the same girl, and they dance the night away and in the morning they're too tired to visit again, and they're too late. Her father contracts their wealth away by marrying her off to someone else. Two girls fight for the hand of the richest man, whether they like him or not, so they can live as they like until they die. It's all work."

Jona watched for Salvatore to make his real move. Salvatore slipped a string of pearls off the neck of his dancing partner fast as a hummingbird's wing. Jona wouldn't have seen it if he wasn't watching close for just that.

The red-haired girl with the huge, beautiful laugh approached an older man who wasn't dancing at all.

The girl offered her hand to be kissed. The man scowled like she was a fool. She spoke.

He responded rudely.

The girl smiled. She swayed her hips to the music.

He huffed at her.

She spoke, and poked him in his fat stomach. People around them laughed.

His face lowered to a glare. Red spread up the back of his neck.

Salvatore took the red-haired girl's hand, and swung her into the dance. The necklace Salvatore had stolen passed from his sleeve to her bosom. They parted, with their eyes still locked.

She danced away from him with an adolescent boy looking up at her like he was in love. She was laughing and laughing and sharing long glances with Salvatore over the young boy's head.

The dancers stopped to breathe. Servants with drink trays fanned out through the crowd. The musicians bowed to applause.

Rachel sighed, amazed at how beautiful everything was. She leaned deeper into Jona's arms.

Jona didn't notice. He was thinking about killing Salvatore.

Rachel pecked Jona's cheek.

Jona blinked. He leaned into Rachel's ear. His mind returned to the creature in his arms.

"My mother makes most of those dresses," he whispered, "She doesn't recognize the girls unless she sees them in the dress she made. She never knows who's pretty or who isn't. She just knows whose dress cost more, and who's always sending the dress back to let out a seam. Girls get fat quick if they aren't careful."

"That's a horrible thing to say," said Rachel.

"No," said Jona, "Don't miss my meaning. Not all girls, just these kind. Never missed a meal in their life, and their only work is handing babies to a nurse."

"It's still not very nice, Jona."

"They're not very nice. Only rich. Without the money, they're nasty, lazy, and fat. You're beautiful, and you don't have anyone to buy you pretty."

The music started again, a languorous waltz. The girls in dresses like cotton altars, and the men in their stiff suits spun around and when Jona closed his eyes a little, just to a squint— and he couldn't really see the money hanging off of every limb in silk and gold thread—then the waltzing crowd looked just like the Nameless' dancers underground, bobbing and weaving around. Jona squinted at the crowd, and tried to pretend like he'd open his eyes and be underground.

He had this sudden urge to escape into the darkness, and hurl his body against other bodies, against the giant drums. He wanted to jump and push and dance where dancing hurt. He gritted his teeth. He looked at Rachel's face while she watched the ball.

Rachel was in bliss. She leaned into Jona's shoulder. She sighed into his chest, again.

❦

*How do you get the power of the wind? What do I have to understand for the wind?*

*Power? It's not really power over the wind. It's more like... like a silent sound.*

*Well it looks like you control the winds.*

*I can tell you the koan. A student of the Unity heard of a Senta who could make ribbons dance like ghosts. The student sought out the Senta. The Senta stayed in his hut, and when someone knocked on his door, he always grabbed any visitors quickly by their hair, shouting at them to speak. The first time the student tried to see the master, the master grabbed her and shouted "What is it?!" and before the student could speak, the master threw her into the yard. The second time the student tried to speak, she was thrown further, against some rocks. This bruised her badly along her back. She rubbed her back in pain and tried one more time. She knocked on the door. The master grabbed her and threw her as hard as he could. The student shoved her foot in the doorway before she could be thrown. When the master slammed the door, the student's footbones broke like glass. In that moment of pain, the student understood the master's lesson, and the gasp of pain in her chest swallowed the sound in the air with the wind.*

*Rachel, you know that sounds like nonsense, right?*

*Well, it may sound like nonsense, but when you understand it, it will fill your chest with pain, and the sound will bend to you, too.*

*Pain. I understand pain.*

*You only think you understand pain, Jona.*

❀

Jona's mother stirred the porridge for her breakfast. She hummed to herself while she stirred.

Jona sat drinking tea behind her. His uniforms were all on the roof, drying in the winds. He had washed them last night with the rest of the clothes, mostly naked and standing on the roof with the night breeze running over his sweaty back over the washboard. The uniforms took forever to dry in the wet air. Jona leaned against the chimney, and then he paced over to the uniforms and tested them with his fingers—still wet. He went back to the chimney. He paced.

He snatched the uniform from the line. He pulled it over his body damp.

He went downstairs, where his mother stirred porridge. She daydreamed a little, she hummed a little, and she stirred porridge.

"Hey, Ma," he said, "I'm thinking of grabbing a chicken. Want me to bring back a chicken?"

"Rather you didn't. It's so much trouble to pluck them and gut them," she said. She tested the porridge, and frowned. Too hot. She took it off the fire, and kept stirring. "I'm getting some sausage on the way back from the shop."

"Oh," said Jona, "that stuff's all sawdust and gizzards."

"It's cleaner and easier than chickens."

Jona stood up. He held out his porridge bowl. "Ma, I can afford a chicken now and then," he said. "We don't need to eat shit sausage all the time."

She filled his bowl with the slightly burned porridge. It smelled sour. "Better set the money aside, Jona," she said, "Today we can afford chicken. What about tomorrow?"

"Tomorrow I'll have enough for another chicken. Ma, I'm sick of sausage. We make good money between us. Let's get a real chicken now and then."

"Good money?" she said. "You think we make good money?" She poured the rest of the porridge into a slop bucket. She dumped the slop out the window, into the gutters of the street. She slammed the window shut. She sat down, and picked up her cup of tea. The cup was beautiful, laced with gold.

"At my wedding," she said, "each and every guest had goose liver, and chicken, and fruit from across the sea like sweet jewels. I wore silk and velvet, all of it red with gold thread. And when your father brought me into his home, we rode a carriage through the trees that used to be outside these windows."

She looked out the kitchen window, and a shop girl glanced in the window with her cart of flowers. She gestured to Jona's mother to open the window to buy flowers. Jona's mother glared at the girl.

"Ma," he said, "what's wrong?"

"Stay safe out there, Lord Joni," she said. "You're all I have in this world." She placed the bag with her sewing needles over one shoulder. She walked out the door.

Jona looked at his porridge on the table. He poked at the porridge. It smelled terrible.

🐾

Jona slipped Aggie a bag of coins to keep in her cell.

"Lotta good that does, Corporal," she said. "Let me just hop off to the kiln for a bite, mayhap I get my own meat-pies."

Jona nodded. "Never know when a few coins come in handy, girl. Fellow might turn a blind eye, or encourage another fellow to turn a blind eye. Maybe bring something to you that you won't want to ask me about. Never know when a little bit helps."

"You can't bribe me," said Aggie. "These letters you bring me are all fake. Salvatore's not the kind of man that writes letters."

"I wouldn't know about that," said Jona. "Maybe he don't write them. I don't know where Salvatore gets them."

"Well, they're fake. Salvatore could be here if he wanted to be here. An Anchorite convent was no barrier to him, and a prison has to be easier than a convent."

"The convent was no barrier to you," said Jona. "You're the one who escaped it. Not him."

She covered her eyes with her hands. Tears crept through the cracks in her fingers. "Leave me alone," she whimpered.

"You know folks're going to come and check you out soon," said Jona. He reached out to her hair. He stroked it. "Your belly's not growing. Then, they'll make a decision and everything will happen fast."

She pushed his hand away. "I'm sick of blood pie," she said.

"You want something else?"

She ignored the question. Already her mind had drifted away into the ether of the pinks that she had devoured. "I pray to Imam when you aren't here, Corporal."

Jona listened to her talk, and fade into dreams.

"I pray to understand the perfect love of selflessness with Imam, the fountain of all joy and sorrow. This prison is the whip to purify my love so I may die in peace."

Jona said nothing.

"When I see you, I doubt my god. I turn instead to the heat of pain that keeps my soul locked inside this incarnation of my undying self. I will throw my soul away from Imam to see my love again, Corporal. Bring him to me. I must see Salvatore again."

Jona stood up from the edge of her cot.

He bowed slowly, like a courtier.

He backed out of the cell, and shut the door.

Rachel was waiting in Jona's dining room.

His mother was at work, and Rachel should've been at home, asleep, but she couldn't sleep, so she came to his back door. She knocked on it. He opened it. She said she was having bad dreams.

This was the second time she had been inside of his house.

And he let her in. He was off today, and he was reading an old book of fables he had liked when he was a kid. He was waiting for nightfall, when he was catching a night shift out on the Island district, arranged by the Night King to let him kill an important man.

They sat in the dining room, and he made her a nice lunch, and they drank cheap tea. She poked through his bookshelves and read an old seamstress' guide, unbound, to the dresses of a season long past. He casually picked up the book of fables from his childhood. They read like easy koans with animals. Rachel and Jona talked in bursts.

Pieces of the conversation stick to his head. He said things, but he was only saying anything to keep her talking to him.

She responded as if he really meant what he had said, when he couldn't remember it the moment the words passed his lips.

She said to him, "You don't know what it's like underneath. You've seen my arm, in the dark. You've never seen the rest."

"We're being beautiful fools," he said. "Perfect fools. You're leaving soon. I know it. I know you'll have to leave, and I'll still be here." He was rubbing his thumb over her hand. They were holding hands, and he was rubbing his thumb over her hand. Her gloves were off, and her collar was loose, and her hair was all over her shoulders in a beautiful disaster of clean, dry tangles.

"I am not," she said. "Do you know what happens to a woman? I know what happens to a woman."

"What are we doing? What are we to each other?"

"I don't know."

"I like you."

"I like you, too. I'm going to miss you."

"Then, don't leave."

"It isn't my choice. You should come with me, but I know you won't."

"I can't leave my ma. I can't leave my responsibilities here."

"Right. I'm not really pretty, am I? I mean, not like a real person. I'm a monster."

Jona took a deep breath. He let go of her hand. He stood up. He tugged at his collar. He pulled the uniform jacket off his shoulders. Then he pulled his filthy grey shirt—it was white once—from his back. He stood over her, with just his pants and boots. He turned around. He looked over his shoulder at her.

"See these scars?" he said. Across his shoulder blades, skin had been ripped away in two jagged curves down his whole back, leaving deep, dirty scars.

"It's not the same. Men are supposed to have scars. Djoss has lots of scars. Women are supposed to be pure, and beautiful. And besides, I'm not just talking about a couple scars. I'm talking about…"

"So," said Jona, interrupting her.

She halted. The tone of his voice wasn't pithy. He was trying to lead her somewhere. She knew where. "So… So, what?" she said.

"So show me," he said.

"What?" Her hands trembled.

"Let me see you," he said, again. He put a hand over hers.

"I'm… What?"

"Stand up," he said.

"It's all scales and they make sounds when I move and it's awful."

He touched her cheek with his hand. He pulled her eyes up to his. He let go of her hands to unbuckle her belt.

She dropped her tea cup and tea spilled over the table. They both ignored the tea. "So, you…" she said, "You think you…"

He nodded. He pulled her to her feet from her belt. She couldn't keep her hands on her buttons. She was trembling too much.

He took her hands in his. He helped her hands unbutton the buttons on her jerkin. He looked directly into her eyes. She was gasping for air.

"I've never…"

Then they were kissing. Her lips tasted like purple gold.

She unlashed the laces along her jerkin, and threw it off. The shirt came next, and Djoss saw this woman rising up from her serpent skin. Her breasts were human, enough, but below her nipples thick scales reflected light like obsidian. Above, the line of scales at her nipples, scales splashed, like pockets of freckles up to her neckline.

He touched the scales along her stomach, smooth and hot. He ran his hands up to the human skin at her shoulders.

"I'm ugly," she said.

"You're an eclair," he said. He tugged at her skirt. "A beautiful, delicious eclair." He leaned into her chest.

She leaned back and closed her eyes. "What's an eclair?" she said.

Jona stopped kissing her. He pulled away and looked her in the eyes. "You've never had an eclair?"

"What is it?"

"It's the best dessert in the world," he said, "Soft and sweet and expensive. I'll have to get you one."

"Tomorrow," she said, "Not now." She grabbed him by his hair. She pulled him close.

※

Poor hearts, that never reach true love.

# CHAPTER XI

The carpenter opened crates of marionettes made in the shape of animals. Cows, dogs, pigs, horses, cats, rats, all white wood and bright paints and jointed like insects in the camouflage of mammals.

Jona didn't help. He sat at the table, sipping some brandy. These two men never met each other until the toymaker handed Jona a letter in the middle of the street. Jona read it fast, and nodded. He followed the toymaker to the back of his workshop.

Jona sat down on a counter covered in sawdust, and he waited.

"What's your name, anyway? What should I call you?"

The carpenter said nothing. He made Jona wait until he had a crate open. The carpenter piled wooden marionettes in a heap on the floor. The strings twisted together in a net over the rigid body parts connected by tiny chains. Beneath the marionettes in the crate, pieces of a hookah were hid. The puppets were all just filler to hide the hookah. The carpenter pulled the parts out while he talked. He put the hookah together casually. Underneath the hookah and the marionettes, piles of demon weed lay like giant, pink tea leaves.

"Come on," said Jona. "I don't even know what to call you."

"Yeah? Well, don't call me. I'm almost done. You want to know what this is all about, all that you've done? Here it is. This is the stuff that owns the city. Where it moves, whole communities crumble. Where it is pulled away, strong men make money moving it in. This is the answer to all your questions."

"My only question is who you are."

"I'm this stuff. It's all I am."

The carpenter kicked the marionettes into a fire pit, and put together a hookah and put it over a fire like he was going to use it. He started the fire and said what he said while the water warmed. Jona said nothing.

*Been fixed. Chief Engineer's gotten in over his head, and it's time to blood him. Simple plan, but hard to pull. Jump the coachman after the Chief gets in from the bear-baiting. Drive the carriage to the alley just south of the old brewery, at the edge of the animal pens. You know the one, right? Right. The empty warehouse—the one with the old crane—will be open and waiting. Move fast else the other coachman will know what's going and catch up with you. Shut the doors behind you. Bar them. Slice the horses' throats before they know what's what.*

Jona closed his eyes and nodded. He visualized the furious ride through crowded streets. People jumped out of the way of the carriage, and some people fell under the wheels. Jona'd have to jam a tooth into the bench and hang on for it else the bumps would bounce him. Then, the alley.

Then, the horses. They would jump, and kick, and scream. They would die in moments, with deadly hooves flying.

*Wait for the Chief's boy to pop out.* The people in the carriage will be annoyed at the coachman for the crazy detour, and the younger one will jump out ready to punch the coachman.

*Tooth him in the lungs, so he can't scream.* He'll make that weird sucking noise people make when they got a tooth deep in their lungs, like they're trying to breathe from the hole in their side with all that blood drowning them.

*The old Chief will have his defenses, and who knows what he built in his work room. Don't attack him at all. Shut the carriage door. Tooth it jammed if you have to. Anything. Hook the yoke with the old crane's chain. Grab the other end fast, and let the crane carry the carriage into the canal where the ships used to dock. Cut the counterweights. Let the carriage sink to the bottom and the Chief drowns. Stick around, and make sure nobody escapes. Push the other bodies—horse and man—into the water. Dump your clothes, and hop the rowboat home. There'll be a rowboat there for you.*

*Simple plan, Cutter. One blood monkey, and three to bleed with the horses.*

Jona took a deep breath. He nodded once, slowly. Jona asked about what to do if something went wrong, or if the engineer was with someone important.

*Improvise, blood monkey. It's what you love to do, isn't it?*

Jona had only one thought in his head, right then. The Chief hadn't been alone last time, in the animal pits. If Lady Sabachthani was with him this time, he wouldn't be able to follow orders.

And Aggie, he asked.

*Do the job, and we'll see. She isn't burning yet, and that's us saving her. We're thinking on it. Could go either way.*

✦

Jona traded for a night shift on the Island District, at the station next to the ferry.

The estate guards worked the Island District. The city ran a patch of ground where the ferries landed, and nominally managed the empty streets between the walls.

Usually old Sergeants got the post. No ferries ran much after a bit, but the Sergeants waited until morning. Mostly king's men just slept until something woke them.

Nic got the letter with the shift change, and he asked Jona if Jona got in trouble where Nicola didn't know about it. Jona shrugged, and said it was a favor for a friend.

✾

Lady Sabachthani had smashed her levy again tonight to bring the Chief to her estate. She had done it before Jona's shift. Jona saw the workers coming down the road for the last large ferry.

The Chief Engineer's carriage rolled to the ferry pulled by two brown mares. Workmen with huge tools trudged behind the ferry. A haze of sweat steamed off their bodies. Saltwater mud trailed their dirty boots.

Jona tapped the other king's man on duty, Christoff. Christoff ceremoniously closed his eyes and pretended to snore.

Jona jumped onto the ferry next to the worn-out workmen and their huge tools and their saltwater mud. He pushed to the front of the ferry. Men pushed long sticks to clear the delta and sandbars back to the mainland.

At the mainland, the workers shuffled north to the warehouses where they slept with the tools. The carriage rumbled away east.

Jona jogged south.

A dry sewer grate was jammed open just for him, with a big stick between the lip and the lid. Jona shoved the stick and kicked the lid open. He dropped down into the dry stink.

He waited until his eyes adjusted to this new darkness. He saw the sealed box of clothes. He tore open the box. At the bottom, there were new clothes and knives with forearm holsters.

Jona dumped his king's man uniform. He wrapped a large Senta jerkin over himself, with the red X on grey suede across his chest. He pulled a hood over his head. He slipped a grey mask over his mouth to hide most of his face.

Jona ran east fast through the rats and the puddles.

His boots knew these limestone and brick corridors better than he did. Jona ran hard to the pits. This time of year, this particular sewer line ran dry. In the winter, it was knee-deep in water. Light trickled in from the street from between the sewer grate's bars. The light spilled on the dead animals and the mounds of trash and filth. Closer to the pits, a few bodies were down in the grates. Jona jumped to avoid them. Once past the light, his boots found nothing but solid limestone.

✦

Jona emerged from the sewers in the middle of a busy street. He was panting from the run. Underneath his heavy Senta leathers, he felt weighed down with the loam of suede sweat.

Jona knew the area. He ignored any eyes that might have been watching him. He pushed into the crowd of sailors drifting in and out of the taverns and bathhouses and brothels. Jona walked down an alley, and ducked behind a sailor's bath house at the top of a hill. He had a view down this tiny hill to where the carriages waited out the owners that had gone into the pits. The entrance for the richer folk was cut into the side of an adjacent hill.

Jona was thirsty. He slipped into the open back door of the bath house. All that heat coming out of the kitchen, they had to keep the back doors wide open.

The dishwasher looked up at Jona, a Senta with a hidden face. The dishwasher didn't seem bothered. He looked up, but his hands kept scrubbing. His face was numb—no surprise, no anger, no fear. Jona nodded at the man. Jona made the universal gesture of drinking alcohol. The dishwasher stopped scrubbing long enough to snatch Jona a bottle of piss gin from a crate behind him.

Jona took the gin back into the night. He didn't pay anyone for the gin. Nobody stopped him. The dishwasher returned to his dirty mugs. The bath house staff bustled none the slower for the loss of one bottle of piss gin.

Jona found a shadow along the edge of the wall. He pulled down his facemask. He drank the gin. It burned all the way down.

Jona watched at the bottom of the hill, where the coachmen congregated around a few half-empty flasks. They talked. They laughed. They kicked at each other's shins. They waited for animals to die and pugilists to pass out and rich men to return to their carriages.

Jona fingered the two knives up his sleeves. He just had to clasp his arms to come out cutting.

He wondered if these two knives were enough.

Coachmen carried whips and clubs and sometimes small swords. They usually had crossbows hidden up on the roofs of the carriages.

Every now and then a coachman left the group to walk down the rows of carriages, looking for trouble. The coachman took turns walking down the carriages. Jona counted out how long it took for one man to finish his walk and another to take his turn.

Night crawled forward.

Jona improvised.

He waited until the coachman passed beyond the hill. Jona jumped fast down the hill to the horses and carriages. He pressed his back against a carriage, keeping the carriages between him and the coachman. Jona heard horses whinnying. They smelled the sewers and the of-demon sweat.

Jona walked softly along the back of the carriages until he reached his mark. He peeked around the corner of a horse at the group of bored coachman. A coachman balanced an empty bottle on his head while drinking a flask. The men cheered for their acrobat. None had walked the line since Jona had descended from the hill.

The engineer's carriage only had one door.

Jona leaped around the side of the engineer's carriage with the door. It wasn't locked. He jumped in fast. He closed the door gently behind him.

Jona held his breath inside, holding perfectly still, listening for an alarm.

He listened. Not even the horses sensed him now.

※

Jona knelt down on the floor. He held the knives tip down so he could jam the pommel forward at whoever entered first. He didn't want to have to think about who might receive his first blows. He wanted to move so fast that no one had a chance to think.

Jona cooled his breathing. The piss gin reached his ears. Hints of camphor clouded his head behind the alcohol buzz—maybe a touch of belladonna or pinks had hidden in there, too.

Jona had never been so close to a carriage floor before. He looked down at the planks of wood, and noticed where the knots cracked the smooth joints. Little points of dim, reflected moonlight slipped into the black shadows from the puddles in the muddy field. Drinks spilled in the rolling carriages. Cracks in the floorboards meant spilled drinks fell out on their own. Piss, too, if it came to that.

Jona stood up, turned around, and put his knives away. He urinated into the back of the carriage. He turned back around to face the door, and he knelt down again, knives in his hand and ready to jump. He tried to keep his hands off the ground on account of the piss. The smell lingered. Jona listened to the liquid dripping down into the mud below the carriage.

He tried to breathe quietly.

Time passed. Somewhere else, the city breathed bodies in and out of taverns and brothels and homes and ships and theatres and apartments. Money changed hands. Lovers met for the first

time, made love, fought, and fell away. A city reached vast ten-
drils into the world along the roads and rivers and sea currents.
A thousand upon a thousand minds dreamed of better lives in
dark bedrooms and smoke-filled backrooms. A thousand upon
a thousand voices spoke of their dreams with others, and these
dreams were more important as hope than as reality, because
in the morning there was only work and nobody spoke their
dreams out loud when they were earning their little corner of
the city in coins.

Jona stood alone in the dark, in his own stink. He thought
about Rachel. He was about to make hope real for his own night
bosses, and all he thought about was making his dreams real
with Rachel—dreams that would never be real.

Then, he heard men muffled by the wooden walls. Too much
laughter from too many voices emerged from some distant
crowd. Men came closer, talking too loud, like drunks. A woman laughed.

The carriage door opened. Jona jumped.

A flash of wind and cloth.

A woman screamed.

The butt of Jona's knives together against the man's temples
knocked the coachman into a heap. Jona flipped the knives in
his palms. He jumped around the coachman's crumbling body.
The Chief had his hands on a veiled woman. The Chief pushed
her behind him. The Chief turned his back to shield her with
his own body, as if she was the one who needed protection.

Jona jumped. The left knife caught the Chief in the side of
his neck. The knife tore through meat. The tip thumped spine.

The Chief's hands flew up to his neck. Blood sprayed like sick
fireworks.

The second blade tore into the Chief's right kidney.

The old man fell forward, arms flailing, into the veiled
woman. Blood sprayed over her silks and satins from the neck
wound. She held the man up by his arms.

Jona hugged the body away from the woman. He jammed his knife in and out of the Chief's stomach three times from behind. He wrapped the other knife around the Chief's throat to slice the jugular clean. The head only hung on from spine and small ligaments. Blood poured from the neck. The body was all limp, now. Jona, holding up this bag of spraying blood in his arms, held still. He, the veiled assassin, looked into the veiled woman's sad eyes.

She nodded. She turned away.

Jona heard the cranking sounds of a crossbow from the high seat of the engineer's carriage. Jona hefted the Chief's limp body around to take the bolt in the chest. The tip of the bolt nipped at the leather jerkin, but didn't pierce the red X.

Men were running at Jona.

Jona pushed the body aside. He ran between the coaches, and back up the hill. He jumped into the back door of the bath house.

Behind him, men called out in alarm.

Jona jumped through the kitchen, through the cauldrons boiling clothes clean and warming water on large, smoking racks of coal. He ran around the attendants with their huge buckets of soapy, hot water.

He heard bustling behind him, and shouts. He hefted a giant soapy cauldron over onto the tile behind him. He ran through the curtains to the sailors scrubbing away in their neat rows of cast-iron tubs sitting on hot stones. The men watched from their tubs, impotent and naked.

A man shouted something and waved his arms at Jona. He stood in the doorway. Jona lowered his shoulder and tackled through the poor man. They both tumbled out the front door, into the street. Jona leaped to his feet and ran into the mud and the ruins.

Jona bobbed and weaved through the crowd of indifferent sailors until he hit a dive with a rabbit on a pike and rotten instead of a sign. No bouncer worked the door. Jona ran inside.

Eaters—sailors, gangers, and warehousers—munched on the raw pink petals and leaves of the demon weed. Rough gangers working here passed around piss whiskey cut with hookah water and got more blasted than their customers.

Jona sprinted through the room, to the stairway. He wanted anyone following him in anger to have to get through this room alive.

By the time Jona was through the room, weapons were out and red drunk gangers had their boots on the ground, ready for a stomp with the Senta that had run through their private spot of the city.

The men chasing Jona ran into an angry mob.

More people died this night.

The real demon weed smokers huddled around the hookahs in the basements and back rooms. Jona only had one bouncer to pass—an old rowdy with no ears and no nose. Jona reached out with one hand as if to hand the fellow a fist of coins. Jona's other hand darted under the man's rib. Jona jammed his blade into the lung. The bouncer gasped for air. Jona shoved the bouncer into a wall.

The sick haze of smoke and demon weed stink made running down the hall feel like running through a long, silk veil.

Behind him, Jona heard the fighting. Jona didn't even stop to look. He ran forward. He saw a door to the edge of the canal down a long hall drenched in pinker piss and flies. Jona jumped down the hall. He kicked open the door—the wood was all rotten and the metal was rusted through. A small landing jutted out over the water.

There was a rowboat.

This empty rowboat, moored with ratty rope was unguarded, oars and all. Whoever had brought this boat here had fallen into the hookahs and forgotten their boat.

Jona cut the moor rope and kicked off into the water.

From the four corners of the district the riot bells rang like temple minarets—all king's men to post, and every decent citizen off the street. The ruin with the dead rabbit hanging from the door all full of pinkers and gangers had been surprised by the men chasing Jona. When surprised, they fought. When they fought, they fought everything that wasn't one of them.

Even more men died tonight in this little riot, some of them king's men.

But Jona wouldn't die. Jona paddled with the currents to a fork in the canal. Then, he dove into the water in all those heavy Senta leathers. He dog-paddled like dancing in quicksand. He struggled into the Old Brewery's port.

(The knives had fallen out of his gloves in the swim. The blood on the daggers swirled like small ribbons to tease the sharks in the shallows.)

Jona swam into the open dock. He pulled himself up into the shadow of the old crane. The Night King had emptied this room of transients tonight. Jona had a change of clothes, and a new rowboat resting against the wall.

He stripped off his wet Senta leathers. He dropped them into the water. The leathers floated away like a dead body, all bloody and heavy, with long sleeves.

(Probably sometime in the night, a curious guardsman might fish these out of the canal and get mad that they're just rags, throw them back in, and then another guardsman does the same, and then a sailor or two, until a ragpicker finds them floating and turns the leathers into the paper I use to write these memories down.)

Jona stood, glistening and naked in the reflected moonlight off the water. He rummaged through his new clothes carefully. He had trouble identifying the different pieces.

The warehouse was closed tight, with no windows at all. Light ruined beer, made it skunky. The only opening in the brewery was this gaping hole along the canal and a few doors that had been sealed shut tonight, and one door with fellows outside waiting uncomfortably for a rampaging carriage that would never come. The moonlight and lamplight reflected off the water. The crane had a shadow among these shadows.

Sometimes a lone river ship slid past outside. Night watchmen sang out in the dark to let other ships know the speed, the direction, and the size. Men with long poles trudged, half-asleep, up and down the deck, pushing the ship along.

Jona didn't dress right away. First, he slipped back into the water naked, and he scrubbed at his hands and face. He didn't know if he still had blood on him.

# CHAPTER XII

The sea breeze licked at the jewels of river water all over his body.

He needed to dry off, and put some clothes on, and row back to his post at the island before the morning shift change.

He didn't have a towel, so he just pushed all the water down with his hands until he felt merely damp.

He found one leach on his leg. It was dead already from his demon blood. The leech hadn't let go when it died. He pulled the squishy black creature out of his skin, and tossed it into the water.

He used river water to rinse the bloody spots on his leg from the leech's teeth. Jona had to wait for the wound to clot before he could touch his clothes lest the blood burn through the new uniform. He didn't mind. He wanted to be drier. He wondered if he had a leach dead on his back that he couldn't see, but he couldn't do anything about it now.

He had to get back to his post. He pulled on his new clothes, and now he was a river tout, ready to give directions around the canals for a coin to the other ships, and sometimes a lift to a fellow left by a ferry that didn't mind paying a bit more for the hurry.

He tied a ratty bandanna over his hair, and smeared some fresh mud on his face and arms. People see a dirty river tout, they don't look twice at him.

He shoved his new rowboat into the water. He jumped into the boat so his momentum pushed it out of the black and into the water. He rowed silently. He dodged the few ships running through the canals without a singsong cry about his own presence on the water.

He had to go down the canal, into the bay, and north to the island, where he'd change clothes one more time tonight, back into his uniform, and sink this little rowboat with the clothes inside of it.

Jona wasn't far from the edge of the canal, where larger vessels full of fruits, fish, vegetables, and wheat unloaded precious cargo into the flat canal vessels. Perishables usually ran after dark, to get to the markets by morning light.

Jona turned the corner to the bay, where bustling brothels and bars spewed disease and terrible music like a house vomiting buckets into the gutters.

Someone cried out for a river tout. Jona didn't look up. He was going to keep rowing as if he didn't hear. Then, the voice cried out again, and Jona recognized the voice.

Lord Elitrean's son in a sailor disguise waved his arm at Lord Joni, whose tout disguise was better. The boy had draped himself in filthy rags like a sailor, and wore rags over half his face like a wound. The boy was not covered in filth or mud. His skin was pure and white, as if he had come directly from a bath, and no salty sea air or sunlight had browned his white skin.

(I think everyone puking in the gutter, and spinning to foreign noise among foreign prostitutes was a noble in disguise. Even the prostitutes were bored rich wives, looking for some excitement, unconcerned about passing down the face of the father to the sons and daughters.)

Jona slowed his little boat. He shouted to Elitrean exactly what a tout should shout. "What, you?"

"Ahoy, tout," shouted Elitrean. His accent was all wrong. He sounded like a nobleman trying to sound like a sailor. "Run me to my boat," he said.

"How much you got?"

"I got enough, tout. Nine do it for you?"

"They foreign coins or local?"

"Local."

"I'm your boy," shouted Jona, "Nine'll get me all night. Something wrong with the ferry?" The ferry would recognize him, and report his travelings to the boy's father, especially after dark. Jona knew that.

"Something wrong with nine coins?" said Elitrean.

"Nothing wrong, then, sailor," said Jona.

Jona rowed the boat to shore, and held up his hand to this boy who did not know he would be king.

Lord Elitrean's son plopped on the damp bench across from Jona like he had never been in a boat before, but he was just pink and uncoordinated. The boat rocked. Jona held out his hand to the passenger. Jona put the nine coins into his pocket. He dropped his oars, and pushed off the sidewall of the canal. He rowed into darkness. He didn't say a word. Jona aimed his boat where he was told to aim it. Lord Elitrean's son was heading for the Island, not some boat.

Jona imagined Lady Sabachthani in a red wedding dress, lifting her veil to this fellow that Jona had thrown out of a whorehouse once. She wasn't pretty, and she was twice as old as him. She was smart enough to know the hollowness of men's smiles.

And the rumors are out there, this boy picking his teeth with the jagged end of his little signet ring (a better disguise would have hid the ring), his eyes swamped in pinks and his body the victim of every disease that washed into the brothels from the sailors' ships.

Jona said to himself that he didn't care. Then, he asked himself why he had to say to himself that he didn't care.

For all her wealth and power, Lady Sabachthani may never know the joy of love. Even if she were naked, she would have more armor wrapped over her flesh than Rachel's warm scales. She had stood in the night, stared into her betrothed's assassin and stepped, calmly, away.

And Elitrean's son would never know love. He could not separate his own desires from his self. Beneath the surface of his skin, this noble child was unformed, all impulse.

Jona was impulsive, too.

Jona pulled one oar from the water, and swung it into the rowboat next to the boy's leg.

The boy looked at Jona. "Something wrong, tout?"

Jona nodded. "Oar's broken."

"Looks fine to me."

"You can't see it?" said Jona. He pointed at the edge of the oar in the boat.

Elitrean leaned over the oar, frowning.

Jona swung the other oar with both hands.

Elitrean's eyes rolled like marbles. He collapsed into the floor of the boat.

Jona swung again. The skull cracked like a jar. Inside, the boy was unformed. Globs of brain and chipped bone pooled on the floor of the rowboat like spilled soup.

(Jona saw Tripoli's death in his mind, and choked down bile that suddenly jumped in his throat. Tripoli lying in a puddle of his own intestines and liquid shit and weeping blood and screaming.)

Jona placed the paddles back into the water. He started rowing again, blood from his oar trailing behind in the water.

Jona reached the tall reeds at the edge of the island. He slipped Elitrean's signet ring from his finger, and pulled off a rag to use as a rope. Jona tied the ring to a heavy stone from the shallows. He tossed the ring and the stone deeper into the bay waters.

Jona slipped Elitrean's own knife from the boy's boot. Jona cut off most of the clothes. He wanted this body to look like exactly what the boy was in life: a foul, murderous, bloated dog. If the body managed to float far enough towards the shore, he'd be buried in a pauper's grave, or burned with the dead in the sewers. The body floated off into the currents.

Jona kicked a hole in the bottom of his rowboat. He lashed the oars down to the boat with the rest of his canal tout clothes. He had a uniform near here, placed just for him. He pushed the sinking little boat into the bay currents.

Jona walked through reeds at the edge of noble compounds. He strolled back to his post, through empty streets. He felt eyes on him, and he didn't care. Estate Guards wouldn't think much of a king's man walking through the king's streets. Night birds and insects sang moon songs from the gardens. A few stars pushed through the night clouds and city lamps.

Jona looked behind himself every few steps. He half-expected the Night King herself to be standing there, or Lady Sabach-thani's men. The further he walked, the more he was afraid. He slowed down so he wouldn't look conspicuous. He choked down his own heartbeat.

Jona felt safer when he returned to his post. His alibi had fallen asleep.

Jona kicked Christoff's chair. Christoff startled awake, reached for his weapon, but saw it was only Jona. Christoff stretched and yawned.

"Don't snore," said Jona, "It's unbecoming of an officer."

"I'm no officer," said Christoff.

"Sleeping's what officer's do," said Jona, "Corporals don't get to sleep."

"You all right?" said Christoff.

"I'm starving. Do we have anything to drink?"

"I got some rum," said Christoff, "but it's piss water. Foul stuff."

"I need something."

"Cool yourself," said Christoff, "Lots of night left for you to piss me off. Don't need to make it all in one go." Christoff slowly pulled his leather flask from beneath his chair. He tossed it at Jona's head. Jona caught the flask in the air. He tugged at the stopper and drank as much as he could in one swig.

Christoff leaned back in his chair, and let his eyes drift closed again.

Jona sat down and watched the night. He thought about what he had just done, and it scared him.

Sunlight threw a lonely eye over the city from the east. Jona kicked Christoff's seat to wake him up again before they got relieved. Jona thrust the rest of the rum back into hiding under Christoff's chair.

Relief came, and he and Christoff went back to their stations to report and sign off.

Then, Jona walked home. He filled up a bath with hot water, and rolled into it. He closed his eyes. He tried to imagine that he was sleeping.

He wondered if he would face the souls of all the men he killed in dreams like a normal blood monkey if he could only fall asleep.

Killing was so easy without dreams to wake the dead.

Then, Jona thought about love.

Another conversation, hidden in many corners inside the of-demon's mind. Two voices, bodiless, but clearly Calipari and a mixture of other men, and other times. A sea of tobacco smoke, and sweat. I'll call the other fellow Jona, because Jona was one of the voices, once or twice.

"How in Elishta you meet Franka, anyway?" said Jona.

Nicola leans back in his stool. He looks at the horizon past the tavern walls. "Oh, I was out inspecting the guard towers," he said, "Ran into her on the way out. She's been a barmaid at Bill's place for as long as she's been walking. We hit it off. This was four years ago? About four years ago. Her kid was still a runt back then. He's still a runt, but he was a punier runt back then."

Jona squints. "You know the boy's father?"

"Nah, but I know he ain't around anymore. I think he's dead. And if he ain't dead, he better not come around again after walking on Franka like that. I'll kill him." No hint of exaggeration in Calipari's voice. He wasn't just talking, he meant that he'd kill the man as easily as men mean to wear a jacket on a cold day. "I like the boy, though. He's a good kid, and it's all Franka's doing," said Calipari, "When you and me walk about, we run thugs and rollers and drifters and ragpickers born just like Franka's boy and their mothers drifted off like nothing happened, and the kid's just sitting there by his lonesome turning into trouble. Franka kept her boy, and damn to them that'd shame her for it."

Nic took a long drink of something. Brandy. Wine. Ale. Piss Gin. "Anyhow," a pause to cough away strong liquor, "We both trade time so sometimes she comes around here, and sometimes I'm out there. We write letters. She can't read, but some of the folks read letters to her. They write them back to me, what she tells them to write."

Jona shook his head. He shouldn't have said it. But, he's drunk, so he said it. "You trust her out in the traveler's bar like that and her already with one kid? I couldn't do that. I just couldn't. I'd go nuts."

Nic was calm. He looked at Jona with a little squint in his eye. Jona knew he had crossed the line. Jona wouldn't say it again.

He'd never forget the answer.

"I trust her," said Calipari, "You've never met Franka. You'd trust her if you did."

"Yeah, you're right," said Jona, "You'd know if she wasn't honest."

Nic said nothing. He just looked at Jona with that tiny squint. Nic threw the last of his drink back. He coughed at the strength.

"When you retiring, anyway?" said Jona, "I heard you got the land already."

"Yeah," said Calipari, "In the winter. I've already got my parcel assigned. I just have to not get kicked before winter, and I'm a farmer with my good wife and a good son."

"Sounds nice," said Jona, "You know who'll be taking your corner of the pigshit?"

"Maybe Geek will. He's ranking Corporal around here. Maybe one of you boys will get some stripes 'fore he does. That's the Lieutenant's problem, though. I'm just trying not to toss the place before my time is up, or roll into the bay," said Calipari. "When you up for that stinking fleur, anyway?"

Jona shrugged. "When an officer kicks. Then, I can test for it," he said, "Until then, I'm your boy."

"You up for a little trouble?"

"I'm always your boy. What you got?"

"Everything in the city. Anything at all. I'll miss it when I'm gone. I hear some fellows are racing ducks at this tavern. We bet on the ducks, then we eat the loser."

❖

Jona tried to hold the image in his mind of the moment the Chief died. He tried to recall the precise moment the Chief believed in his own death. At one moment the face slipped from shock into a death mask. Jona tried to remember that final face, when the face was still alive.

Jona wondered if death was like sleeping. Dead people looked like they were sleeping, sometimes.

He figured he'd ask Rachel about it, later.

He couldn't remember when he was going to see her again.

He wanted to see her again, soon. He wanted to hold her warm body in his while she slept, so he could share her dreams with the messy words that mumbled out from her lips.

❈

The King, himself, through his own hazy fog, called down the law on all Sentas. Bring all Sentas in, question them, and kick them out of town.

In practice, guards got burned pretty bad over it, if they got too rough with their fists. Most Senta just kicked town alone as soon as they heard, wearing someone else's clothes for a while.

Rachel didn't know. Down in the Pens and the warehouses and where the big ships stripped their cargos out along the flat river boats, nobody threw anybody out of town.

Sergeant Calipari had called all his boys together at muster and told the Pens District to leave the Sentas be for now. The guard was too busy watching out for real sneak thieves and rollers to worry about useless laws that'd be forgotten in a few weeks.

Anyway, the king's men all knew that a fellow probably wore Senta leathers to let the Senta take the blame. Everybody hated foreign religions.

Then before Jona could leave with the boys, Nicola pulled Jona aside.

Jona yawned. He asked to be a scrivener for a day on account of how tired he was.

Nic handed Jona a pass. "Go home," said Nicola.

"What?"

"You worked all the other night, and if I know you, you spent all day and night in trouble, and you still need some sleep," said Nicola, "Don't think my eyes and ears in the city don't tell me about your wanderings. Take two days off to get your head back. Sleep in. Sergeant's orders."

Jona scowled. "I don't get paid at home," he said.

Nicola rolled his eyes. He held the pass out further. "You don't get paid if we kick you on account of disobeying," said Calipari, "Get out of here, Corporal. Go home. Sleep. That's an order."

Jona shrugged. He stretched his hands over his head as if he was tired.

Jona signed his pass. He turned to the door. Nicola clicked his tongue at Jona's back. Jona turned. A large bottle of red wine soared towards Jona's hands. Jona caught the bottle. He read the label, and nodded at Nic. "Thanks, Nic," said Jona.

Calipari winked, and shooed Jona out the door.

※

And the engineers kept working. A new fellow found the mantle of Chief on his shoulders. He hid in the palace.

Chief Mishle Leva's funeral was lavish. Lady Sabachthani, in black, stood on the front row, gently weeping behind her thin, black veil.

And down where the porters pulled crates from the ships and loaded them into the flatboats near the rivers and animals in crates rolled in from all over the world and passed through the slaughterhouses at the Pens and all the vendors walked barefoot in mud and ragpickers picked through the piles of trash and Jona and his boys walked about and Rachel lived and Djoss lived and thousands of people quietly tried to find their little piece of happiness—down there—no one batted an eye if they heard the news.

Didn't bother the Pens and Docks and Warehouses a bit if some fellow got rolled. People got rolled everyday.

# CHAPTER XIII

Jona took Calipari's wine to Rachel's apartment.

He wanted to see if she was home alone. He had been to her apartment a couple times. Her lock was worthless. He shook the handle and lifted it up until the old gears fumbled loose. When he opened the door, he saw her dozing in her bed. She hadn't even looked up at the door noise.

Jona had never seen her brother, but he had seen the signs of the man. Bread, half-eaten, staled and molded on the counter. Huge, mud footprints led to his bed. His sour sweat smells spread across the room from his filthy bed on the other side of the apartment. Djoss wasn't home now. He was rarely around in the daylight, unless he was sleeping.

Jona placed the wine on the floor next to Rachel's bed. He sat down in front of her. He watched her eyes moving behind her eyelids. She was dreaming.

On the other side of the room's wall, a young boy read aloud to an old woman. The old woman kept correcting the boy's mistakes. Farther away in the building, a baby cried, a man snored, and even farther, women shouted gossip between windows while pulling in their wash. All around them, people were falling in and out of love, behaving lewdly, and everyone ought to be ashamed of themselves, because there was gossip about everyone.

Jona couldn't find a corkscrew in the kitchen. He couldn't find wine glasses, either. All he found were little tea cups and a tea pot with no smoke stain on the bottom like every other tea pot in the world.

He gave up. He pulled off his shirt. He slipped into bed next to her.

She smelled him. She woke slightly. She nuzzled into his neck, and drifted off again.

❁

*What do you do when you're alone and don't know what to do with yourself?*

*Nothing.*

*When a Senta doesn't know what to do, the Senta closes her eyes. The Senta tries to breathe carefully and continuously. Each breath must fill the lungs, burn a little, and then fall like liquid from the mouth in a steady, flowing breeze. To seek the Unity, first the Senta seeks to find the places inside that are unharmonious.*

*Sounds like doing nothing to me, but I'm no Senta.*

*Sit up straight, allow the blood to flow freely, and feel the breath seeping in through the body to each relaxed finger and toe. Close the ears next. Close the skin. Seek a heartbeat, and the swell and sink of the lungs like bellows. The Senta seeks to purify the being into Will alone. In a limitless universe—our unbroken one—the center of the universe is the point of strongest Will.*

*I bet it's nothing like a good bottle of wine. Do you have a corkscrew?*

*Listen. Look at your hands. We of the winds and the sun do not*

*question Will. We see it in our hands. We see that animals have feet,
teeth, hair, milk, faces, shit, sex, and blood. We see that only monkeys and men have hands. Monkeys use their hands to climb trees.
Men use hands to cut down trees, or plant them new.*

*So, you don't have a corkscrew?*

*When I dreamcast of monsters, they are men with giant palms,
all colored pink or black or red as blood. When I dreamcast of the
dying men, their bodies end at the elbow. Blind men see with their
hands. Deaf men talk with their hands. Men with no corkscrew use
their hands. Use your hands, Jona.*

*I don't think I'm strong enough for that.*

*Well, I didn't really want any wine, anyway. I don't want to work
drunk. That place is unpleasant enough without an unharmonious
mind.*

*This bottle will never open without a corkscrew.*

*Then, the bottle is empty of wine. It contains only the hope of
wine.*

*If we go to my place, we'll have a corkscrew.*

*I will stay here and sleep some more. I am not like you, Jona.*

*Do you want me to go?*

*Yes. Goodbye. Knock, next time. My brother might be here, you
know.*

◈

Aggie with her sad eyes, and her face all dirty and her nose a
bit crooked, and her hands reaching out for Jona's gifts. Letters,
blood pie.

Blood pie laced with demon weed, and demon blood.

She ate the pie, and opened the letter and didn't speak to
Jona. She read the letter again, while finishing the pie.

The letter was a forgery Jona bought from a professional let-
ter-writer who wrote what Jona told the fellow to write and
made the letters romantic and hopeful and said Salvatore's coming to save the girl.

Then Jona took the letter to Salvatore at his café, or his ball or his tiny little rented room, and Salvatore fumbled for something to write with. Salvatore read the letter and shrugged it off and made his mark.

And Jona took the letter here.

"Imam, I am too grateful for this torture," she said. She fell back to her cot, her eyes glazed and the letter pulled against her chest.

Flies and gnats swarmed all over her filthy, thinned face. She didn't bother knocking them away. When her mouth dangled open—while she read—flies landed on her teeth. They sucked at the thin, sick rot with their greedy little legs.

Jona washed her face off with a bowl of water while the demon weed held her mind still.

One time—just once—he touched her breast through her rags. He frowned at himself afterwards. He cursed Salvatore. He stood up over her. He watched her sleep, until he couldn't stand it anymore. He walked out of the room. Her soft warmth lingered in his palm, like a rash.

He tried not to think about the girl.

Instead, he thought about killing Salvatore, just like he had done Lord Elitrean's son.

Jona slipped into the door at evening twilight, a little juiced from the liquor and the duck sausage that was barely cooked and mostly made of bloody oats all drenched in malt vinegar. He shoved his way in, kicked his boots off in the foyer, and stretched his arms over his head.

"Ma, I'm home!" he shouted.

And the old woman, like a sparrowhawk, landed on her son from the kitchen hall. Spit-wet fingers scrubbed at Jona's cheeks, and fixed his hair. Spindly seamstress fingers scurried over every wrinkle in his shirt.

Jona winced. "What the…? Ma! Back off!"

"Lady Ela Sabachthani is sitting in our kitchen."

"What?" said Jona, "What's she doing here?"

"Offer her something to drink. Offer her something to eat. She won't accept it, because she knows we got nothing, but you have to offer, anyhow. Anyhow, behave yourself, Jona. Are you drunk? You smell like liquor. Sober up. Hold still a minute. Let me adjust your shirt. What is this, blood?"

"It's duck blood," said Jona.

"Why you always get so much blood all over your shirt all the time? Is it your blood? Whose blood is it?"

"I told you," said Jona, "It's duck blood."

Lady Ela Sabachthani touched Lady Joni's hands. Ela smiled at Jona.

"Milady," said Jona's mother. She pulled away from Jona.

Lady Sabachthani took over for Lady Joni's hands, adjusting Jona's dirty, bloody, wrinkled uniform. "Lord Joni, I haven't seen you in some time. Is there somewhere we can talk alone?"

Jona looked at Lady Sabachthani standing in his foyer in her fine dress. He bent down at the knee, stiffly, to pick up his boots. He nodded at her.

"Well?" she said.

"The roof, milady," he said.

"The what?" said Lady Sabachthani. She leaned forward, like she hadn't heard.

Jona pointed up. "We'll go to the roof," he said.

Lady Sabachthani cocked her head. "The… roof?"

Jona smirked. "You've never been to your own roof?"

She straightened his collar one last time. "Of course not," she said.

Jona gestured to the stairwell near the door. "Well, I'll show you mine. Just climb the stairs up. Keep going until you run out of stairs, and you're there," he said, "You want something to drink? I don't think our tea is as fine as yours, but I bet we got some brandy hiding somewhere."

"Anything will be fine."

Jona's mother rushed off to the kitchen to find brandy. Jona knew he had already drunk all the brandy, but he wanted his mother to disappear awhile looking for it.

At the roof, he walked her to the edge. They looked down at people bustling. Singsong cries of the street vendors rose above the dwindling birdsongs of early nightfall. All the parasols in the misty streets like confetti-colored blood pulsed through the city's black dirt veins.

Jona turned his back to the city. He placed his boots on the ground next to his bare feet. He leaned against the boundary wall. He looked at Lady Sabachthani in the lamplight spilling up from the street. "I'm glad you came, but it scares me that you came here alone. People will question your motives. That heart of yours..." he said. He shook his head.

"What about my heart?" she snapped back.

"Well," said Jona, "your heart is a deadly thing to give to a man these days."

She smiled, sadly. "Not my heart, Jona, just my hand," she said. "My heart is the only thing that keeps me alive, sometimes, through all of this."

"Right," said Jona. Jona looked past her, at the door where he worried his mother might be eavesdropping. "So, let me get this down solid on account of my ma's ears. You aren't here to ask me to take that deadly little hand of yours, are you?"

Lady Sabachthani placed her hand next to Jona's on the wall. She leaned over, looking down at the street. She sighed. "Not today, Jona. I've been playing a few suitors against each other, all convinced the throne is theirs once I settle a few accounts in the city. Two of these suitors are gone. One is dead, the other missing. I have to find out if young Elitrean is still alive. He is the most-logical choice, considering his wealth and his father's prestige."

Jona moved his hand away from hers, into his own lap. "You would let yourself be rumored into a marriage with that disgusting thing?"

She nodded. "No. His father would be too much trouble. If I don't marry before the king dies, I don't know what will happen," she said, "The council won't vote for just a queen. Once a king is chosen, his hand is his own, and he might never marry. I am not beautiful enough to have royal bastards, Jona. Elitrean is a powerful man, even if his son leaves much to be desired."

"So, you want me to find out about Elitrean's boy for you?"

"I do," she said, "I need someone I can trust. You've been out of all this mess, but you know all about it. And you know Elitrean's other life better than anyone else I trust. I need you to find Elitrean, and bring him to me alive."

Jona took a deep breath. He furrowed his brow, and looked her, carefully, in her face. "I can't do that, Ela," he replied.

"Why not?" she said.

"Elitrean's made his share of enemies. You can't protect me in the Pens," said Jona, "Where I walk about, they don't even know your name. And if someone dropped the Chief, they might have dropped Elitrean, too, and we just haven't found the boy's bones."

"Jona," she said, "I need to find him alive."

"His children won't be clean."

"Then he'll die, and they'll die, and a new king with clean heirs will mount me before it's too late."

"You think you got time for two husbands?"

"I won't if we can't find Elitrean soon. I am not a young woman, Lord Joni. I know this better than anyone in the world. I am also not beautiful. Men tell me I am beautiful, and I know that what is beautiful to them is my title, my lands, and my family's power. Lord Joni, do you think that I am beautiful?"

"I'm the wrong fellow to ask."

"Do you think I'm beautiful, Jona? You would never lie to me. You would tell me the truth. Am I beautiful, Jona?"

"Why do you want it from me, Lady Sabachthani? I can't be honest with you."

"Every woman wants to be beautiful to someone. You're avoiding the question, and you will be honest."

"I think you're beautiful sometimes, and then sometimes you're not."

"How can that be? Isn't it all or nothing with men?"

"When it's just you and me here like this, talking like real people and being honest. Then, you're beautiful. As soon as you get in front of a bunch of other people, it's like your skin is the same, but the person inside of it is different. And you're all haughty, and you let maids do everything, and you let people bow and scrape all over you and you show off your father's... Anyway, right now, on my roof, and it's just you and me and we're being honest and nobody's looking—here, you're beautiful." He was lying, of course. She might have believed him.

The corners of her mouth turned up. She kept watch over all the people below her, living their lives and none even looking up at the two nobles on the roof. "Thank you, Jona," she said. She turned to him. "Thank you for that."

Jona turned away. "What will you do if Elitrean has gone for a swim?"

"A marriage with a king is a difficult thing to arrange."

Jona laughed. "I was talking to my Sergeant about him and his lady, Franka, today. They met at a pub, and she's got a kid by someone nobody even knows who, but they're in love and marrying. Sergeant Nicola Calipari and his barmaid. Love and marriage and nothing else in the world matters and it's as natural as breathing."

"Is he a good man?"

"Nic's tapped as a keg, but he's a solid fellow."

"Send him my regards."

"You met him once," said Jona, "Remember the fellow with me when we came about the dog?"

"Oh," said Ela, "Yes."

Jona clenched and unclenched his fists. Lady Ela Sabachthani looked below at all the people walking, and in her mind she was probably wondering if any would ever be her royal subjects. Either that, or she was thinking about kissing Jona. Maybe both.

Jona broke the silence. "Look," he said, "I can poke around a bit, but I wouldn't hold my breath. Best case, Elitrean's kid wasn't the one who rolled the Chief, and he jumped town thinking he was next. Worst case, Elitrean rolled the Chief and died in the riot when he was trying to escape."

"I'm sure you are capable of finding out more than I am," said Lady Sabachthani, "My father and I have our ways, but they are imprecise, like the Sentas."

Jona shrugged. "I don't know about that stuff. What I know is, if I was Elitrean and I didn't roll the Chief, I'd be on a slow ship to Galvez with someone else's name and not even my father knows about it until you're married and on the throne."

"Someone always knows," she said, "You'll find the one who knows, if anyone can. I trust you."

"You say you trust me, but I bet you don't trust anyone."

"Not even I can go through life alone, Jona. I have to trust someone, sometimes. You've never lied to me before. You've never gotten involved in these little diplomacies of marriages."

"I haven't?" said Jona, "Good luck to you trusting me. My take is drop the crown, and go find some nice old guy who takes good care of you. Have kids before it gets on too late. Most girls your age are working on marrying off their daughters, not on having them."

Her lips pressed together, cold. "I am aware of my age, Jona. Please don't remind me. Just tell me that I'm beautiful, and that you'll help me."

Jona sighed. He rubbed the back of his head. He stood up straight. He bowed to her, like a barefoot courtier. "I'll help you," said Lord Joni, "And, I guess, right now, you're beautiful."

"Thank you, Lord Joni," she said. She turned, abruptly to the door.

Jona watched her leave and couldn't help but feel this weird lump in his throat. Not like crying, but still a lump. A little, harmless, weird lump just sitting there in his throat, dry as a bone—but weird.

# CHAPTER XIV

My papers are covered in rocks to hold them in place, in their order. My papers are piled in a corner away from the door. I finish a page, dry it, and place it facedown in the corner beneath the rock.

The rest of the room is smothered in Calipari's clean lines. A huge map in dozens of pages covers the inn room's floor, with all the corners in their place, and all the places merging into the center, where—in place of the King's Palace—we place the pile of Calipari's introductory letters. My husband stomps in from the streets. He jumps on tip-toes across the corners of the papers. In the center of the room, he rummages for the right letter. *We should've put this somewhere else,* he grumbles, *or gotten a larger room.* I wave him away. I'm writing.

Then, he hops back to the door, and leaves again. *Good-bye, my love, and stay safe. When half a heart dies, the other half dies, too.*

Guard Captains and Nobility may serve us, but the people do not believe we tell the truth. Unless we throw the wolf upon our backs, we remain just faces in a crowd. Even as wolves these city sheep would be too afraid to obey. They'd run and ring their bells in fear.

Sergeant Calipari's clean black inklines cut mud-wonderful streets into corners, and rivers, and valuable informants' daily routines.

My husband returns and tells me that the church record-keepers have found the old woman alive.

I must fly with my husband to the house in the center of the city. Calipari had left the Joni estate and the dressmaker shops off his maps, and we did not push the man. We did not need to force the issue. My husband located the house on his own.

Quill, I put you down today. I shall return to you when I can. May you remain as sharp as the wit of a wiser woman while I am away.

I pick up my pen, again.

The Joni home smelled like the sloughed skin of the family. The scent pounded into the pillows, and the scent pressed deep into the rugs and wooden walls. When people came home, the familiar smell brought them peace.

Familiar dishes seeped into the woodwork—oatmeal, and old milk and cheap sausage fried in oil and lumps of bread and boiled oranges in molasses.

I smelled her skin, too, below the lost food. Jona's mind, from beyond the frayed sea wall of my consciousness, reached out with her memory. I saw her in my mind the way Jona saw her. A mother pushed a wooden spoon around an iron pot. Her delicate white skin draped loose and cold over eggshell bones. She smelled like spoiled milk and citrus. I saw her in her plain brown dress, dingy ash at her neck. Her face was a pinched squint that never smiled. Fuzzy thread and powdered indigo puffed in clouds from her stained clothes when she moved—a dressmaker's aura. The job is in their hair, their fingernails, and their smell like a fine linen powder.

She smelled this way her whole life. Leaning over the boy's bed, she smelled this way. Dressing her son for temple school, she smelled this way.

The house shrank in Jona's mind as he grew up, but the memories held the walls farther apart than they really were. When my husband and I found the Joni estate, the rooms were smaller than Joni's mind recalled.

We let ourselves in at a back window.

The house smelled like dust and candle smoke. The rooms were empty. The walls were smoke-stained white. The windows were dingy and muddy. I asked my husband if he was sure someone lived here. He said that he had seen an old woman coming in and out of the house, and the stink of Jona's taint all over her.

I sniffed the air around the doorways. She had been here recently.

My husband waited near the front door, wrapped in shadows in a corner. I hid near a back door. We didn't know when she'd come home, or if she was even still alive.

Night fell. Nothing happened. The sun rose.

The street sounds outside the walls drifted away into the songs of birds singing down the moon.

We waited for three days, taking turns seeking food from the street vendors. (A hot corn girl and an apple girl and a hot sausage boy all saw us each day, amazed at the coins we handed to them like nothing at all.)

A lock turned in a key. A door opened across the house. I walked through empty hallways. I felt my footprints born in the dust.

She saw me before she saw my husband behind her. This woman was thinner than Jona remembered her.

She screamed. "Who are you?" she shouted, "Why are you in my home?"

The demon-stain had aged her. Her veins showed through her skin like a wet map hung to dry on wicker bones. She was younger than my husband, but she walked with death.

"Lady Joni," I said, "My husband and I are Erin's Walkers. We must speak with you about your son."

She breathed heavily. Her lips curled in pain. "My son," she whimpered. Her words coughed up from a clenched throat. "*My son?*" she repeated.

"Yes," I replied.

"Lord Joni's dead," she said, "All the Lord Jonis are dead."

My husband loomed behind her, part man but mostly wolf. "Who carried the stain?" he growled, with a human tongue "Are you like him?"

Tears welled up at the edge of her eyes. "Please, just leave me in peace," she said. She walked to the kitchen.

I held my hand up at my husband. *Let me.*

In the kitchen, she had put the kettle on. "I assume you're going to be here a while," she said, "I'm making tea. You're from Erin's temple, right? Wolves come from Erin."

"We're the Walkers of this region. Thank you for the tea," I said, "but we must test your blood, and we will not drink the tea in this tainted house."

"My blood?" she said. She looked me in the face. "If you prick me, I'll bleed to death. I'm old."

"Who was the demon?" I said.

"Why does anyone care?"

"Please," I said. I pulled a knife from my belt. I had the heartwood paper in my hand.

She sat down at the table.

"Can I have that knife?" she said.

I flipped the blade in my palm. I held it out to her. She took the handle and held it in front of her. She gazed at her reflection in the steel. "I used to be so beautiful," she said, "and I had a rich husband. I had a wonderful son who loved me. Even when

I didn't have a rich husband, I had a wonderful son who loved me." Her lip trembled. "Will you be arresting me or taking me to the guards or anything like that?"

"We will," I said.

She looked over at the teapot heating up to a boil, breathing deep and controlling her tears. "Do me a favor," she said, "After you're done, will you burn down this house for me?"

"We will," I said. I pulled a second knife from my boot. "Do you want my help?" I said.

"No," she said, "I can do this myself. Will you be burning my blood?"

"Yes," I said, "I have heartwood paper with me."

"All right," she said. She held out her hand for the paper. "I carried an of-demon inside of me. I washed his clothes and threw out his bathwater and turned his bed in spring. When he was sick, I cleaned up after him. I drank holy water to stay alive. My husband taught me. I'm probably poison. I feel like I've been poisoned. I drank holy water every day since my wedding, but that isn't enough."

The water rose to a boil. She poured the kettle into an iron pot. She pumped water from the sink's water pump into the pot, testing with her hand for the temperature. Hot, but not too hot.

I stood up to keep a close eye on the woman. I wanted to make sure she was cutting herself, and the blood we'd be testing was hers.

She rolled her sleeve up her arm. She didn't shake. She looked me in the face. Her stern squint dared me to step in. The knife touched her skin near the wrist. Her jaw clenched.

Her hands shook hard. She quickly put the knife in her bloodied hand. She tried to slice her other wrist, too.

I stopped her. I snatched the knife away. I placed her bloody arm over the paper for her blood. I stole a dishtowel to wrap her wounded forearm.

"Please," she said. She leaned into my shoulder, crying.

"No," I said, "Dogsland must have her turn with you, enemy of life."

☙

I tested her blood over the iron tub of water. The blood burned so hot, that I had to let the heartwood paper fall into the water. The water swallowed the flame. If she had been of-demon, the fire would burn as hot inside the water, too.

After this test, we bandaged her arm. We walked her to the Captain of the Guard.

(She knew her fate after how her son had died. She knew, and felt no will to flee or start again. She waited for her own destruction, getting out of bed, washing her hands and face in a basin of holy water, pushing needles through the hem of dresses, cooking cheap sausage for herself alone, and talking to the son that wasn't at the table anymore—but still she talked to him. She heard his voice in the gaps, evading her questions. She was too tired to walk home sometimes and slept in a tavern near her work to save up the strength to walk home. Since his death, she had been so tired.

Then, we finally came to send her skull to the spikes along the city wall. She was Lady Joni, once, and rich and beautiful. Now she was just another skull along the wall.)

☙

My husband and I didn't use just fireseeds this time. We over-turned barrels of kerosene across the halls, down the muddy stairs, and into the basement. We placed fireseeds at the win-dowsills so the sudden flames would blow new seeds out into the streets.

I went to the back door. My husband went to the front. We both dropped our matches. We ran through the streets to our inn near the docks.

Houses all around caught the flame. Men screamed as their shops burned to the ground. Women tore their hair. Dogs screamed at their gates with nowhere to run.

Fire companies flocked to the site, ringing bells and dragging their pumps like a parade, buying the burning buildings for almost nothing before they raised a finger to help push back the flame.

My husband and I watched from the window of our inn near the docks. The smoke drowned out the sea clouds. Old demon stains burned strong. Let this whole city burn down.

My husband spread dandelion seeds on his windowsill. He blew them into the wind.

*We should burn the whole city.*

*We are executioners, not revolutionaries.*

*We were executioners. We did not kill this woman who had done such evil things for so long.*

*Did you want to kill her?*

*She was not a child of a demon, only the mother of one.*

*No one was looking. We could have killed her. People were hurt in the fire. They died in it.*

*Erin, be merciful, I pray that our holy task is judged righteously done when our soul rests in Your cold embrace.*

*Erin, be merciful.*

The buildings that burned opened a new canopy for the seeds of life. New men would rise from the mud to grasp at the sun over the canopy. New homes and new shops and new streets would bring new hope to people that needed hope after such an awful fire.

Ragpickers dug through the remains as soon as the trash was cool enough to touch. Ashen rags became grey paper. Paper got sold. The paper described the transaction of items passing from one boat to another. These passing items, with all of their papers, eventually fell to the ground as rags. The ragpickers took them to the ragmen, and spent their money on the things that spilled in from the seas.

Imam's flock seeks to pluck the ragpickers from the streets, house them in dormitories, and educate them so they might be more than ragpickers.

The paper their Temples use to write such missions come from the very ragpickers that need to be saved.

※

Where did I leave those three blighted of-demons during their time in this city?

The memories hiding in my skull blur together, and I struggle to follow threads of life with this quill.

Quill, together, let us go dancing at a ball. I seem to recall that such a thing was next enough.

# CHAPTER XV

Work isn't bad. It's just work, you know. I work, and I make money, and then I go home.

*You said that you meditated while you worked.*

I do. I reach for the Unity while I work.

*What is that? What's it like?*

Well… Let me think of how to explain it. Hm.

*It isn't really important. I'm trying to talk about something, is all. I hate sitting around in silence.*

*I understand. I think I can explain the Unity. Last night, I looked down at these wet little wads of ratty hair on my mop. These frayed bits did not see their path across the floor. I couldn't see their true destination until after I swung the mop. And the Unity was the handle. The Unity was my hands pushing the mop. The Unity was the destination. The place that was out of my hands was the thing I controlled. The room was, regardless of me. The floor was, regardless of me. The little white-grey mop-threads splayed everywhere with each flick of my wrist, pre-ordained but also not pre-ordained. And then, I wondered if I had everything backwards, and each one of my fingers was the true population of the metaphor. I couldn't see where my fingers shoved the mop. And that started to make sense. And I thought about other kinds of fingers shoving other kinds of mops. And then, there's this woman— we'll call her Jess, because they all pretend their name is something cute like "Jess"—and she clomps up and down the stairs ready to roll a fellow with her bat. The bat crosses the same air, and the same heads got smashed—because all heads looked the same to Jess, who was not cute like her name. And I knew her life. The Unity unfolded like a flower. Jess hadn't touched a drop of liquor since her daughter died. Jess' daughter, like a smaller, prettier Jess (but she wasn't really that pretty), took up with a mean fellow for a while. Jess was too drunk to notice what was happening. The fellow beat the girl up so bad she could barely walk home to Jess. Jess broke off the leg of her kitchen table and carried it to the man. Jess came down on him. She took his own knife and claimed both of his ears, his nose, and his tongue. She threw the man out the back window from three stories, and figured he'd bleed to death before anybody helped him. She was right. When Jess got back, her daughter was dead. Jess put the pieces of the dead man in a pickle jar in her cupboard, and she buried her daughter. Now Jess kept the girls safe. And that's Jess. And the Unity brings the threads of her life into focus.*

*That's a horrible story, Rachel.*

*Well, it's a horrible place. I work, and I go home, and I don't think about anything when I'm there but my faith.*

*I want to take you somewhere beautiful, Rachel. Please, let me take you somewhere beautiful.*

᎗

Jona rummaged through his mother's closet for her old dresses. He needed something long-sleeved, with a high collar, and gloves. He wanted something green to match Rachel's eyes. He wanted something simple that would be easy to sew into the right size.

He found something jet black, long and elegant and fringed with white silk ribbons. He pulled it out from the closet and carried it downstairs. He held it out to Rachel. "Put this on," he said.

"What?"

"It's my mother's dress."

"I'm not getting in that thing."

"You are, and then you're going to help me fix it to fit you where it's too big on you."

"Why?"

"Because every beautiful lady needs a beautiful dress."

"I don't need anything like that."

"Come on, it'll be nice, and then tomorrow I'll take you somewhere you can wear the dress."

"I'm not going anywhere in that thing."

"It won't be dangerous, I swear. People'd notice a Senta, but they wouldn't notice you in this."

"I don't like to go places Senta aren't welcome."

"It's not that, it's just that you'd be the only one in the place, and everyone would notice you."

"Where?"

"Just this party, and you'll love it. We won't stay long. Then we'll go about town pretending like we're both rich nobles, and everyone will believe us because they'll see you in your dress, and me in my dress uniform."

"The dress is beautiful."

"Do you want to try it on?"

She frowned. "I do," she said, "I really, really do." She pulled off her Senta leathers, with a frown like she hated what she was doing. She wasn't going to stop.

Rachel walked like a peasant in a dress. Jona pressed a hand on her hip.

"Like this," he said.

His hands moved her hips under the fine black satin. He put his feet behind hers. "Lift up from your body."

She put her hands on top of his. She looked over her shoulder at him. He pressed his lips into her ear. "Like this," he said.

His thighs pressed into hers. He pushed her with his own body. He held her hips in place.

"Like this?" she said.

She stepped away from him. She took two steps, before her boots clipped each other. She stumbled, laughing.

"No," he said, "just try your best. You're beautiful enough, and you're with me, and no one will really notice."

She couldn't take off her boots. Underneath the hem of the dress, her muddy, dank boots clomped inelegantly. None of the nice shoes fit her demon feet. Even if they did, they would only make her step worse because Rachel'd only ever worn these strange kind of boots that hid her deformed, bestial feet.

Jona asked her where she got the boots, and she said that her brother made them for her from other boots. If they ever tore, Djoss took care of it.

Then she changed the subject in the same breath.

"This is a terrible idea," she said, "Please don't make me do this." She pressed her face into his shoulder. "I've dreamed of this as long as I knew what people with money did, and I can't wait to go, but it's a terrible idea. We're going to get caught."

"We'll be fine," he said, "Rich people will never admit that two of-demons—and poor of-demons at that—crashed their ball. Anyway, the true measure of a grand ball is how many illicit guests sneak through the gates. We won't be surrounded by the rich. We'll be surrounded by people just like us. Merchants, maids, guardsmen, nobles, and anyone else with the juice to wear nice clothes and hop through a window. Free food, and fine dancing, and everyone is lying about who they are except for the people that don't need to introduce themselves. Even they're mostly faking."

"Faking being rich and powerful?"

"When a rich and powerful person lies, you can't just call them a liar, right?"

"You can't?"

'No. Look, just pretend as much as you can, and try to follow my lead, and do what the other ladies do. If they catch us, they kick us out the back door. I do this all the time, you know."

"Do you?"

"My mother did, too, when she met my father. Remember who I am. I am Lord Joni. I may be poor, but I am still a nobleman. I must jump these things and wow some ugly horse of a girl who can buy herself pretty to take me to her bedroom and call me her husband."

Rachel coughed. "Charming."

"I'm never actually going to do it," said Jona, "If I wanted to do it, I'd have done it long ago. Rich is nothing. Money buys ugly girls pretty, and stupid men smart. Rich ruins a good fellow."

"I'd love to get myself ruined like that."

"Rich people get complacent, and they don't see the problems hanging all around them. Happened in Galvez across the sea, and a bunch of them rich folk died and didn't see it coming. We poor saw it coming from here."

"Djoss and I don't stick around to let things happen to us. Usually fellows can see it coming, whether they dreamcast or not."

"Rich people don't see it. They smile and dance until the rope bites their neck and rolls 'em. Happens everyday."

A long pause.

Her hands brushed along the dress. His fumbled in his pockets like a fool. Her eyes looked down at herself. His looked at her face.

He realized that he had stood her in front of a mirror, but the only thing in the reflection was her clothes, and some malformed shadows instead of a face.

I suspect Rachel was thinking about Jona's father, and that's why she didn't say anything after his speech.

※

Jona rubbed Rachel's shoulders, above the skirt of scales hidden in the folds of her dress. He kissed her neck. She stared out the window of the carriage, to the street, and all the people walking and walking and walking. "When we get there," said Jona, "you're a vacationing Duchess from the Brendt Islands, near Galvez. Your family resides in…"

"I'm a dispossessed duchess, with no holdings at all, and I came here on your arm because I'm trying to find a rich husband to rebuild my family name. My parents are dead. When they were alive, we were from Batriva, in the north where it snows all seasons."

"Have you ever been to Batriva?"

"I lived there for almost a year."

"Perfect. If anyone asks can you talk about it?"

"Me and Djoss had to jump out a second story window to escape with our lives. Mud and a mattress saved our lives."

"Don't talk about that. This is going to be lovely, I promise. No mud, no mattress, no second story window."

"I'm terrified. I can't wait. Please, let's not stay long. I just want to see it, dance once, and then make our grand escape. Do you think they'll send hounds after us?"

"I can ask them, if you want, if we get bounced."

"I hope they don't send hounds after us."

※

The carriage stopped at the rear gate of the compound. Jona

and Rachel were nowhere near the grand entrance where line after line of carriage waited for a grand introduction through the main hall.

Jona shook hands with a man in a smoot-covered apron smoking a pipe at the gate. Money passed between their friendly palms. The man held the back gate open for Jona.

Jona turned back to the carriage. He held up a hand for Rachel.

She emerged from the carriage into the night like a raven bursting from a treehollow, long hair like a ruffled train of feathers and flowing trails of white ribbon and black satin. She stepped down carefully, pretending like she wasn't wearing thick boots inside the hoops of the dress.

The man with black apron and pipe held his breath when he saw her.

Jona nodded at him. Rachel's skin was a smooth, nocturnal alabaster. Her imperfect face made her like a monument, where time's fingers had carved new, soft nuances into the stone. She was as gorgeous as anyone could hope to be.

Jona took her arm. He led her through the gate. Jona knew the way. They strolled under a small stone arch, into a maze of low flowers. They walked around a pond covered in paper lamps like burning lilies, and into a large hedge maze. Jona stopped her once to kiss her. She leaned back into the branches, and then she shoved him back. She smacked him because he was messing up her hair.

Jona helped her prod her hair back down. He led her through the maze to the main lawn. Paper lanterns hung from trees like giant fireflies, flickering. Already, people milled about—so many people, and all so beautiful. The men wore black and dark purple and uniforms with ribbons and medals. The women wore everything else, and black and dark purple. Every face was pure. Every smile was truthful.

Servants in white moved through the crowd, with liquors on trays. Guests reached up and selected from the different colors of liquid. The sips were small like their small laughter, all delicate like crystal.

Rachel clutched Jona's arm. He led her towards the raised dais where a group of musicians tuned.

Jona leaned into her ear, and cupped his hand over his mouth to hide his lips. "In another hour or so, this whole place will be stuffed with dancers. Everyone will be spinning around the dance floor like it's nothing, but nobody dances with the fellow they came with," he whispered, "Let's go meet someone. I'm looking for this fellow I know."

Rachel leaned up to his ear like she was going to kiss his neck. Instead, she cupped her hand over her own mouth and whispered back to him. "Are they all crashers, or is there someone you see that actually belongs here?"

"This rabble?" Jona gestured to the people all around. He didn't bother to whisper. "Mostly crashers," he said, "Mostly. Come on. Let's meet some people. Duchess Rachel Batrilander, I presume?" he offered his hand.

"Oh, goodness! You must be Lord Joni," she said. Rachel raised an arm at a passing waiter for a glass of liquor and quickly selected something in a bright shade of blue. She swallowed it fast and looked around at all the beautiful people walking through the lawn from the house. She put the empty glass on another passing tray.

Jona looked at her wide eyes, her smile. He introduced her to the first man he saw. He kissed Rachel's naked wrist above her glove. She laughed. The man's beard tickled.

Jona walked Rachel around the room, introducing her. The names, like a foreign vocabulary rolled over Rachel's ears. She let the men kiss her wrist, right next to her pulse. After a few men had kissed her, a spike of fear entered her. She might smell like bleach. Her hands must be too rough, after all that cleaning.

She wrapped her arms around Jona, and refused to let anyone else touch her.

Women curtsied, and she copied them as best she could in her heavy boots. The bottom of the dress, where the hoops brushed the grass, was already damp with dew. Jona had lowered the hem all the way down to hide her boots. The hem dragged over the grass, picking up every tiny drop of dew.

Another man kissed her wrist before Rachel could stop him. He said his name. Rachel stuttered her own invented title. Jona asked her if she wanted something else to drink. She nodded her head. He pulled her back to the edge of the crowd.

Before they could return to the edge of the garden, gorgeous people poured out from the sprawling main house, and Jona looked up at the crowd. He pulled Rachel's arms off of his body. He looked up over the crowd strolling down from the main house. He muttered something to Rachel, but she didn't hear it. She fell back from him, and tried not to look too conspicuous.

Rachel followed Jona with her eyes. She saw him stop a thin, pale man in a purple topcoat with black, silk pantaloons. The man smiled at Jona, but Rachel couldn't see Jona's face. She saw Jona's head leaning in close and firm, like he was saying something important. She walked as gracefully as she could across the crowded yard. She had to dodge circles of old friends clumping together as the two crowds from the house and the garden merged.

She took Jona's shoulder. He turned with an angry face at her. He took a deep breath.

A red-haired woman touched the shoulder of the pale man with whom Jona had been speaking. The pale man snatched the woman's arm from the air, but let the woman walk away from him. They both held their hands up, reaching after each other in the crowd.

Jona shoved the man's hand down. "Hey, have you met the Duchess from Batriva?"

The man cocked his head. "No," he said, "I can't remember meeting her at all." He squinted. "You look familiar," he said.

"I'm sure we've met at some lovely party in Batriva, where I am from originally," said Rachel. She recognized the man, too. He could've been a patron at her brothel, or a man about the streets in her neighborhood.

He had a familiar face.

"I'm sure we might if I had ever been to Batriva."

In the distance, a band began to play a slow, majestic march. Ruffled dresses and shining pantaloons meandered out to the center of the lawn and bowed gracefully at each other. The people danced with their hands quite nearly touching, spinning stately circles.

"My name is Sir Salvatore Fidelio," said the pale man. He reached for her wrist. She let him take it. She looked back from the dancers. He kissed her, and he did not let her go. He stayed there, with his face against her glove.

"I am the Duchess Rachel Batrilander of Batriva," she said. "Pleased to make your acquaintance."

"I wish to dance with you," he said, "if you wouldn't mind…" He looked at Jona. Jona nodded, and bowed to the man.

Rachel clutched at her own dress.

She had never thought so much about her boots before, like heavy chunks of lead beneath her dress.

Salvatore took her out among the spinning circles, and found a place for them in the swirling lines. During the marches, men took the outer circle and women took the middle. They took simple, slow steps spinning in time with the music with their palms out, nearly touching. Then the men stepped backwards at a turning of the melody, and the women swelled forward following a reed flute's mournful wail. The men gracefully spun together to the outside of the circle of women. Now the women were on the inside, and the men pulled the women back from the center to where they were before. The steps repeated with a new partner. Though it was mostly movement, women put themselves into the motions, swaying their hips or twirling their fingers like snakes.

Rachel danced stiffly. The men looked her in the eyes, and sometimes one slipped his hand too close to hers and brushed at her skin in a lithe stroke. Rachel knew what they wanted to tell her. *Put your body into it, darling. It's simple, but so is true grace.*

Rachel smiled and looked away. Her stomach danced more than she did.

When the song ended she was with Sir Salvatore. He bowed to her. She curtsied.

"Milord," said Rachel, "This dancing has parched my throat. Please, take me to find a drink."

"Of course, milady."

She took his arm and let him lead her past the crowd.

"I've forgotten your name."

"Sir Salvatore Fidelio," he said, "and you are still the Duchess from Batriva?"

"I am still. Ask me later, I might be someone different. What do you know of Lord Joni?"

"Him? I know he wasn't invited."

"Are you sure?"

"Quite. That's alright, it doesn't reflect poorly on a man to seek to improve his station."

Sir Salvatore gestured over his shoulder. Rachel turned, and she saw Lord Joni dancing a graceful waltz with an older woman, as graceless as Rachel, but with wider hips.

Salvatore snorted at Jona. "He seems to be doing quite well for himself."

"Oh..." said Rachel, "Who is that woman?"

"That is the daughter of Lord Sabachthani. Not even the king is richer than her, I hear. Certainly, no one is as beautiful."

"Well, I'm sure he's just being polite," said Rachel. She turned back to her companion on whose arm she was.

"Frankly, I don't think he stands a chance."

"She's a bit old to be dancing vigorously, isn't she?"

"I would be careful before I discuss the hostess at her own party, Duchess. Have you been here long?"

"Here? I came with Lord Joni."

"No, no, girl. How long have you been in Dogsland? Has it been for the whole season, or did you sneak in to catch the final hours before the rains?"

"Oh, I just came in from Batriva three days ago. Where are you from, Sir... I forgot your name again."

"Salvatore. I have been here all the days of my life. My father was a soldier who earned our minor nobility during the war, but he died rather quickly afterwards. Fortunately, the title is hereditary. I have been seeking my fortune until recently, and therefore have not been attending many of these lovely affairs."

"Oh, and how is your fortune... Where do you..."

"I am a speculator in the wool market."

"Are you rich?"

"I wouldn't be here if I wasn't, would I?"

"Of course not. Where's my drink?"

"Excuse me?"

"I really am thirsty. Find me a drink. Something tight. Last thing Jona brought me wasn't tight enough. It didn't even buzz me."

"I'm sure one of the servants will get around," he said, "They seem determined to ignore us. Perhaps they suspect us of being crashers. I hate to break it to you, but everyone knows Jona is a crasher, so we all suspect you are a crasher, too. They won't kick you out if you behave yourself, but they certainly won't pay any consideration to you when you show up on his arm."

"My name's Rachel Nolander. That's my real name. Send the hounds after me if you want. What's your real name?"

He smirked. "I'm Salvatore Fidelio, no 'Sir'."

"Nothing wrong with a fellow trying to improve his station. Tell me, Salvatore Fidelio, have I seen you before tonight?"

"I can never remember anyone. I have a terrible memory unless I really know someone."

"Well, Jona's left me for the hostess, so I guess it's only you." Rachel looked over Salvatore's shoulder, "So dance with me on the other side of the lake. I can't handle the crowd. I'm scared to Elishta about all of this. This was all Jona's idea."

Salvatore bowed. He took her hand. He walked her around the lake. When they reached the edge of the light, Salvatore bowed, again. He held out his hand to her.

Instead of delicately touching her for a decadent waltz, he pulled her close to him like a peasant girl. She rested her head on his shoulder. He spun her in his arms around the edge of the lake, far from the crowd.

⚜

And Jona saw the two dancing. He bowed to Lady Sabachthani, and begged her forgiveness. She rolled her eyes, and looked across the lake. "We'll talk more later," she said, "Don't kill any of my guests over some peasant girl, Lord Joni."

Jona ground his teeth. "I'll do what I like," he said, "If we're being honest about it." He pushed through the dancers like he was a king's man closing in on a street tough in the Pens. People cursed him for his rudeness and he didn't hear them.

He walked quickly around the little lake to Salvatore Fidelio spinning Rachel.

Jona clenched his fist. Rachel laughed at something Salvatore said. Jona hopped a little, almost running now.

Jona grabbed Salvatore by his ear. Rachel scowled at him. Jona tossed Salvatore into the shallows of the lake.

Jona pointed down at Salvatore like Imam's own Inquisitor. "You're coming for Aggie, or else you best learn how to swim."

Salvatore looked up at Jona. He sat in the lake, and splashed his hands among the shallows like it was a joke. "If you wanted to cut in, you should have asked, Lord Joni." Salvatore stood up. He walked back to the shore.

Jona lifted a boot to kick at Salvatore's face.

Rachel grabbed him. "Jona!"

Jona pointed his thumb at Salvatore. His face twisted. "If you knew that fellow like I know that fellow, you'd do the same thing. Maybe worse." Jona spit on Salvatore's shirt. "Aggie's counting on you. All you have to do is show up on time, and take her. After that, you can dump her anywhere and walk away. But you have to show up first. Here you are, like nothing happened. Have you gone to see her? She won't even talk to me, anymore. She won't do anything but ask for you."

Salvatore stood up from the shallows as gracefully as he could. "You're the one who told me to do that to her."

Jona walked out to him. Jona jammed his finger onto Salvatore's chest. "I told you I'd do my best to save her, too," shouted Jona, "I told you I would. And I did. And now you have to do your part."

Salvatore brushed water from his hair. He looked at the green algae on his palms from the bottom of the pond. He rubbed it off on Jona's lapel. "I can't even remember her face," said Salvatore, "Did I love her? I don't know. A woman I loved would never have done what she did. I don't know her. I don't know anything about her."

"She's going to die!" shouted Jona.

Servants walked around the lake casually, ready to intervene and throw both men from the ball. Lady Sabachthani stood at the edge of the party, watching this scene with her arms folded.

"People die," said Salvatore, softly, "but I don't unless the king wills it."

Jona grabbed Salvatore by the lapel of his fancy coat and threw him into the lake, again. He took Rachel's hand and pulled her into the hedge maze.

Rachel touched her cheek where the lake water had splashed her, but it wasn't lake water. It was tears. She was crying. Her sleeves melted in the acid, like smoldering paper. Her eyes widened. "Wait!" she said, "Wait!"

Jona turned.

She bent over. Her tears fell straight down into the grass. A small stench of burning grass and death followed her tears.

"What is it?" said Jona. He noticed her clothes were melting here and there.

Rachel breathed hard. She tried to clamp down on the lump inside of her. She tried to close her eyes so tight that no tears could slip out.

Jona didn't say anything. He rubbed her back. He looked at her, mystified by what was happening. She choked hard on her own sobs. She clamped her eyes shut, and tried to hold all of her tears inside. She held her breath.

Where tears fell, a section of hedge browned at the edges, and grass melted at her feet.

They walked back through the maze. Her clothes continued to burn off from acid. She spit on her hands and patted at the edge of her new holes. "It's my tears," she said.

Jona took off his jacket, and put it over her shoulders. He didn't care if his dress uniform burned. He never wanted to wear it again. He had made her cry while wearing that jacket.

In the carriage, Jona held her hand. "I'm..."

Rachel put a finger on his mouth. "Hush," she said.

She leaned into his shoulder. She ran her hand up and down the side of his face with this burning smell between them—the brimstone, acrid smell of acid-burned clothes.

❊

Rachel got back to the apartment in her own familiar Senta clothes alone. Djoss sat on a chair, nursing a bottle of piss brandy. He looked up at her. "Hey," he said, "Where'd you go?"

"Oh, I was just out a bit."

"Where did you go?"

"I went out."

"Okay, and when you do that, where do you go?"

"I go out. That's all. Look, Djoss, I don't ask about your women. Don't ask me where I go. I won't be found out. I'm careful."

"Rachel… I just want to know where you go. I get worried sick when I don't know where you are."

"You think I don't worry when you're gone?"

"It's different for me."

"Why? Because you're human?"

He looked up at her like she was a child. He spoke softly. "Because I'm a man," he said, "Because I can always walk away with nothing inside of my belly."

She snapped her fingers. A spark of flame jumped into the air. "Elishta on you and your belly."

Rachel snapped her fingers again, and the brandy burst into flames. Djoss cursed. The bottle fell to the floor. It shattered. He jumped up from it. He stomped on it with his boot before the fire spread.

Rachel grimaced. "Why do you have to worry about where I'm going all the time?" she said, "Can't I have my own life, like you do?"

Djoss spit on the spot of singed floor. "What if we have to break for it?" he said, "I need to know where you are in case we have to break for it. You tell me the same thing."

Rachel rolled her eyes. "Well, I'm going out. I don't know where I'm going. I don't know when I'll be back."

Rachel stomped out the door. She slammed the door behind her hard. She fumed all the way past all those noisy rooms.

Djoss was behind her. He called out to her.

She ignored him. She turned two corners, walked past the large slaughterhouse, and through the human bottleneck from the workmen building the new canal. She turned a corner, and then another corner, and then another. She didn't know where she was, anymore, and she had never been there before.

# CHAPTER XVI

I know Djoss looked for Rachel in the stockade because he met Jona there. I don't know precisely how his feet carried him over the streets.

I know he was chasing after Rachel, but she was so fast through the evening crowd returning home and grabbing the meat for their dinner from the butchers near the Pens and no one knew her, really, so how could he find her?

Djoss could find Turco faster than Rachel. Djoss didn't know where she went. He walked down the road. He asked the vendors and shopkeepers if they saw his sister.

"What did she look like?"

"A Senta, about this tall, and pretty as a flower with mouse brown hair."

He cursed when he saw where she worked. He went inside, and told the women there that they'd have to find another maid for the night because Rachel was sick and wasn't able to get out of bed at all. He didn't know if she'd ever come back, but if she got better she'd come by.

They shrugged. They put the sign looking for help in the window. Djoss asked if that ever really worked. The owner said that the people who worked there couldn't usually read, but having the sign up still seemed to work.

Djoss walked up and down the street, looking for her. They hadn't been going out together lately, and he didn't know where she was going now. He stopped ragpickers that he knew. They didn't even know Djoss had a sister.

Djoss tried to find the few places he had taken her when they had gone out together, but they were anonymous places, where people don't tend to remember anything.

He stopped in at the tavern where he still bounced when there wasn't any weed to burn and he asked around if anyone had seen his sister. This time of day, it wasn't crowded yet. People were still home eating dinner, pretending to talk to each other, and no one had hit the streets, yet.

Yet, the boss told Djoss he needed to work later. Djoss told him his sister was missing, and he needed to work on finding his sister. The boss told him to go get somebody to cover his shift for him, and Djoss grabbed the first big fellow he saw come in the door, and Djoss offered him a few coins to pick up the shift that night. Djoss told him he could take the night's wages for the shift, too.

The fellow shrugged, and figured he might as well.

Djoss hit the streets, with no idea where to go, except that he had to keep looking. He walked and walked, searching the crowd, until he was completely lost. He stopped in a tavern for a drink. He didn't have lots of money on him. He bought the cheapest thing on the menu, and he drank it fast so he could get drunk quickly. He did it until he was out of money.

He stumbled back into the street. He was drunk enough to

shout his sister's name while he walked, like seeking a lost dog. Angry men threw trash from the windows. A jar of pickles broke on Djoss' forehead, cutting him. A woman cheered from her window. Djoss tumbled into a ditch, overwhelmed from the alcohol and the vinegar. He turned onto his side to vomit.

When he woke up, a city guardsman was poking at him with a sharp hook. Djoss groaned. He looked up at the man standing over him in the early morning light. The guard shouted something. Djoss couldn't understand it because it hurt his head so much. He rolled to his knees, and the motion rolled his stomach into his mouth. He poured more vomit into the street.

Then he heard what the guard had said. "Get out of the street, fool. Be drunk somewhere you won't get trampled."

Djoss clutched his stomach and staggered into an alley. He threw up one more time. He sat in the alley for hours, waiting for the worst of the hangover to pass. He stood up and trudged towards his home. He squinted into the light and took a wrong turn.

He heard a town crier screaming about the executions slated for tomorrow. Robbers, thieves, rapists and none of them wealthy.

The town crier called out about an of-demon girl to be burned alive.

Djoss stopped in his tracks.

He turned towards the town crier, up on his little pillory. He walked closer, slowly, with a new sickness all over his face.

"Hey," shouted Djoss, "Hey, what was that about an of-demon?"

"I only know what I shout," said the crier, "Ask a gossip about the of-demon. I'm an honest fellow!" and he went back to his litany of criminals.

"What's her name?" said Djoss.

The crier ignored Djoss. The crier kept calling out new names. He had finished the executions, and was now listing the people to be locked in the saddles and ridden about town. Djoss stopped the first person he found. "Do you know the of-demon's name?!" he shouted.

"Toss off!" said the man. He pushed away from Djoss.

Djoss grabbed another person, a woman. She slapped him.

Djoss shouted at the crier, "Hey, you!"

"Toss off!" shouted the crier, "I'm working!"

"Where do they keep the ones they're going to kill?"

"Don't you know? See me there soon you keep bothering me. I'll smash your head up. Head to the King's Old Palace, other side of Dogsland River."

"What's it look like?"

"Stick around a little longer and I'll show you."

Djoss asked everyone around him for directions. They pointed North, across the river, and into the mainland, where the swamp mingled with the city and the wall.

Djoss ran.

Three different layers of king's guard let Djoss through to see the girl. They didn't even ask for bribes. Corporal Christoff didn't look up when Djoss clumsily tried to sneak past his desk in the last room.

They were expecting some tough to rescue the girl. They assumed Djoss was their fellow.

Djoss climbed down three flights of stairs following the directions he got from the third guard. He made it all the way to the bars.

Jona was sitting next to an open cell. He looked up at Djoss. "Salvatore send you?"

"Who?" said Djoss.

"Worthless sneak thief, that Salvatore. Can't even save his own girl," said Jona. "Has to send someone. Right then, go on. She's in there."

"Who is?"

"The girl. Salvatore's girl. You're here for her, right? Go on in, and get her."

Djoss had been around enough to know he'd best hop in and check the girl out, and the rest of the mystery was best not unraveled right then. Djoss set his eyes low, walked in, and aimed at the shadow weeping in the back of the room. There was a girl, long black hair and puffs of dust when her chest heaved. Her hair was black, but in this filth it could've been anything wrapped in black filth.

He saw it wasn't his sister from where he stood. He went in anyway. He wanted to see the second of-demon he'd ever seen in his life.

She took a deep breath at Djoss' footsteps behind her. Her tears dried up, and her face chilled pale. "Did Salvatore send you?" she said. She looked up at Djoss with plaintive eyes, her hand upon his filthy boot.

"He did," said Djoss.

"He should've come himself. Why didn't he come? Who are you?"

"I'm Djoss Nolander," he said, "pleasure to meet you." He offered his hand.

The girl looked at it like a dead fish. "Where's Salvatore?"

Djoss sat down across from her in the straw and filth. "I don't know," he said.

"I want you to go find him, and tell him that he has to come for me. I know he'll come for me. I just know it. He loves me. He would never leave me to die like this. Imam'll find a way. He'll save me when I least expect it. When will he save me? You have to know him. You must know him. I won't leave without him."

Djoss leaned forward and looked at the girl, closer. "I'll find him," he said. "Where can I find him?"

"Don't you know?"

"I'm sorry…"

"I will not leave this cell. Without Salvatore, I am a dead woman, and all glory belongs to Imam. I know Salvatore'll come for me. And if he doesn't, I won't…" she started to sob again, "I won't know a body on the streets. I won't know a soul, without him. I'll have nowhere to go…"

"You can come with me, if they'll let you," whispered Djoss. He touched her face. "You're not alone, you know. There's another girl like you. I was looking for her when I found you."

She threw his hands away. "Get out!" she shouted. "Don't touch me!"

Jona leaned in at the two in the cell. "Hey, street meat, you saving the girl, or what? All I hear is talk talk talk in there, and nobody's saving the girl."

Djoss stepped out of the cell, his face pale. "She's the of-demon?" he said.

Jona nodded. "Tested her blood myself, twice. Beautiful thing, yeah? Never know how evil takes in a body. Probably all rocks and brimstone inside of her. Bet she has beast guts, or all teeth between her legs."

"I bet," said Djoss, "You know this Salvatore fellow?"

"What's it to you?"

"Do you know him?" said Djoss.

Jona nodded. "I know him," he said, "She won't leave without him. I told the girl her fellow was waiting upstairs, but she wouldn't believe me. She won't leave unless he comes for her. Silly thing, to burn a girl just because she was born a little evil, if you ask me. Plenty of people are born evil, right? I can walk a block and tell you every kid that'll hang before he's got a beard. Don't roll 'em, before they earn the rope, right?"

"Well, the girl…"

"Well, the girl's a dead woman if Salvatore doesn't come for her." Jona stretched his neck. "Look, I don't know you, fellow. If you don't know where Salvatore is, best to walk the job. I wouldn't get involved in this, were I dumb like you. Nasty, nasty."

"I'll take her with me," said Djoss, "I'll take her over my shoulder and kicking, but tell me where Salvatore can take her off me."

Jona stopped. He cocked his head. He looked up at the hulking figure of the dirty, pens-stinking bouncer. Jona stood up. "That's your game?" He whispered, cruelly. He pushed Djoss against a wall, hard. Djoss bounced back and put his hands up. He was smart enough not to punch a king's man in the king's prison. Jona kicked and shoved Djoss back up the stairs. "You want to see the of-demon up close before she's burned? You want to taste a spot of evil, just to see? See if she'll ride you one last time? That what you think? An ugly sack of street meat like you, and you think some condemned of-demon might ride you just for kicks? Think you save her and she rides you? Take her off and have her and then let the some monkey buy her off you?"

Djoss didn't mind getting hit by a king's man. He stepped backwards up the stairs where Jona, muttering and striking, pushed him. Djoss was back in the streets. His body was puckered in bruises from Jona's sharp fists. Djoss jogged away into the night, alone.

"You go find Salvatore," shouted Jona, at Djoss' back, "If you don't, I'll hunt you both down myself."

❖

Djoss did the only thing he could think of. He went home.

It was a long walk.

When he got home, no one was there. He got water from the well. He watered the flowers and set the rest to boil some water for rice and tea. He had a few sausages left over, made with pork and some berries and lots of sawdust. He ladled out the boiling water for his pot of tea, and then he threw the sausage and the rice into the rice pot.

He ate alone, staring at the door. When he was done, he laid down in his bed. He closed his eyes, and breathed deep.

Djoss pulled himself from the bed. He rubbed his forehead. He looked around to see if Rachel had returned. He had cooked enough rice for them both. He didn't know how to cook just enough for one. He ate most of what was left, and covered the rest with a cloth in case Rachel came back later.

He looked outside at the street below them. He called out to one of the street vendors, and he asked the vendor if she had seen Rachel. The vendor didn't know who Djoss was talking about.

Djoss took more money from his little stash. He hit the streets again. First he swung down to his tavern to grab another lay-about to pick up the gig for just one night. The boss told Djoss that if Djoss kicked one more night, he'd be gone. Djoss told the boss off and stuff the lot of them.

Djoss hit the taverns he knew, and the cafés he knew, and the places he thought she might know. He found a few familiar faces, but that's all. They hadn't seen the girl.

He figured he should retrace his steps into the city. He went back to the first apartment, at the baker's shop. He hopped inside, and caught the baker's wife sweeping up and closing down. He asked her if she'd seen Rachel. The woman said, "Who?"

"My sister," said Djoss, "We lived here a while ago. Thought she might turn up for some bread or something."

"What she look like?"

"Senta, and a woman like a younger, thinner, prettier me."

"No Senta came in today. You buying anything?"

"No."

"Then let me finish up. We're closing down for the night. Be open tomorrow right at sunrise. Fresh bread, then."

He stepped out of the place and looked around. He wanted to

go back further, to Turco's crate city. The closer he got, the more it occurred to him that there probably were no crates anymore. That kind of home is ephemeral, and rain and rot and sickness swept in and melted the whole thing into the sewers. The place was probably just a mudpit now, where Turco lit cookfires at the edge of a river and a few stalwart vagabonds lingered around a fire in a muddy field.

Djoss stopped at a street vendor and tossed a coin and said the name, "Turco, the fellow from Dunn. One of them Three Kings painting three crowns. You seen him around?"

The vendor nodded. He pointed towards an alley. Djoss nodded. He walked towards the alley, and he remembered it now. This was the place where there had been crates. Now, he could see the rotten wood in heaps, fallen and covered in thick, green moss. Turco smoked a pipe against a warehouse wall. He smiled at Djoss. "Hello," he said, "You've been missing, Djoss. Dog's been counting. Didn't know he could count, but he's been doing fine, I think. Mudskippers help him."

Turco reached into his pocket for an extra pipe. He offered it to Djoss.

Djoss took the pipe. "Thanks," said Djoss, "Where're the fellows? Where's Dog and the mudskippers?"

"Out and about," said Turco. Turco pulled a match from another pocket. He slipped some spare weed into the pipe, and flicked a match. He held it out to Djoss.

Djoss took one puff, and knew he had made a mistake taking the pipe. He coughed. His head spun. He leaned back into the wall. He shoved the pipe back in Turco's hands. "Thanks," he said, "I needed that."

Djoss slid down the wall. He looked up at the sky. It moved. He felt coughs rising up from his chest like sweet butterflies. "Elishta," he said, "What kind of weed is that?"

"Good stuff. Not the common stuff we been smoking on the corners, all mixed up with lettuce and chicory and whatever else to fool us with. This is the stuff we run around to the pipes. This is the raw demon. This is the burnt tongue of Imam and Erin all in you."

"I've never had any that tight before," said Djoss. He looked at his hands. His hands seemed far away. "Nothing that tight. Where did you get that?"

"You've been running it out and about with the mudskippers. Three Kings, three crowns rolling a racket with this stuff. Good stuff, right? This is off the tip top."

"Amazing," said Djoss. He watched his hands shrink in front of him. The sky was purple. The air he breathed was thick with joy. His coughs faded into a hum in his throat, like a hiding smile on the back of his tongue. "My sister'd kill me. Headcheese can break a fellow's skull. Break it in half. Amazing stuff."

"Right, that. You ready to help cut it?"

"No," said Djoss, "You see my sister anywhere?"

"No. I know a fellow who might have seen her."

"Really? Who?"

"Don't know his name. He knows everyone in the city, though, if they're worth knowing. He's a Senta, too, but he keeps his head growing and growing with the names and places where people are, and this good stuff." He lifted his pipe to his lips. "Good stuff, yeah. He knows everyone to know, and everything, too. He knows me. He knows you."

Djoss held out his hand for the pipe. "Hey, let me try that again."

"Careful," said Turco. He handed Djoss the pipe.

Djoss took a long hit, until his lungs burned and he coughed away the pain until the glow rolled in like a cool breeze on a hot day. He smiled. "Where is this fellow?"

"I'll take you," he said, "How much money you got?"

"Some," said Djoss, "How much it cost?"

"We'll see when we get there," said Turco, "Finish that pipe for me and we'll go."

Turco took Djoss by the hand, because Djoss wasn't walking straight. Turco led Djoss to a tavern by the water. The sign out front had a picture of a woman standing next to her own head. *The Silent Woman*, it was called. He led Jona inside. Turco waved at a fellow behind the bar, and the fellow waved Turco past the bar, and into the kitchen. Once there, Turco knocked six times on a wall next to the counter. The wall opened. Turco took Djoss' money from Djoss' own pockets and handed it to the bouncer of the lower room. The bouncer counted the coins, nodded, and gestured down with his thumb.

Candlelight surrounded a pool of pillows. Men and women lay in heaps on the pillows. They clutched at the thin ends of a huge hookah, like a giant glass tree reaching out rubber branches to the men laid low on the pillows. A mound of slowly churning pink weed smoke bubbled up through the water. Men sucked on the little hoses.

Turco snagged one of the limbs, and handed it to Djoss. "Here," he said, "Try this."

Djoss took a drag, and the universe opened in his skull. He fell backwards onto the pillows. His mouth opened.

Turco laughed. "Welcome to Elishta," he said, "Folk like us only get one shot at the right life. This is it."

Djoss slowly dragged himself up to sitting. He took another quick sip from the limb of the tree. "Where's the fellow who knows where Rachel is?" he said, after three tries at speaking.

Turco looked around. "I guess he isn't here, yet. Just stay tight. He'll get here." Turco slipped a limb off the hookah. "Everybody says this stuff is bad. I don't know why. Way I see it, we spend our whole lives wishing for happiness and never getting it. Here I am, and I drink the smoke of this here wishing tree, and I wish for happiness and I get it. Where else guys like us be happy?"

"When will the fellow get here?" said Djoss, like he hadn't

heard a word.

"Relax," said Turco, "He'll get here."

⊞

Whether the fellow ever arrived or not is unknown to everyone. Turco had used Djoss' money to buy himself into the hookah.

When Djoss came back down from the bliss, he was lying in a gutter, in a hard, cold rainstorm, in the middle of the night. Muddy water full of all the filth of the city streets flowed past him. He was choking a little on the rain. He sat up, soaking wet.

He tried to remember where he was. He looked to one side, and saw the ocean on the other side of the street. He looked the other way, and saw a tavern. He stood up, but his legs were full of smoke, and he had to sit back down again, splashing, into this tiny street river. He waited until he could feel the blood in his body. His whole body had fallen asleep, and he had to let the blood return to parched limbs.

He stood up. He stumbled over to a wall next to him. He leaned into the wall. He staggered back to his apartment, stopping for directions twice. He didn't know what day it was. He stopped to puke four times. His whole body ached. He wanted to buy some food, but he couldn't find any money in his pockets.

On his way home, he passed the square where they had burned the girl. Rain poured over the smoldering ruin. Two king's men—privates with barely any facial hair—stood next to the damp, burned corpse, throwing dice to see who had to actually touch the corpse when they cut her hands free, and they needed to pull the melted flesh from the stake where it had melted in like glue.

Djoss sat down and looked up at the body. He sat there, and thought about his sister. He thought about the girl he saw, in the prison. He thought about his mother.

He broke down into tears. His tears weren't acid, but they still burned down his face like every one of his nerves was broken and burning.

The rain stopped. The seasons turned, but they didn't turn fast. The rainstorms would return again, but for now, they were only an occasional force off the ocean.

# CHAPTER XVII

*When we leave this city, we won't know where to go. We haven't made any plans.*

*Don't leave, then.*

*We will, Jona. I should find a way out while we still can.*

Rachel walked in a straight line, looking for the city walls. When she got frustrated with that, she turned a corner. Then, she turned another corner. She walked up the first hill she encountered, climbing up and towards a river on the other side of the valley. This river had a large bridge, overgrown with city life and lined with low huts and tents. Shrewd men lined the edges of the bridge with outhouses that hung just over the lip of the bridge, available for a fee. Steady filth dripped in bursts onto the river boats like a slow, oozing waterfall.

Rachel walked over the bridge, past the many dirty shops and hot corn vendors and tinkerers selling scrap warped into tools and baubles and the ragmen with their cheap used cloth and cheap paper.

She was hungry, and tired. She stepped into an inn on the other side. She invented fortunes for strangers in the inn's tavern until she had enough money to spend the night.

She could barely make out a glimmer of the Unity. She was a charlatan to these drunk men and she didn't care. She had a room on the second floor of the inn. It had a bed, and a bathtub. She didn't have enough money to take a bath—nor did she want to risk a servant's assistance—so she fell back onto the bed and stared at the ceiling. She listened to two people making love through thin walls, and it reminded her of Jona. She clutched at her stomach, and thought about him.

She didn't sleep well. She dreamed of darkness.

In the morning, she left the inn and looked at all the people bustling off to their normal lives.

She closed her eyes, and imagined all these people who just wanted to be happy. They wanted to lead spectacular lives. They dreamt of winning prizes and the love of someone beautiful and conquering the enemies of their way of life. Every single one of them wanted to be rich, beloved, and peaceful before they died.

In her mind, she reached out into the Unity, searching for happiness. She wanted to find one happy person in the push of bodies.

Perhaps it was the stink of demon taint that kept her back. All she felt were horses pulling carriages with a numb, animal bliss. Sometimes a whip cracked, and the spark of joy faded a while, but it came back soon enough. The horses were happy.

She opened her eyes. She walked aimlessly through the streets until nightfall. She found another tavern. This time she was able to see a few actual prophecies in the cards. She didn't earn as much tonight. People paid less for bad news.

She made enough to eat and get drunk. She staggered into the alley near the tavern and found a place to lean against the wall that was mostly hidden from the street. She pulled an empty crate over her body, and closed her eyes, curled up inside this empty, wooden box.

In the morning, she was stiff and sick. She staggered into the light, and followed the crowd to a town square.

The crowd screamed and threw rotten bits of food at a beautiful, pale girl tied to a pole.

Geek and Sergeant Calipari stood on the platform beside the girl. They looked sad about what they were doing. Geek stared at his boots. Calipari held a single torch in one hand, smoldering quietly in the sun, and in the other he held a scroll. He read the scroll, and Rachel threw up when she heard.

The girl was going to be burned alive. She had bled true for Elishta's demon stain in her blood and she was going to be burned alive.

Geek walked over to the girl. He unsheathed his blade. He lifted her chin with the tip, and got her to look hatefully in his eyes. "Hold still," he said. He jumped, spinning, and he slammed the flat of his blade across the side of her skull. She sagged under the blow, unconscious.

The crowd booed.

Calipari shook his head. "She's supposed to be awake for this," he shouted.

Geek shrugged. "I guess the terror made her pass out," he shouted.

Calipari squinted. "Guess so," he shouted back. He pulled a black hood over his head. He placed the flame at the pile of kindling wood bunched at the base of the kindling.

The crowd cheered. They threw pieces of wood and coal at the girl, now. The bottom of her ragged dress caught fire. Her legs reddened as the fragments fell off in bits of black ash. Then, her dress was almost completely burned away, and she was naked from the waist down and her skin was all blisters and boils like an overcooked chicken and the fire kept growing higher and higher and the skin flaked off in grey clusters. The crowd cheered when the last remnant of her dress melted into her ruined skin.

Her eyes fluttered open. Her head rolled to one side. Her hair had burned into a jagged mess.

She screamed.

Her body was blackened bones below her waist. Her chest charred from the smoke. The stink of cooked fat hung in the air. She pulled at the bonds over her head, pulling herself up higher and higher out of the fire. Her hands were still human. They reached and reached up. Rachel watched the girl's hands. In the back of her mind, an old rhyme popped up, unwanted.

*Hands are the things that make us men,*
*Deaf men talk and blind men see with them*
*Dead man reach hands up to the sky*
*Grab that soul that's flying by.*

❖

The crowd was gone. Only a few morbid stragglers and ragpickers remained at the fringe of the square. Calipari used his sword to cut the bonds over her hands.

The cooked cadaver crumpled into the pile of burned wood. Calipari chopped off the girl's head with one stroke. He poured fuel over what was left of her. He covered the girl's body in a thick yellow soup of whale oil and kerosene. He reached for a new torch. He tossed it onto her. He bowed his head and prayed quietly to Imam.

The remains of the demon-touched body couldn't be buried. It had to be burned completely away.

Calipari and Geek tossed their swords into the flames. Calipari turned his back on the fire, and looked around at what remained of the crowd. He needed to make sure no one disturbed the fire until the body was burned away to purity. Then, the body would be thrown into a deep pit and burned again and again, until nothing remained but a black stain on the steel.

That's how demons are killed and their poisonous bodies are removed from the world of men.

❧

Rachel's guts were in knots as tight as rigging. She walked to Jona's house. She got there by sunset. She knocked on his door. An old woman answered.

"I'm looking for Corporal Joni," she said.

"Are you, now?" said the woman, "and what about?"

"Please," said Rachel, "It's important."

She sniffed at her. "Some Senta demanding my son. Have a prophecy about something, you want to share with my boy?"

Jona appeared behind the old woman. He pushed past her. "Ma, it's fine."

The old woman walked back into the house. "I'm going to bed. Be careful with those Senta, Jona. They can sniff things about people you'd rather they didn't know. And be sure to do the dishes before you leave."

Jona brought Rachel into the kitchen, and what was left of dinner. She sat down, and poked at some leftover noodles. "Mind?" she said.

"No," said Jona. "Don't you have to work tonight?"

"I don't think I'm working anywhere right now." She didn't see any silverware, so she reached into the bowl with just her gloves. She slurped at the noodles, unashamed.

"Are you alright?" said Jona.

"Why did you have to ruin my night like that?"

"What? What did I do?"

"You didn't even dance with me."

"Oh," he said, "You never dance with who you show up with. I told you that."

"I'm not some noble hussy. I wanted to dance with you because it's every girl's dream to go to a ball with a handsome lord and dance into the night. And when I had someone to dance with…"

"Salvatore sold out his partner, and now she's dead. She was just a kid, too, younger than you. Hey, how old are you anyway?"

"I don't know. I'm exactly as old as you. How old are you?"

"I'm twenty-six."

"I'm not that old. I'm trying to be mad at you, Jona. I'm trying."

"Be mad. I was a bastard."

"You were."

"It's probably the blood to blame, not me."

"If the blood makes someone evil, how come I'm not evil? I just know I'm not evil. I don't feel evil. Who says we're evil?"

"I think… I don't think it works like that."

"Well, how does it work, then?"

"I think it works like… I don't know."

"Imam tells us that all we do in the world will be brought back to us seven-fold. If I do good, then that good will come back to me, and I will be good."

"All right, well if we do both good things and bad things, will the sevenfold cancel each other out?"

"No. Maybe. I don't know."

A knock on the door. Jona looked past her. "A minute. That's going to be my Sergeant."

"Get rid of him. I want to talk with you."

"I'll try," he said, "Not easy to get rid of Nic."

Jona walked out of the kitchen, and opened the door. Calipari let himself into the kitchen in an instant, digging through the pantry for some tea to drink like Rachel wasn't there.

Rachel looked at Sergeant Nicola Calipari. She heard his name being said, and took his hand and shook it. She looked right at him. She washed her hand in the sink, and stormed out.

※

Nicola gestured at the slammed door. "Pretty thing, but weird in the head. What'd you do to her?"

"I told you not to come in, Nic. You weren't listening."

"You hit her, yet?"

"Of course not."

"Well try not to hit this one. I know a few fellows that like to keep a lady in line. If you need to hit her, you've already lost, I say. I went about with a Senta once, when I was your age. It was great until she prophesied I'd end up with someone else. Then she left me. You haven't been doing any prophecy with her, have you?"

"Of course not. You know I don't believe in any of that. Imam."

"Hope you don't tell her that. Drives Sentas crazy, crazy. Hope she hasn't done it on her own, either. Prophecy's not a good idea. I don't know why lovers do it, but lovers are always dumb. Providing the livelihood of many a Senta, but that's the way of things."

❧

When Djoss got back, Rachel was there, asleep. He grabbed her boot and wanted to wake her up.

"Hey!" he said, "Rachel! Wake up!"

She groaned. She sat up. She looked at him. "What?"

"Where'd you go?"

"Nowhere. You?"

He snorted at her. "I went nowhere, too. Didn't see you there."

"Well, that's too bad. That's where I was. I guess I didn't see you, either."

"There was this girl," said Djoss, "They burned her. For a while, I thought…"

"Well, it wasn't me. It wasn't anyone I knew."

"I wish…"

"You're a mess. You're sopping wet, filthy."

"I was in a gutter when I woke up."

"Oh?"

"Yeah."

"Drink much?"

"Something like that. Lost all our money."

"Better get back to work then. Those mudskippers still running your little packages?"

"Yeah. You should go back to work, too. I think you lost your job, though. You'll have to find a new one."

Silence hung in the air like a low fog, filled their lungs, and filled their eyes. They looked away from each other.

"Elishta, Djoss. What happened to us? I don't remember when we last talked to each other. When's the last time we just sat down and talked to each other?"

"What should we talk about?"

"I don't know."

"Anything."

"We'll talk in the morning."

"I'm worn out."

"Go clean up. You're a mess."

# CHAPTER XVIII

J ona scrubbed his uniforms in the basement. He brought
hot water down from the kitchen, and poured it into his
own private tub. His father used to sleep in the basement,
alone.

When Jona's father slept, he walked in his sleep. All the urges
of his darkness took over his body, and his dreams were of being trapped inside of a monster, looking out from this monster's
terrible eyes. The monster was chained down, in the basement.

Two strong stone pillars with many heavy chains kept the
monster locked in the basement.

Sometimes the man had drifted off to sleep somewhere, alone,
and he woke up covered in blood with a full belly on the grounds.
Servants were warned about the Lord's sleepwalking, and they
were urged to wake the man up with loud noises and slaps.

Jona stripped his uniform off his body and ran it over the
washboard. He scrubbed it and scrubbed it until it was mostly
clean. He had a couple spare uniforms, but they were down

here, too, tossed over the stone pillars and stained with mud and blood.

Jona had to wash them all. When he was done, he poured the water over his father's mud grave. Jona collected his wet uniforms in a basket. Then, Jona walked naked up the stairs, to the roof.

Jona stopped in his tracks. He moved the basket in front of him quickly.

Lady Sabachthani stood up, bowed gracefully, and turned her back to him. She looked at naked streets, devoid of life at this late hour.

"Good evening, Lord Joni," she said.

"Ela," said Jona, "I wasn't expecting you." Jona quickly pulled wet pants on. "May I offer you something to drink?"

"No, thank you," said Lady Sabachthani.

"I'm wearing pants," said Jona.

Lady Sabachthani turned back around. She sat on the edge of the roof, again. "I've seen men naked before, Lord Joni. I thought you might show up," she said.

"Did my mother let you in?"

"Oh, I found my own way. I had hoped there might be some news about my suitors."

Jona sighed. "I don't know who the killer was," he said, "but I know who ordered the killing of the Chief. Someone didn't like the idea of a commoner on the throne."

"Who?"

"A friend of Lord Elitrean," said Jona, "but not a friend of his son. This fellow is best left alone. I may buy the blood monkey's heart for most, but this fellow is untouchable for all but the king. Oh, and Young Elitrean didn't know a thing."

"And have you heard anything about my other suitor?"

"Well, rumor says…"

"I've heard plenty of rumors already," she said, "for instance, that we were in love. What do you know?"

"I know nothing," said Jona. Jona pulled up a uniform shirt. He threw it over the line. He reached back into the basket for more clothes. "Elitrean's boy seems to have dropped into the water. Best I can figure is he was in disguise and he got rolled. They tossed him into the river. I don't know what disguises he liked to wear, but that's the best I can figure it. He isn't smart enough to hide this long when people are really looking. Think about it. Rumors sound good, this time."

"Please keep looking for him, Lord Joni," said Lady Sabach-thani, "and when I am queen, tell me who ordered my friend's death. No one is untouchable to the queen. Not even the kings of great nations are untouchable to the queen of Dogsland."

"I will, milady."

She stood up from the edge of the roof. She walked towards the stairwell.

Jona kept putting his uniforms up on the line. He didn't turn around to watch her leave. A hand touched his naked back, where his back was scarred from the demon wings that had been cut away. For a moment, it felt like Rachel, but Jona knew it wasn't Rachel. He turned around. Lady Sabachthani was close to him, looking up at him.

"Thank you," she said. Her hand remained on Jona's shoulder. "When this is all over, I won't forget you. You can dance in the finest balls with me, and then you can dance in the worst of the sailor pits like you belong there, with no mask or hired guards or fears. You know how to find murderers and thieves, and you know how to make people talk. My throne will need men like you in the days to come."

Jona looked away. "It isn't your throne, yet, Ela." He stepped back, into his own wet clothes. "I don't help you because I want something from you. I'm doing it because you asked me to help you. That's all. I don't want a thing. I do just fine by my own. If you want to do me a favor, just forget me. That's the only favor I want. When you're queen forget me. I'm happy just living my own quiet life."

A cool breeze washed over Jona's naked back. He shivered. Ela smiled, mysteriously. She backed away. She stepped into the stairwell. She closed the door behind her.

⟐

A pub—any pub—full of people covered in the remains of their professions. Dock workers drenched in sweat, sea spray, and splinters. Factory workers stank of stale wool. Sometimes musicians played if they weren't too busy drinking or pinching after the girls. The two genders mingled freely after the inspector's bell. Women flocked to a corner to have their fortunes read by a man with tarot cards.

Rachel's breath stopped. She grabbed Jona's collar. "We should go," she said. She leaned into him, to hide her jerkin's red X on charcoal grey.

"What, why?" said Jona.

Rachel gestured where only Jona could see. "There's a Senta telling fortunes in the corner. I don't want him to see me."

Jona looked over his shoulder. "What's he doing down here? Sentas don't usually come down here except for you."

"Let's go, Jona."

"No."

"Please," she said, "I just want to go."

"He won't do a thing with me. If he tries to do something, he'll get bounced or I'll arrest him. Besides, if he's down here, he's probably just faking. He'd make better money by the city walls."

"Jona…"

Jona sighed. "Fine," he said. He drank the last of his rum. He drank the last of hers, too. "We'll go somewhere else, then." He tossed some coins at the barman, and grabbed Rachel's shoulders. "Where do you want to go?"

"Anywhere but here," she said.

Jona and Rachel had to pass the Senta's corner to maneuver through the crowd. Jona stopped Rachel right next to the fellow. Jona looked over his shoulder at the old man flipping cards.

"Hey, Senta," said Jona.

Rachel's fingers tightened on Jona's hand.

Jona sneered. "I'm looking at you, foreigner. You hear me?"

A seamstress, in the middle of her fortune, scowled. "He's busy, king's man. You got your own Senta."

"Yeah, and I'm taking that one with me, lady. Your Senta looks suspicious to me."

The Senta looked up at Jona.

"Come with me, old man. We've got business outside."

"I have no business with you."

"Take your cards and come with me. You'll make more money with me than you will with her."

"I am not a greedy man."

"Never knew a Senta that didn't turn a card for the right coin. Well, finish up with the lady and meet me out front. I won't hurt you. I promise."

Jona walked to the door. Rachel's nails dug hard into Jona's palm. Jona ignored her.

"Look," said Jona, "you can't live in fear of these folks. Let's test them. Let's see if they can really see us for what we are."

"They can. Let's go home, Jona. We can just leave."

"He'll get here, else I'll send a bouncer after him. He's a faker. I'll show you what I mean. Lots of grinders find the clothes somewhere, and they run a little grind at the docks where nobody knows better."

The Senta didn't come out; Jona tossed the bouncer a few coins, and told him to fetch the old fellow telling fortunes for a king's man.

The bouncer returned quickly, with one hand on the old Senta's shoulder.

"Thanks," said Jona.

The old man folded his hands. "You need something, king's man?"

"Yeah," said Jona, "Thing is, when fellows show up down here in a dive like this and start reading fortunes, they're usually a grinder in someone else's clothes. So, I want you to show me that you are what you say you are. You got any fire, or ice, or wind?"

"I have studied the koans," said the old man.

"So, show me."

"No," said the man.

"So, you're a faker. I'll toss you in the tank, and you can think about what you're gonna wear when we strip those clothes off you in the morning."

The old man pulled out his cards. "A student of the koans came to an old Senta," he said, "A Senta older than I am. The student asked for the old woman's assistance with some of the more difficult teachings. She hit the student over his head, and hobbled away from him. She shouted 'I will do what I like.' The young man, thinking on her words until he understood them, looked down at his hands, and saw that he had aged, too, even older than the old woman had been. He became one with the Unity not long after."

The old Senta turned back towards the pub. The bouncer blocked him. The bouncer looked up at Jona.

"I've never heard that koan before," said Rachel. Rachel snapped her finger. A flame jumped into the air. She held the fire in space, like a floating ball of burning paper. She called the winds to carry the fire to the old man's face. Rachel, concentrating hard, wrapped the fire in a ball of ice that spread inward. The ice snuffed out the fire, and fell into the mud, lifeless and melting.

The old man didn't blink.

"I told you he was a grinder," said Jona.

"Would you like your own fortunes read?" said the man.

Jona laughed. "If that's all you got, you're going to be sleeping in the tank tonight."

The old man looked at Rachel. "I can read your fortunes if you like, just as I have read the fortunes of the poor folk in this blighted tavern."

Rachel nodded. "Fine," she said, "but not here. Jona, do you know somewhere we can go that will be private?"

Jona looked down at Rachel. He huffed at her. "Sure," he said, "We can go to the Old Brewery. It's big, it's mostly empty, and I don't think the rats will pay us any mind."

※

The Old Brewery was open to the night. The street doors, unlocked let in the animals and homeless drifters collected in the corners, mostly sleeping, like bits of paper blown in off the street, accumulating in damp piles. In the center, the huge crane, leaned over the water like a limp fisherman's pole.

Jona led Rachel and the old Senta to the center of the brewery, near the crane.

"We're mostly alone," said Jona, "but eyes are watching us here. Try anything funny and word will get back to the people that can do something about it."

"This spot will do just fine," said the old Senta. He pulled his cards from his belt and shuffled them in the dark. "Funny thing, the future. So strange, yet so easy to see. People don't see the patterns of their own life. Do we even need the cards or do we use them to help the one who seeks the future? What do you seek, young one?"

"I am not your pupil, do not address me like one," said Rachel.

"You can call upon the sound in the air, but you cannot call what connects them. I shall draw a card for you."

The man pulled a single card from the center of the deck.

Rachel snapped her finger and the card burst into a ball of flame. "I've changed my mind," she said, "I know my future. Do you know yours?"

"I shall remove my clothes and give them to you. I shall walk away. I'll die in these streets. I have embraced my place in the Unity. What have you embraced, young one?"

"I am not your pupil," said Rachel. She turned away from the man. "Do not address me as one. Now take off your clothes. I need them."

Jona, confused observer, said, "Rachel? You think his clothes will fit you?"

"I'll make them fit when I get home."

The old man stripped. He folded his clothes, ceremoniously. He placed them on the ground in front of him.

"Let him go, Jona," she said, "And don't ever do this to me again."

Jona's mother stirred the porridge for her breakfast. She hummed to herself while she stirred. Jona was on the roof, listening to his mother through an open window. The street had only just awoken, and Jona leaned over listening for his mother.

His uniforms were all on the roof, drying in the winds. He had washed them last night with the rest of the clothes, naked and standing on the roof with the night breeze running over him.

He didn't tell his mother about Lady Sabachthani's visit.

The uniforms took forever to dry in the wet air. Jona leaned against the chimney. He stood up, went to the uniforms, and tested them with his fingers. Still wet. He went back to the chimney.

He gave up waiting. He snatched a uniform from the line. He pulled it over his body, still damp.

He went downstairs, where his mother stirred porridge. She daydreamed a little, she sang to herself the songs of her youth, and she stirred porridge. She wasn't singing because she was happy, but because she was trying to push something away from her mind, and Jona knew it because he knew his mother.

"Ma," he said, "what's wrong?"

"Stay safe out there, Lord Joni," she said, "I'll see you later tonight." She placed the bag with her sewing needles over one shoulder. She walked out the door.

Jona looked at his porridge on the table. He poked at it. It tasted terrible.

# CHAPTER XIX

*What do you want to do?*

*I want to go to bed. I'm tired. I'm so tired. I worked all night.*

*Do you think your brother will be there?*

*No. I haven't seen him for two days. He's running with gangers now, you know. I don't think he bounces anymore.*

*Everyone's in with the gangers these days but you and me. Nothing to do. Maybe he'll turn around on his own.*

*Maybe. We need some lemons. We're out of lemons. Go buy some lemons.*

---

The lazy sun, falling slowly through the sky while clouds rushed past, reached one sleepy finger through the window and onto the bed. Rachel curled closer to Jona to escape the hot sun. Jona stared at the ceiling. They had made love. They had talked. Rachel had fallen asleep. Rachel had woken up when Jona tried to move to escape. Rachel pressed into him. Her warm scales funneled Jona's sweat into her mattress like tile roofs guiding rain to eaves. The scales nipped at his damp skin when she moved. If she pressed hard enough she might scrape him.

Jona ran a hand over her face. He could see that her eyes were open, looking down his naked body.

"The hottest part is almost over," said Jona, "Dogsland'll start cooling off soon."

"Good," said Rachel, "I'm so hot I can't move."

"When it cools off, the rains'll come. Places'll flood. People will drown in their own homes. Not really, but it'll start to rain a lot, again. No one will drown. They'll just wake up wet if they didn't get their house ready. Roofs might cave in. Foundations carved bad might bust. Won't stop the city. We'll walk around with parasols and go on like there's no rain. We'll scrape out boots at our doorways and pretend there's no mud. Ships'll come just the same. Ships'll go just the same. Things will go on until Adventday, about when the rain lets up a bit. Then it'll come back, but it won't be as strong. Then the rain will fade until it's just the sun. But it will rain a while first."

"When it rains everyone will be all muddy," said Rachel, "and the stinking meat and blood will wash away so fast that the Pens won't stink at all."

"Oh, the Pens always stink. But you get used to it."

"You should go. My brother might show up sometime."

"I should. Let go of me, and I will."

"I can't let go of you, Jona."

"I'll stay, then."

"But I should."

The sun patch slowly crawled over the thin sheets. Rachel crawled with it, deeper into Jona's skin.

The walls leaked the noises of the people in the building. Unconnected clanging of pots or boots or the creaking of footfalls or the chairs. Muffled voices—mostly women—spat gossip from window to window. Children in the narrow street, banged cans with sticks and sang songs.

A key in a lock.

Rachel's eyes opened. Jona grabbed at his pants below the foot of the bed, but he was too late.

A giant stepped in from the street. A cloud of alcohol sweat spilled into the room behind him.

Rachel had the sheet pulled over herself. Not even a hooked toe peeked out from the edge of the bed. She looked up at her brother, her face pale. "Djoss," she said.

Djoss took one step closer to the bed near the window. His fists clenched.

Jona grabbed for his boot. He had a knife in his boot. He jumped down to the floor, grabbing for his boots. He found one. He jumped up with the boot in his hand.

Djoss took one more step. He raised his fist. His face was blank as death.

"Don't hurt him," said Rachel.

Jona jammed his hand into his boot. He quickly felt around for his knife. "Tell him to stop and I won't," he said. No knife. He had the wrong boot.

"*I wasn't talking to you!*" said Rachel.

Djoss took another torpid step. His lip curled.

Jona grabbed his other boot. He shoved his hand inside for his boot knife. He grabbed the handle. He whipped it around between him and Djoss. The knife was still stuck in the boot. The boot waved in the air. Jona flipped the button that held the knife down. He threw the boot at Djoss. Djoss knocked the boot away with his fist. He raised his fist.

Jona knelt down low with his knife in his hand, ready to lunge.

Rachel snapped her fingers. Fire spread over Djoss' face.

"I said don't hurt him!" she shouted.

Ice followed the fire, encasing Djoss' head like a helmet. He punched at his head. A wind blew him back, through the open door into the hall. The door slammed shut.

"Jona, get dressed," she said.

"Will he..."

"Jona, just get dressed. He won't hurt you. Just get dressed and go."

"What about..."

"Do it!"

Jona grabbed at his uniform. He put his boots on first. Then, he took them off, threw his pants on. He grabbed his uniform shirt.

The door opened again. Djoss stood there, burning. Tears welled up at the edge of his eyes.

Jona stood, looking at him in the doorway. Rachel shouted at Jona to go. Jona looked up at Djoss' red eyes. "I'm sorry," he said. He stepped into the hall.

The door slammed behind him.

He stood in the hall, listening at the doorway in case Djoss attacked Rachel. Rachel said, through the door, "Where have you been?"

He couldn't hear Djoss' answer. Then he heard a deep bass voice, like a human bear, "I'm going to get some sleep. Burn those before somebody gets sick. Is he sick from you?"

"No. He's like me."

"He says he is."

"He is. I know he is. It's all right. We're careful. We're more careful than you."

The sound of a giant falling into a mattress. Leather pulling over skin. The sounds of the rest of the building overwhelmed the sounds from Djoss and Rachel's room.

Jona walked down the hall. He pulled his shirt and jerkin over his shoulders. He realized that he had left his knife back in her apartment. He couldn't go back for it.

He found half a small lemon in his pocket, still fresh and leaking bitter juice. He sniffed it. He bit it. He walked down the stairs, sucking on the lemon. In the street, he threw it into the gutter. He looked up at her window. He saw lines of laundry drying, dancing in sea breeze. He heard the street. He heard the wind blowing in from the ocean.

He waited, looking up at her window. Then, he walked away.

❦

Jona was sitting on the fence again, waiting for her to come out with the wash. He sat there, waiting, and when he saw the night maid come out with the wash, it wasn't Rachel. It was this other woman, with fat arms. She looked up at Jona, sneered at him, and went to work. "Nothing to steal round here, king's man. Even the women are too cheap to steal."

"I wasn't trying to steal," he said, "Looking for Rachel Nolander, the maid. She's Senta. She here?"

"No," said the woman, "She's off."

"Oh," he said. He swung down from the fence. "Tell her I was looking for her."

"I ain't saying nothing to nobody," said the maid.

"Yeah," said Jona. Jona tossed her a coin. "Well your kind don't count as somebodies, so you tell her."

# CHAPTER XX

Sergeant Nicola Calipari and Geek bit thumbs at each other and laughed because of a joke they had just finished about a fellow that'd answer every question they asked him by biting his thumb at whoever punched him last. Jona walked in at the end of the joke with Jaime. Jaime clomped his heels and saluted.

Sergeant Calipari jumped to his feet. "What was that, Corporal?"

"Corporal Lord Joni and the Corporal Kessleri walked the Pens, sir!"

"Excellent, Corporal!" said Calipari, "Are the livestock safe in those Pens?"

"Sir, no sir!" said Jaime.

"What?" Calipari leaned into Jaime's face, spitting on him a little, in good fun. "Why aren't the livestock safe, Corporal?"

Jaime choked on laughter. It took him two tries to spit the words out with gravitas. "Any pig in a pen isn't safe, sir! Pigs in pens are lunch, sir!"

Geek burped.

Jona grabbed the reporting papers from the desk, and moved items around the duty desk so he could sit down and write report. The worst he saw was some kid smugglers. When they were ghosted by the guard, they cut cargo and ran. Jona let them go. He dumped their lost pinks into the river.

Jona cut a goosefeather quill, and dipped it in the ink. He scribbled his report. Jaime waited for Jona to finish.

Jaime was telling the crew about this thing his kid used to do. Jona didn't want to listen. When Jona finished his report, he handed the paper to Jaime. Jaime scanned quickly, while talking. Jaime initialed at the bottom, and placed the paper on Calipari's desk.

Sergeant Calipari took the paper, initialed it, and stuffed it into a large envelope with all the other reports. He looked around him for a spare body. Jaime and Geek had both disappeared into the holding cells to drink brandy in an empty cell.

Jona held out his hands. "Sergeant," he said, "I'll take it in."

"Corporal?" said Calipari. He leaned back in his seat. "You sure you don't want me to get one of the scriveners?"

"It's fine," said Jona, "Let the kids go home early."

"*You* want to run papers?" he said, "Look, if you got nothing going on, want to run a den with me and the kids instead? We bust one of the dens, we smash the pipes, and we run anyone we catch into the tank. Then we file a few reports. A little fun for the scriveners, huh?"

Jona nodded. Jona stood up. He unsheathed his sword, and checked the blade for imperfections. He flipped the blade back into his baldric. "Bats or teeth?" he said, "And you know how I feel about just bats."

"I know, Corporal. Sorry, but bats. You can keep the teeth in your pants," said Calipari, "You never know."

Jona pulled a club from off the wall. He hefted it in his hand. He didn't like it. He put it back for a different one, thinner with more weight at the end. "I'm not sitting with a scrivener," he said. "Get me killed."

"I'll sit the scriveners around front, and you'll watch for the back way," said Calipari, "Always a few like to run for it. Break them. I'll meet you in the middle."

"Aye," said Jona, "Which hole?"

"The Three-Legged Dog."

"That pit?" said Jona, "Back way's a pit, too. Easy to roll a fellow there."

"Soft on me, Corporal?"

"Never," said Jona. He gestured at one of the scriveners. "Just give me the new one. He's fresh from training and still strong from it."

The scriveners sat up taller hearing about the evening's plans. Their quills slowed, and their backs straightened.

Jona caught the youngest private's eye. Jona and the new private shared a grin. "Pike him and he'll watch my back," said Jona, "He'll like pikes better than teeth."

"You'll be fine on your own. I'll run through and let the kids break the guts of the place. Any trouble should break quick."

"Right," said Jona, "If some tough breaks me, my mother'll come looking for you, Nic. I'm an only son."

"You'll do fine, Jona," said Calipari, "You live for this stuff." Calipari snapped his fingers at the new private, who would be running reports at the end of the day. "If you get back in time, you can come along, Private."

The boy, for he was still a boy, dropped his quill where it sat and ran for the central station, reporting envelope in hand.

⟡

*He doesn't tell me anything about where he goes. Nothing at all. It makes me sick to think about it.*

*I could probably tell you.*

*Don't. Please, just don't.*

Turco and Djoss cased this huge warehouse from the back.

The warehouse had one whole wall open to the canal, where water and ships ran straight into the warehouse like needles docking in old veins. These flatbeds with heaps of damp wool belched back into the canal.

Turco and Djoss stood outside the arch where the wall opened to the canal. They were on dry land. Turco pressed against the arch, his head shooting around the beams to peak inside. Djoss was just behind him.

Six workmen moved wool from the heaps on the land to the heaps on the boat.

Turco grimaced. Djoss shook his head. Djoss pointed again. Turco looked in, and saw workmen. He punched Djoss on the shoulder. Turco tried to walk away. Djoss grabbed Turco's cloak. Djoss shook his head. He gestured to the ground with his open palm. *Wait.*

The next riverboat piled with wool disengaged from the docks, and drifted into the canal. The drivers pushed the boat along with long poles across the bottom of the river. One man stood in back with the rudder. Until the next boat came, the workers sat down on the wool, and passed different flasks around.

Djoss pointed again. The wool on the boat had been blocking a small, red door on the other side of the warehouse. Card games are behind red doors.

Turco nodded. He wrapped a dirty red rag over his face. He slipped a small crossbow from his cloak. He strapped three bolts to the string, ready to shoot wild. "You were right," he said. He grabbed the edge of the wall and swung around, howling.

Djoss winced. Too soon. Djoss tugged a brickbat off his back, and swung into the warehouse on Turco's heels.

A worker looked up at Turco. "What you want?" he snorted, "You stealing wool?"

Turco stopped in his tracks. "Pardon us, gents," he said. Turco bowed gracefully.

Turco kicked open the red door. Inside the room, six men sat around a table, and a seventh held a bottle of brandy.

Djoss filled the space behind Turco.

The gamblers looked up at Djoss, a huge gorilla of a man, with arms like bags of meat. Turco waved his crossbow around the room like a child with a toy.

The man with the brandy placed his cup onto the table. He placed the bottle next to it. He raised his hands. The other men put their cards facedown on the table, and raised their hands in the air.

Djoss had the brickbat in one hand and a damp red rag over his face, too. Djoss closed the red door behind him. "Well," he said, "Keep your hands up, and don't get killed."

Turco moved to the edge of the room. He howled and hopped. Turco threw his cloak on the floor next to the table.

Djoss swept one hand across the table, and threw everything there onto the cloak—card, coin, cup, and pipe. He grabbed the corners of the cloak together in a bunch, and swung the make-shift sack up to his back.

Djoss and Turco backed away fast, and by the time they got to the warehouse again, a new boat had been half-piled with wool. Turco jumped onto the boat, and he crawled over the mountain of wool to the other side of the boat, the edge of the warehouse, and escape. Djoss followed over the wool, too, because he didn't want to run through the workers with the money.

The workers stayed out of the way.

The man with the brandy probably alerted the improper authorities. Djoss and Turco had to get off the streets. They moved ten blocks fast, sticking to the alleys as much as they could. They didn't run, but they didn't linger. They lost their red rag bandannas. When they got to the tenth block, they were at the kind of tavern where no one had eyes.

The place used to have a sign of a black dog over it, until a thug had broken the decrepit sign and the dog had lost a leg.

Now it's called the Three-Legged Dog.

Djoss paid cash for a room upstairs. While there, they'd both split the bounty, and take their prize downstairs to the limbs of the wishing tree. They'd smoke everything immediately.

By the time they finished counting, Turco's hands were trembling, and he sweated pink blood. He fingered the pipes from the table, searching for the right kind of smoke. The pipes leached black ash.

"You," said Djoss, "Get your hands out of the way."

Turco pushed aside cracked glass from the cups and bottles, and the edges cut his hands, but he had to get to the next pipe. He didn't seem to mind the tiny lines of blood on his hands.

Djoss slapped Turco's wrists. "Hey!" he said, "Look out, alright! I'm trying to count the coins! People don't smoke the real stuff at the tables."

"Never know," said Turco.

"They don't, all right?" said Djoss. He pushed Turco back from the pile. "Relax. Let me finish counting. We can't rent a room for the ragpicker pipes with what's left."

"If they don't throw us out together, I'll cut off your fingers."

"I'm almost done counting."

"Did you hear me?"

"Wait..." said Djoss. He looked down at hands, befuddled. "I lost count. Let me count. Go spit out the window and see if you hit anybody."

Turco threw his hat off his head, and let his scraggly, black curls swing free in the wind like ruined rope. He wiped at the pink blood seeping from his trembling skin. He leaned out the window.

Djoss finished counting. He pushed a pile of coins across the floor. "Hit anybody good?"

"No," said Turco, "I haven't been spitting. There are guards down there."

"What? How many?"

"Lots."

"What are they doing?"

"They're standing there. And they're talking with a fellow."

"A fellow fellow, or just someone?"

"A fellow fellow. I think it's the innkeeper's fellow. Their watchout man is watching out. Don't worry. Fellow'll bribe the guards. Guards don't really care about this place. Might get killed coming in here, ringing their bells."

"Want to wait a bit?"

"Why?"

"You know, maybe the fellow don't have enough."

"No, it'll be… Yeah, I see the coins. Let's go."

Turco stepped towards the door. He crossed over the coins and Djoss.

Djoss grabbed at his cape. "Wait," he said. "Weren't we going to use this to get some paint, find Dog and get the mudskippers working?"

"We can do that later."

Djoss pointed down at the floor. "Don't forget your coins," said Djoss, "I've got mine."

⸎

Corporal Jona Lord Joni leaned against a wall beside the back door. The Three-Legged Dog squatted on an intersection of three footpaths. Two of those footpaths went to the front door. One went to the back. The back footpath was a zig-zagging mess of old bricks, loose beams, and squatters in the ruins. The front way wasn't much better, but at least the two roads passed between the Pens and the Ferry, and crowds walked on them.

Jona had the bat in one hand and the sword in the other, and he held them up so everyone there could see him.

Among the ruins, hollow eyes looked out from shadows at Jona like he was a piece of raw meat.

Jona knew he'd hear the screams and footsteps pounding up

the stairs, when Calipari struck. Until Jona heard commotion, he watched the crowd around him. Two men in black capes bled pinks. They trembled and passed an undercooked sausage between them. They growled obscenities at each other between their turns of bites of food. An abandoned chamber pot kept a fire burning where six or seven wadded clumps of rag watched the two men with the sandwich. They pretended to ignore Jona.

Jona pressed his back against a solid pillar that used to be a chimney. He kept his weapons up near his face so no one could easily wrap a blade across his throat from behind.

Then, from inside the building, ceramic broke. A woman screamed. The band stopped. A cluster of boots galloped towards the back door. Jona stepped away from the pillar. He held his sword out in front of him, towards the door. He braced himself for the runners.

The first was a puff of cloth and fear. Jona jammed the sword into the man's thigh. The man's face grimaced and he dropped to a knee. Jona pulled his sword out in time for the next man, a Dunnlander that reeked of the pink. Jona caught the Dunnlander tripping over the fallen body with a bat across the skull. Jona knocked the spinning Dunnlander back into the guy behind him. The press of bodies swelled out into the alley. Too many were trying to run for it. Jona swung his sword again, at the air around the Dunnlander so everyone behind the Dunnlander could see it.

"King's man!" shouted Jona, "Stay where you are!"

Sergeant Calipari shouted from inside the Three-Legged Dog. Jona couldn't make out his words. The bodies stopped at the back door, peeling back into the building as the scriveners jammed at them with quarterstaffs and clubs.

Jona kicked the Dunnlander back into the room. Then, he picked up the wounded man up by the hair and threw him into the room.

Jona's eyes adjusted to the darkness. He saw smoke, and motion. Scriveners corralled all the people against one wall, mostly. One of the scriveners prodded at two men grappling on the ground with his boot, without a weapon in his hand. Jona squinted through the haze of smoke. Then he gasped. Jona saw Calipari wrestling with a large man on the floor. The large man had Calipari by the neck, but Calipari was smacking the fellow with his club across the large man's stoned skull.

The large man was Djoss, Rachel's brother.

Jona sheathed his sword and threw his bat at the scrivener there. Jona grabbed Djoss from behind in a hard sleeper. Jona dragged Djoss away from Calipari.

Calipari gasped for air. "Hold him!"

Jona pulled Djoss back into the alley. He threw him past the man with the injured leg, and jumped over his body.

The Dunnlander had recovered some of his consciousness. He was trying to crawl to the river. Jona pulled a knife from his boot, and lunged. The Dunnlander took Jona's blade in his back, right over his hip. The Dunnlander screamed in pain. His blood spurted black across Jona's uniform.

Jona looked up and heard fists slamming into skin.

Calipari had come after Djoss in the alley. Calipari stepped on Djoss's head and snarled.

Jona pulled Nicola back.

"Let this one go," said Jona.

"What!?" shouted Calipari.

Djoss dragged himself to his knees, and crawled down the alley.

Jona had a hand on Calipari's shoulder. "We got plenty, didn't we? What's one more?" barked Jona, "So, let that one go."

"Why?!"

"I know his sister," said Jona

"I don't care who you know!" snarled Calipari, "He had it for me!"

Djoss shook his head. "Listen, I *know* his sister. I can't drag him in. I'm trying to make things right with her, and I don't want to drag him in."

Calipari looked at his boy, in this alley. He cocked his head. "Never knew you to have mercy," he said. He took a deep breath. "Never knew you liked a girl this much. Let him go. But, you owe me one. You owe me big."

Djoss stumbled down the alleys between ruins and river, into the warm embrace of stink that the poor made with their fires burning trash in the night. Let the pinker burn himself in those corners. Let someone else slit his throat. Jona's hands were clean.

Jona collected his knife from the kidney of the howling pinker.

Calipari grabbed the Dunnlander by his sweaty hair. Sergeant Calipari glanced at the wound on Turco's back, and cursed. He pushed Turco to the edge of the river. "You're bleeding black from your liver," said Calipari, "You're a dead man now or in an hour. Hour'd be long with this kind of pain. So…"

Turco screamed for mercy. He screamed so loud his voice cracked.

Calipari pulled a knife over Turco's throat. Calipari pushed Turco's body into the river. Blood fanned out in a cloud. The body stayed afloat, drifting towards the bay.

❀

*Let Rachel find him, thought Jona.*

Her brother was lying in a ditch, all bloody.

She was meditating a koan, and pushing a mop from one corner of a hall to another. A man came by and asked if she could read his fates. She told him that she saw a painful encounter with a mop in his immediate future. The man laughed and went back into the room with the girl he had bought. Rachel looked down on the water, focusing on her koan. *How do I move a ship on the far horizon with only this hand?* She pondered a solution of the pain that moved the winds, how enough pain could pull any ship, anywhere.

And, then she saw her brother in a burst, on the horizon, sinking.

She knew there was nothing she could do until her shift was over. He would survive until the shift is over. And rent money had all been smoked, so her money would be necessary.

After her shift, she walked six blocks south and turned a corner behind the warehouses and behind the pens. She ducked under the pillars of a ruined building. This used to be a house. Now it was the ruin that shared a wall with a warehouse that shared a wall with a tavern so no one could tear it down and no one wanted to pay to renovate. Under the eaves the drifters shuffled into slow death and alcohol.

Rachel wrapped the air behind her with fire to keep the bedraggled night monsters back. She touched her brother's face, and wondered how she'd get him home by herself. She picked up his legs. She pulled him through the mud on his back by his legs. She dragged him out of the mud, to the cobblestones in front of the tavern. She flagged down a man in an empty dogcart, and paid the fellow to help her lift her brother into the back. She hopped into the cart next to the driver.

When the cart reached their little corner of the city, she had Djoss placed gently on the sidewalk, where they could wait for him to wake up and carry himself up the stairs.

She let him rest there, in the street. She took what was left of her night's pay to the landlord, and handed all of it over to him. She went to work. She knew she had to let him heal himself a little. Give him a chance to heal.

She knew it was time to leave this town, and this time it was because of Djoss instead of her.

# CHAPTER XXI

Jona's mother had the smallest hands. She sipped tea. She dipped tiny cookies into the brown liquid and gently placed the cookie on her lips.

"Jona, do you remember what your name was before your father died?"

"Ma, I'm Jona now. This is the only name I've ever known, and the only one I want."

"You should remember these things, Jona. It's important to know where you come from."

"Elishta?"

Her lips pursed. She placed her tea on the kitchen table, and her cookie next to it. She folded her hands on her lap.

"I say something, Ma?"

"You didn't come from Elishta. You came from me. I'm a good woman, aren't I?"

"Ma…"

"I'm no harlot, no harpy. And you're a good man. You're a

king's man. You're a good man. Don't say that you come from some awful place. You don't. You came from my body."

Jona stood up. "My father has been dead a long time," said Jona. "I'm not saying you're evil, ma. I'm just saying how many people did my father kill in the dark? How many died when my father wasn't chained down?"

"He was a good man."

"He was good for a thing like me. And he wasn't even the best there is. I've found some more like me, children of demons."

"They're lying to you."

"They don't know enough to lie."

"They're trying to trick you."

"Ma, they don't know about me. Nobody knows. I don't tell them. I found some more like me because I'm a king's man and I find people. Girl got burned at the stake was like me, but she was better than me, easy. Couple others out and about. One of them's the sweetest girl in the city. She's beautiful, and she's kind, and she's just like me."

"Jona…"

"Don't even say it, I know my future fine. Anyway, maybe we shouldn't worry so much about the past. All the past ever did was break us. Our life's seed has landed here, and we have to bloom where we land."

"Sentas say that. Jona, you know you should avoid Sentas."

"I can take care of myself, Ma. I can take care of you, too. I brought you fine tea, and fine cookies. I got them from the same place the other nobles get theirs. I want you to have them. I know you want them. Don't sit there like you don't have an appetite on account of all this talk."

Jona finished his tea in one burning gulp. He coughed. He didn't want to stop to put his boots on in the foyer. He picked the boots up. He opened the door. He walked down the street with his bare feet until he had gone down a few doorways. He squatted on a milliner's stoop. He pulled his boots on.

All around him, people walked from shop to shop on the land that used to be Lord Joni's garden. Under his feet, the ghosts of tree roots dripped into the sewers. All these people walking on the streets they've known forever didn't know whose land they were on.

And Jona liked them here. This was his garden.

He stood up. He adjusted his uniform on his back, making sure it fell right. He walked to the Pens District.

A handwritten note was tacked to Jona's bedroom door, on elegant paper. Jona knew exactly who had put the message there when he read it.

*Come to the roof, Lord Joni.*

He didn't go up right away. First, he went into his room, stripped off his dirty uniform, and washed his face and shoulders in a bin. He put on a clean uniform. He looked at himself in a mirror. He combed his hair. He touched his cheeks to see if he needed a new shave.

He didn't think shaving would help him look any better. He left his boots downstairs, in the foyer. He went to the roof barefoot.

He saw her, draped in layers of black like a dark chrysanthemum unfolding at her pale face. Jona saw the line on her ear where the powder ended and her skin truly began. Right at the edge, he saw her weary wrinkles of age.

She stood where she had always stood on his roof, against the edge. Below her the city lamplights spilled up across her skin. This only made her look less human, with her gown and her thick layers of make-up.

Jona looked her in the face. He smiled. He bowed.

"You found my note?" she said.

He walked closer to her. "I did," he said.

"Have you found anything about my lost suitor?"

Jona shrugged. "Does it really matter?" he said, "Even if he showed up again, would you want the strange scandal hanging over his head with the sudden death of his rival?"

She turned, leaning on the edge. She looked out at the night city, with the dotting streetlights into the distance like a golden road above the ground. "Of course not. I didn't actually expect you to find anything about him," she said, "I didn't really want you to, either. I just wanted you to look for me, is all. It was important that you look for me, Lord Joni."

Jona looked down on her. She looked so old to him, so tired.

"This kingdom needs a king, Jona," she said.

"You've got plenty that want it," said Jona, "Just hold out your hand and take anyone you want. None of them'd say no to you."

She touched his arm. "I don't just want anyone. I want someone that can be a good king. I look around at all the men I know and all the ones who could be king have already fallen into the bay. I'm not just looking for a powerful husband, Jona. I'm looking for the man who deserves power."

Jona slowly pulled out from under her palm. "Nobody deserves it," he said. He snorted at her. "*You* don't deserve it."

She turned back towards him. "But I have it if I only extend my hand." Her arm rose up, and her fingers extended out to him. "Jona, your mother sewed my dress. Do you like it?" She pulled away from the wall. She spun slowly, letting the silk in the dress dance as she stepped around.

"It's lovely," he said.

She finished her turn. She put her hands on her hips. "Do you really like it, or are you just saying you like it?" She was trying to be beautiful. She was trying so hard to be beautiful, that she looked pathetic to him and looked old. He looked at her, and all he could see were the lines around her mouth, around her eyes.

Jona grimaced. "I think it's lovely," he said.

She smiled at him. She cocked her head. She spoke softly. "Lord Joni, I can get you a fleur with the snap of a finger," she said, "I can return your lands to your family. You can start charging rent to all these squatters outside your door and you'll be richer than Lord Elitrean in a matter of months."

Jona stepped back. "I don't need anything from you. I'll do it on my own or I don't deserve it."

She didn't believe him. She raised an eyebrow, twisting her smile into a wry grin. "Don't you want to be the king?" she said.

"*What?*" said Jona, "No."

She took one step towards him. "Think, Jona," she said, "You know this city better than anyone else who might rule it. You know the lowest sewers and the tea houses and the street gangs and the grifters. You know the seamstresses and the craftsmen and the king's men and they know you. You've been drinking with bakers. You've been living with butchers. You've been fighting the wickedness of the streets instead of hiding from it or riding on top of it or feasting on it from a cloaked carriage." She took another step towards him. "This city would embrace you." She reached up to his face.

Jona pulled back from her hands. "I don't want anything from you, Lady Sabachthani. This city isn't yours to give. The King is still alive. Long live the King."

Now she was angry. Her grin curled into a snarl. "You could place your mother beside the throne in silk and pearls," she whispered, "It's been decades since she's done anything with silk but sew."

"No," said Jona. He took another step back from her.

She stared at him, in disbelief. "You can't be turning this down," she said, "You simply can't. You've worked so hard to achieve this." Her ears slowly reddened. Undoubtedly her cheeks were flush beneath the powder.

Jona took another step back. He was almost back at the doorway to the stairs. "I don't want your life," he said, "I hate that life."

She stomped her foot. She was still whispering. "Don't say

that Jona. What was all of it for if not for this?"

He took a deep breath. "I hate you, too," he said.

She stomped her foot again. "Please don't say that, Jona," she whispered.

He looked away from her, to the empty sky. "Maybe I don't hate you," he said, "When I walk about these streets, nobody who smiles at me wants to stab me in the back." He looked back at her. He felt sorry for her. She'd never know love. "You ever been to the Pens?" he said. "Used to be my father's lands, and I still take care of it. Meals you ate came from here. And you'd eat me, too, and use my streets for your power, but have you ever *been* there?"

Her lips were pinched like the mouth of a closed purse. Her head was down. She kept whispering. "You wear your king's man uniform when you walk about and everyone smiles?" she said, "And you have the sand to stand in this city—my city—and tell me about hating power?"

"I got nothing else for you, Ela. I'm just a Corporal, in it for the parcel. I'll take my girl into the woods and farm the fields and raise my children far away at twenty years."

"So you really hate me, then?"

"I hate people like you," he said.

"But me," she said, "You hate me."

Jona looked her in the eyes. He tried not to crumble.

She waited for him to speak. She didn't move. The breeze blew across her dress. When her dress rippled, her body's stillness seemed to break the breeze.

Jona broke. "I'm in love with someone else, and I don't want you to hurt her," he said. "I want you to leave her and me alone. I'll say anything I have to say for you to leave us alone and away from your deadly hand."

She raised a fist and pounded her own palm, hard. She kept whispering. "If you take that filthy whore's maid to my ball again, I'll toss you both into the river, and we'll see how you swim."

Jona shook his head. He looked at her with open eyes. He knew what to say now, to keep him and his love safe. He wrapped his face in evil. He let evil into his tongue. He looked down on the small, middle-aged woman on his roof. "I pity them that lay one finger on my beloved," he said, slowly.

She didn't flinch. "You must love her a great deal," she whispered. "You must love her a great deal to threaten the future queen over a whore's maid."

Jona laughed at her, cruelly. "You call her that, and maybe that's what she is sometimes, but she's the only thing in the world I want," he said. "If you were as smart as you think you are, you'd forget the throne, and find a nice fellow with a kind face and let him teach you how to love."

She stepped close to him. "Jona..." she said. She reached hands to his face. He slapped them away. "I know what love is," she said, "I have lost more lovers than you have known. This foolishness is just the fire of your youth. What about your mother's love?"

Jona took another step back. "You'll say anything to get what you want," said Jona.

"So will you," she said.

Jona stepped back all the way to the door, never turning his back on Ela. He slipped inside. He closed the door. He flipped the lock on the inside. He went downstairs, pulled on his boots, and fled into his city streets.

⚜

Though I cannot verify my suspicion, I believe that Lady Ela Sabachthani broke down when Jona left her. I believe that she cried all the powder off her face. It melted into the ruffles of her black chrysanthemum gown, leaving trails of white ooze down the center of the petals. The mascara bled, too, two black canals along the white.

I have seen her through Jona's eyes. I am not clouded by the preconceptions of Lord Joni's feelings. I believe she cried on his roof.

⊕

Jona wasn't thinking about what would happen after he had betrayed Lady Sabachthani.

He drank himself into a stupor that night because he wanted to puke thinking about her.

In the wee hours, when even the night in Dogsland grew too long and too calm, he sat in an alley, and stared up at a white moon.

For the first time in his whole wicked life, he knew exactly what he wanted.

He didn't care about the Night King. He cared a little about Aggie, and he loved his mother, still. But, he didn't care if he had to kill people to get what he wanted. He would have killed anyone he had to for his dream of love.

He looked up at the moon, and thought about a life with Rachel, on a farm, raising children and chickens and staying away from all the people that would burn them.

They could live there, and be together, and stay together, and nothing would come for them in the night, leaving cryptic messages or calling upon their sense of duty. They could just live.

Jona loved Rachel. He would do anything for her.

⊕

My husband, sleeping in a heap before the coal fire, was long and lean. All this hunting, and cleaning.

We had spent days interrogating the ragpickers, handing out apples. We had spent weeks pouring holy water over tainted ground. We had burned down the most-polluted place in the city: the home of Lord Joni. We did not even bother asking for the help of the guard to aid us in it, because we knew it was better for the fire to spread on its own, and burn uncontained. There was too much old stain in that ground.

My husband and I were alone in our room, far from the open hills and wild places of the world.

We were no closer to Salvatore, or Rachel.

Jona knew what he wanted. What do I want? I asked my husband what he wanted.

*I want to do something that gets us permanently thrown from this horrible city, that we can go home.*

*Imam's flock would never smell the stain as we do. The poison would accumulate, sicken, and destroy.*

*The trees are patient. What is our hurry? Let them be sick. Let their buildings fall. Let the woods return to this place.*

*You make it sound like it is a holy thing to abandon them to such a fate.*

*It is not holy at all. I know. I know. In the morning, we will go after the greatest prize we have yet found.*

*Salvatore? Do you think you know where he is?*

*No. There is another demon skull to claim, an old one more terrible than any living. We will no longer be executioners chasing after a prize. We will be the fire that purifies this city for a thousand years. Let the rain come and cool the ash from our flame. We were supposed to be executioners. We were supposed to be hunters and killers of abominations.*

*That is why we came, and why Imam allows us among this city that is more theirs than ours.*

*Wolves need not honor the word of dishonest men. We do not belong here, and every moment in this city only makes me angrier at the ones who would keep us from our prey.*

In the morning, we were going after the skull of Jona's father, buried for twenty years beneath his burned out house. We had waited only long enough to follow the scent of the men who came for it, they who believed they could take it from us, who would dig it up at any cost and try to hide it from us. We knew their smell in the ground, the stain's smell from the bones where they took it, and the fate of all their bones if the Blessings of Erin are upon us.

*Do you think I could kill Rachel, after knowing her the way that Jona knew her?*

*Yes. I will if you can't.*

*Then there is hope for us, yet, my love. Erin, be merciful, and let our task be swift in this miserable place.*

*In the morning, there will be so much fire, the city will curse Erin's name for a thousand years.*

*Is that what you want?*

*We must obey Erin's will. The ones who stand in our way...*

*Then, Salvatore and Rachel.*

*Sleep if you can.*

I could not sleep. I might never sleep again if we are stopped before we can do what we must. Death is not like sleep. It is more like waking up.

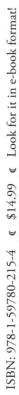

ISBN: 978-1-59780-215-4 ɑ $14.99 ɑ Look for it in e-book format!

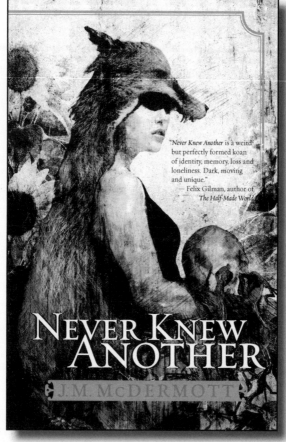

*"Never Knew Another* is a weird but perfectly formed koan of identity, memory, loss and loneliness. Dark, moving and unique."
— Felix Gilman, author of *The Half-Made World*

# NEVER KNEW ANOTHER

## J. M. McDERMOTT

J. M. McDermott delivers the stunning new fantasy novel, *Never Knew Another* —a sweeping fantasy novel that revels in the small details of life.

Fugitive Rachel Nolander is a newcomer the city of Dogsland, where the rich throw parties and the poor just do whatever they can to scrape by. Supported by her brother Djoss, she hides out in their squalid apartment, living in fear that someday, someone will find out that she is the child of a demon. Corporal Jona Lord Joni is a demon's child too, but instead of living in fear, he keeps his secret and goes about his life as a cocky, self-assured man of the law. *Never Knew Another* is the story of how these two outcasts meet.

*Never Knew Another* is the first book in the Dogsland Trilogy.

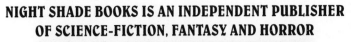

ISBN: 978-1-59780-203-1 « $14.99 « Look for it in e-book format!

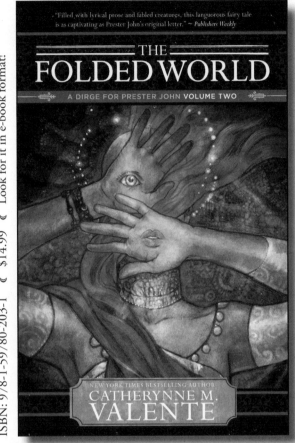

"Filled with lyrical prose and fabled creatures, this languorous fairy tale is as captivating as Prester John's original letter." ~ *Publishers Weekly*

# THE FOLDED WORLD

A DIRGE FOR PRESTER JOHN **VOLUME TWO**

NEW YORK TIMES BESTSELLING AUTHOR
## CATHERYNNE M. VALENTE

When the mysterious daughter of Prester John appears on the doorstep of her father's palace, she brings with her news of war in the West—the Crusades have begun, and the bodies of the faithful are washing up on the shores of Pentexore. Three narratives intertwine to tell the tale of the beginning of the end of the world: a younger, angrier Hagia, the blemmye-wife of John and Queen of Pentexore, who takes up arms with the rest of her nation to fight a war they barely understand, Vyala, a lion-philosopher entrusted with the care of the deformed and prophetic royal princess, and another John, John Mandeville, who in his many travels discovers the land of Pentexore—on the other side of the diamond wall meant to keep demons and monsters at bay.

These three voices weave a story of death, faith, beauty, and power, dancing in the margins of true history, illuminating a place that never was.

# NIGHT SHADE BOOKS IS AN INDEPENDENT PUBLISHER OF SCIENCE-FICTION, FANTASY AND HORROR

ISBN: 978-1-59780-213-0 ❧ $14.99 ❧ Look for it in e-book format!

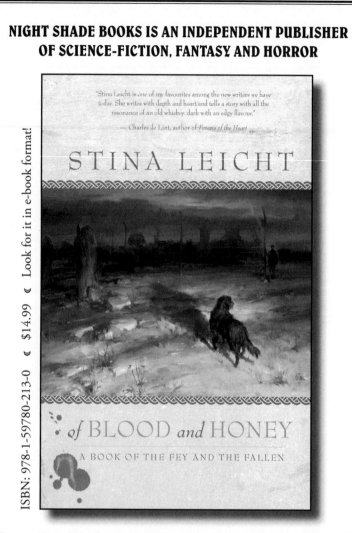

Fallen angels and the fey clash against the backdrop of Irish/English conflicts of the 1970s in this stunning debut novel by Stina Leicht.

Liam never knew who his father was. The town of Derry had always assumed that he was the bastard of a protestant—His mother never spoke of him, and Liam assumed he was dead.

But when the war between the fallen and the fey began to heat up, Liam and his family are pulled into a conflict that they didn't know existed. A centuries-old conflict between supernatural forces that seems to mirror the political divisions in 1970s-era Ireland, and Liam is thrown headlong into both conflicts.

Only the direct intervention of Liam's real father, and a secret catholic order dedicated to fighting "The Fallen" can save Liam... from the mundane and supernatural forces around him, and from the darkness that lurks within him.

It's November of 1977: The punk rock movement is a year old and the brutal thirty-year war referred to as "The Troubles" is escalating.

According to Irish tradition, the month of November is a time for remembrance of the dead. Liam Kelly, in particular, wishes it were otherwise. Born a Catholic in Londonderry/Derry, Northern Ireland, Liam, a former wheelman for the Provisional IRA, is only half mortal. His father is Bran, a púca—a shape-shifting ghostlike creature—and a member of the ancient Fíanna.

Liam must dodge both the Royal Ulster Constabulary, who want him for the car bombing that killed Constable Haddock, and the Provisional IRA, who want him for the deaths of Éamon Walsh and several others found ripped apart in a burned down farmhouse in Armagh. Fortunately for Liam, both the Ulster Constabulary and the Provisional IRA think he's dead.

The clash between The Fallen and The Fey intensifies against the backdrop of the Irish/English conflicts in *And Blue Skies from Pain*, Stina Leicht's follow up to her critically acclaimed debut, *Of Blood and Honey*.

# ABOUT THE AUTHOR

J. M. McDermott is the author of five novels and a short story collection. His first novel, *Last Dragon*, was shortlisted for a Crawford Prize. He lives in Decatur, Georgia, in a maze of bookshelves, coffee cups, and crazy schemes.